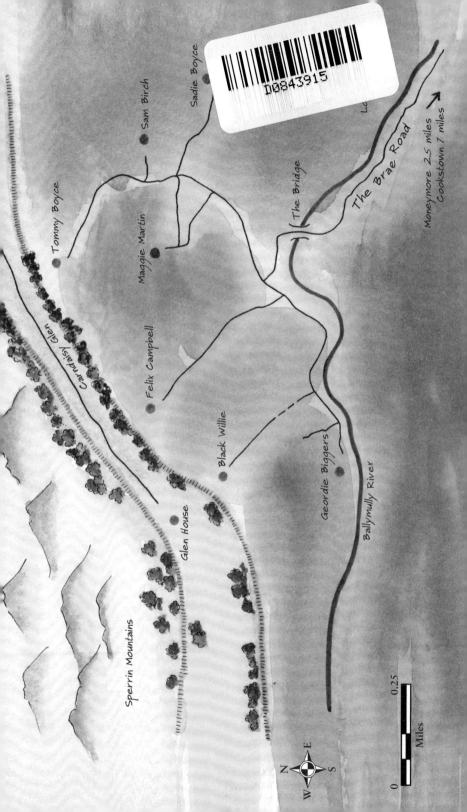

Sadie Boyce

Sam Birch

Tommy Boyce

Carnasky Glen

Maggie Martin

Felix Campbell

Black Willie

Glen House

Sperrin Mountains

Geordie Biggers

Ballymully River

The Bridge

The Brae Road

Lo

Moneymore 2.5 miles
Cookstown 7 miles

N
W E
S

0   0.25

Miles

Anne Barnett grew up in a farming community outside Belfast in mid-Ulster – the area where she has set this, her first novel. Formerly an accountant who travelled between New York and London, she now lives in Belfast with her young family.

the largest baby in Ireland after the famine

A NNE B ARNETT

A *Virago* Book

Published by Virago Press 2000
Reprinted 2000

Copyright © Anne Barnett 2000

A CIP catalogue record for this book
is available from the British Library.

ISBN 1 86049 797 7

Typeset in Berkeley by M Rules
Printed and bound in Great Britain
by Clays Ltd, St Ives plc

Virago Press
A Division of
Little, Brown and Company (UK)
Brettenham House
Lancaster Place
London WC2E 7EN

*For my father and mother Sam and Ella and
for Charlie, Angus and Sarah*

Contents

the largest baby in Ireland after the famine

1

The funeral, 1756

*T*he townland of Ballymully lies between the Sperrin Mountains
and the lowlands west of Lough Neagh. Clouds of flies
*attracted by any light come up from the largest lough in the British
Isles, and darker flies come down from the marshes and small
loughs of the mountain. They drop into the milk in the parlour,
appear on the windows in thick clouds of blackness, and swarm
across yards at dusk, when children say, 'The midges are eating us
alive.' They are the characters of early summer evenings, of hay-
fields and byres and the rumps of fat livestock. Water insects, flies of
the lough, they suit these lands, they suit the flatlands down to the
lough, and the wet marshes up to the mountain, and the deep dank
glens.*

They populate mid-Ulster, the east and the west, the north and the south. Each year they live and die in their millions as they lived and died in their millions before the Scots came, before Normans, and Celts and St Patrick. They came before faith came – before Roman Catholics and Anglicans, Presbyterians and Baptists. Faithless flies, they live for a day.

She was carried down the lane on a bitterly cold day when the wind came in from the east. Her pine coffin raised high to the level of the hedgetops bobbed up and down in rhythm with the pallbearers. All six-footers, their sturdy pace set a distance between the coffin and the mourners dragging behind.

The women stood on the step watching and listening. They saw the men parade her between the old beech hedges, steer her under the laburnums and past the gooseberry bushes. Through bare spots in the hedge, they saw her on the brae. At Archie's sharp corner, she gently slipped then rose again.

They presumed some change of hands.

Maggie Martin, Sadie Boyce and the Gibsons were together again. They were looking down and over the lanes that were leading her away.

She was dressed in brass and wood that gleamed through the faint light of a very short day. They picked her out amidst the mass movement of mourners. Her warm dressage distinguished her still.

Amongst her mourners were sons and daughters, and grandsons and granddaughters, and all other near and distant relations whose family connection was O'Malloran and Duffy and Campbell. In the small confines of house and yard and lane, they seemed a multitude.

Her neighbours were there.

Sadie Boyce commentated the procession. Sadie missed

nothing, she knew every pallbearer, aunt and uncle and cousin. She nor any of the women were going to town. Funerals were men's business. Sadie pasted down her hair and swathed around herself her thick black shawl – in no apron, she hardly recognised herself – and said all her Sadie words about dying and weather and wind. Courageous or mad, she was the only person that day to mention Felix Campbell.

Maggie Martin cried. Her lips, child-like incongruent in her old woman face, quivered, 'A wil' wind,' she said, then turned her ear to the wind. She couldn't help wishing Sadie would shut up just this once, but for Sadie talking was life's only natural activity, she'd hardly abandon it now. Maggie tried to compose herself. She moved away until she couldn't hear a word Sadie spoke, not a breath, sigh nor gasp of it.

There were only three men left behind.

Black Willie stood at the top of the lane distractedly fingering his lapels, gnawing his gums. He'd seen down the hill she was dead, and without second thought, just one foot in front of the other, blind the way we are, he'd walked down the hill into the wake. When she came to the townland – he remembered it vivid, Felix Campbell brought her, waltzed her round the brae – it had been the talk of the land. Even now Felix Campbell wouldn't spare the drop of saliva to save him. Well, now it was different. Out of his mind like a madman. That they hadn't spoken in years was neither here nor there, it's the nearest neighbour you'll fall out with. Willie chewed his gums, and fretted at something unsettling him, like he was in half a mind to follow her. Willie stood his ground so long that the dogs, as at any heat, lay down beside him.

Tommy Boyce sat on the stone in front of the dairy, a group of children before him. Tommy was slabbering, breaking in and out of speech, dancing words to all the voices he heard, soldiers and farmers and bridgemen. 'Aye, Sarah-Ann O'Malloran,' slurred Tommy as the prelude to some great and sad oratory presumed consummated only in Tommy's fertile drink-sodden mind. Sarah-Ann's first words at the bridge were addressed to Tommy, and the spirit of that exchange, its wit and verve, was what took Felix's breath away forty years before. Of all his ramblings, 'Fairies and leprechauns,' in the context he now invoked them, were most rooted in Tommy's experience. He made to go after the coffin, but stumbled.

Immediately she died, Felix Campbell had foreseen the consequences, and was afraid.

All her children, and her children's children, and their children who were her great-grandchildren, would congregate at the same time at the same place. Her large ramified family would attempt to pass through his own small doors. Most had never been over the doorstep. Some he knew only by story or thin snippets of conversation, some he knew by sight. He had his life. They had theirs. Death complicated that simple dichotomy. The living can't ignore the dead. They would all, even those who'd never forgiven her, come to the funeral. They would come from near and far, from morning to night, for three days they would come. Their huge teeming numbers would crawl up his lane, and over his land and fields and all the places he called his own. They would fill the atmosphere with their unspoken resentments. They would grieve at his convenience. Despair rose in him when he thought of it.

Felix imagined then their amorphous multitudinous mass, each face the same as the last, and wished that the thought of no wake had ever occurred to him. Why had it? Why had he tormented himself? Much as he tried, he could not reverse his mind's own history. It was two minds. It was wake no wake, and it construed the impossible as possible, it construed wake, no wake, and it accommodated mutually exclusive worlds. Felix clenched and unclenched his hands, and thought, 'Wake no wake,' until he thought he'd go mad.

The practical problem was how to accommodate them. The house might take a hundred, with forty in the room, another thirty in the parlour, and the same again in the bedroom if they stripped it of furniture. He knew there would be more. Well, they'd just have to stand in the yard. They could stand there, and be beholden to him for opening his house and yard to them to pay their respects to their mother or aunt or grandmother, or whoever they thought she was to them. They'd all be thinking she was somebody to them, more than anybody else. Well, they were nothing to him, and could think and say what they liked. When they asked him how he lived up that lane so far away from anywhere, he'd just answer that there's nothing but yourself at the end of a long lane, and a long lane isn't far enough. They'd know what he meant.

In the event, they stacked up Sarah-Ann's tables and dressers, and squeezed the wardrobe through the too narrow doors, then carted out her table still covered in heart tablets. They sorted through all the worn-out small things, aprons and stockings, tablets, barley water, rosary beads, holy water, that had been the touchstones of her physical existence. Only hours before, she had moved between their material existence, eating her biscuit thinking she'd eat another one, smoothing down her apron with purpose, filling the oil lamp, watering plants between waterings. Then small things had a future. Now small things were pathetic, abandoned. Felix packed them in baskets, and even though she was dead, her things were as real as if she was living. He imagined the last sip of water, the last walk across the room, the last twitch of the eye, the last breath. The last breath was all that separated them. He thought he could feel it still in the room.

Sarah-Ann's daughter Mary came first. She came by car in black. Her hair was a pure soft white as if she'd had a good life, and her face tough and lined as if she hadn't. She wore a black dress of velvet, and matching gloves and shoes, and she stepped carefully as a queen, and said a smart hello, then, like a visiting dignitary, extended her long gloved hand.

Felix followed her directly to the body where she crossed and blessed herself, and wound round her fingers the beads that were round Sarah-Ann's fingers, until the rosary wound round both women, living and dead. Felix looked until he could no longer. Someone sat him on the step, for air, they said, but he slumped forward, as if any moment the formless slackness of him would collapse. Saliva ran down over his old man's chin, and his eyes watered. Already his body had given up its reflex reactions.

No one knew when he went to the glen. When his son, Jim, tried to tell him that the funeral proper was on its way, that the mourners, children and cousins and half-cousins, and priest were at the chapel, he heard nothing, acknowledged nothing, just bent over, even this minute was down there digging, folding out his old gnarled body over the spade, and looking up at the red beech tree, not winter ravaged but how he saw it, spreading out its majestic copper branches to shade her in the summer. He was an old man. She would never again lie beside him.

2

The largest baby in Ireland after the famine

Sarah-Ann O'Malloran's birth was romantic. Or at least the story of it. Or, more correctly, the version of it that, originally propagated by her father, embellished by her grandmother, survived in those old enough to remember it.

Sarah-Ann O'Malloran was born in Cookstown in February 1879 when Queen Victoria was on the throne, Bismarck was in Germany and the Ottoman Empire was in decline. Sarah-Ann made her own history. Weighing in at thirteen pounds, her mother heralded her unique poundage, the locals marvelled at a 'thing that big that couldn't eat solids, potatoes or turnips' and speculated on how she would feed it. Just over thirty years after the Famine of the mid-1840s, her neighbours had never seen a baby so big.

Unharnessed by heritage and unaffected by dietary deprivation, Sarah-Ann made a vigorous entrance into the world. She came kicking and screaming, looking as raw, said her da, as a badly skinned rabbit, but she was the full length of two. They rocked and cradled her to calm her extreme anxiety at being born, and then they washed her and saw that she was really as large a new baby as has ever been cradled or washed. Her face was round and red and covered in fine down, and her legs were thick and solid and long. Her mother thanked the patron saint of child-bearing, prayed to the saint of infants, and the saint of fortune, to guide her from harm. In that order was Sarah-Ann's past, present and future peremptorily, and piously, arranged.

At the time of her birth, weather statistics were collected with care; storms and hottest days, rainfalls and fog were logged and charted, and in February 1879, the century's fiercest snowstorm was recorded. But not the birth of Sarah-Ann. This emphasis on weather is not incongruous: Irish weather is infinitely variable, even in a day, and humans multiply themselves with ease. It was then with perfect ease that Sarah-Ann came into the world.

She was born in a roadside cottage, which had thin stone walls, a wide stone hearth, and two rooms both for living and sleeping. In only one aspect was the house distinguished from a million others. It had a purple door.

Purple is a colour rarely found in Ireland. The Irish are not flamboyant nor given to attention-seeking by means of differen-tiated houses; even today the houses are pebble-dashed bungalows rarely painted any colour except in the occasional seaside town. In 1879, house-dwellers whitewashed their houses every few years according to economy and preference. Their doors they painted less frequently, preferring to expose their red and green eaves to the wind, rain and sun, and, over long years, create a soft weather-beaten look, not in the least conspicuous.

The purple then aroused suspicion. What sort of people were they to differentiate themselves? What had inspired them outside of influence? And the practical question: where had they found purple? Perhaps one of the household had travelled abroad, expanding his horizons, as foreign travels are supposed to? No, the house shared the gross untidiness and slovenliness of the poorest hovels; there could have been no means for travel. All the more bizarre, since poverty and garishness rarely met in bygone days. The colour of poverty in Ireland was dirt-coloured, drab and dreary and grey. Only much later, when past nobility's passion for colour was mimicked in overstuffed rooms, did poverty and gaudiness become synonymous. Whilst the inferior palate of the typically poor results in such lapses in form, this instance was not in that category. The door's beautiful purple jarred with no other colour.

The truth is that Sarah-Ann's family were susceptible to whimsy, and a certain non-conformity. Too, they were afflicted with a burning unconscious aspiration to artistic expression, inadequately satisfied in the minor medium of doors.

Thus imaginations were stirred. Amongst people who lived after hunger, amongst women infamous for shorter lifespans than their menfolk, it is easy to see how the birth of a robust daughter could precipitate an exaggerated response that, leading from one thing to the other, from one neighbour to the next, results in a tale to make things bigger than they are.

3

Felix Campbell, 1916

At forty-three years of age, Felix Campbell, a farmer working a small farm on the upper reaches of Ballymully, was seriously preoccupied with the first major decision of his life. Perforce of character and circumstances, he was making this decision without the counsel or influence of a single human being.

His decision, no doubt a paltry thing to those daily confronted with variety, complexities, possibilities and choice, was for him an enormity. Each morning he awoke empty-headed before the realisation of his situation set in. Each night he paced the room back and forth; fearful to sleep, and fearful not to. He felt his solitude as a terrible bind.

Where he had previously scorned the opinions of others, he now frantically wished for acquaintances whose judgements were available to him. Not that he didn't have acquaintances, of course he had, it was simply that he had never before ventured to request advice of a personal nature. The best type of potato seed, improvements in ploughing or cattle-feed he had consulted on many times, though often more as a matter of courtesy than genuine necessity – he felt himself to be better informed than any other man he encountered. It was another wiser and less practical advice that he now required, and that he so little knew how or where to seek out. That such wisdom as pertains to matters of the human heart was in infinitely shorter supply than the sparse degree of agriculturally scientific knowledge available in the mid-Ulster of 1916 was of only the slightest comfort.

Had he in any way been the type of man capable of exposing his dilemma to the criticism and wisdom of another, he may have confided that he had started to have the strangest dreams about a woman who came to him all dressed in purple, with a half wry smile on her lips, and said, 'How we create our ancestry, how we divert ourselves, how we pervert,' and challenged him to contradict her. But he was as dumbstruck in dreams as in life – he didn't know women. Disappointed in him, the barefoot beauty, her hair caught in briars, disappeared in the undergrowth.

'There is only the ancestry given us,' was his belated response.

Weaned on Protestant Sunday school, the Bible and sword drill, the spiritual dimension to his dream was not lost. He became convinced that, through her, some unknown message was being sent to him, and that he must talk with her. He had no concept of how to achieve such a thing. How could he possibly approach her, let alone confess that he was a man who had dreams, and that she was in them?

Previously a man of solid purpose, his mind was reduced to the contortions and configurations of the indecisive, as if some brain fissure had chopped up his thoughts into a million fragmented pieces. Hundreds of times each day he rationalised that he must speak to her, and that the matter was simple, and each day resolved to approach her, to broach the matter of his dream with her – yes, he would most certainly approach and warn her. Again and again, he worked out in his head the words he would use, sometimes scribbling these into a book, at other times speaking them out loud in a plan for social interaction. Even his practices were clumsy and embarrassing. Just as frequently he realised that the barriers to his communication were insurmountable, floundering him further into indecision.

His three dogs and five cats, companions of a sort, were no consolation. Forbidden to enter the house, they loitered around the doorstep, awaiting their master's presence. Discerning the changes in him, they became resentful. In the late spring they moved to the bottom byre, where they suspiciously observed him and his movements, which, so recently a source of opportunistic feeding, were now a matter of irritation. Against a common enemy they were united, dog with cat and vice versa. But in face of their protest, Campbell was oblivious.

Until his dilemma, his daily circumstances had little changed since the night ten years ago of his parents' deaths from heart attacks. His father's fatal attack was so sudden and enthralling that the sight inspired his wife to mimic him. She died ten minutes after her husband, and had only such time and freedom available to her as to take off the apron she always wore and to scream in agony and desperation. It may even have been relief.

Felix rarely ate with enjoyment thereafter. At the time he conducted himself well, made efficient and practical arrangements. The house was cleaned up, the minister invited, the wake laid out. They were buried on the same day, in the same grave, leaving their only son and heir to make the most of his new-found freedom. 'You kept your head,' said a number of souls anxious on account of his anatomy. This he did, by attempting to maintain as far as possible the customs and routines of his father's house. He rose early as his father had done, farmed the land his father had farmed before him, and went to bed early after studying his papers and books. If he had ever contemplated another method, this impulse appeared to have been truly suppressed.

Felix's isolation, so convincingly explained by himself, may simply have been bad luck. His ancestors had located themselves at the top of a lane at the head of a glen at a time when such a choice would have been admirable. When the Campbells first settled in Ireland, the country was in violent turmoil. By 1916, when times were gentler, a dominant location no longer offered such simple solution.

Reduced, squandered, divided to ninety acres, the present-day farm was bounded to the north by Carndaisy Glen – beautiful, peaceful and tree-covered, the locals attributed its precipitous ravines to the actions of fast-moving streams, though it was the Ice Age made its beauty. To the south, east and west Felix raised cattle, and with more modern techniques had three blades of grass where his father had grown one.

Lugubrious in grey sandstone, the large Campbell house sat square squat into the hill as if it was part of the hill that rose up steeply behind it. It was damp and run-down, and even people well acquainted with it remarked that, from the outside, they didn't know which chimney came from which room, nor which window.

Felix had never married, and, indeed, was blessed, and cursed, with all the appearances and characteristics of an ageing Irish bachelor. That is, he knew nothing of women, and was convinced there was little good to be known. When he was twenty-five, he'd courted his cousin, but quickly grew bored with the palaver of the thing. Social historians would later report that Irish bachelors were a phenomenon, traceable to the aftermath of the Famine, but Campbell, born twenty-three years later, didn't know this. How lucky not to know, and how harsh for the individual striving in his independent fashion to be so regarded.

Always cautious in his affairs with others, he had long held that the extent to which a man's life has value and joy is the degree to which he is free from convention and responsibility. This, he elaborated, can only be truly achieved in isolation and independence from other human beings. True to his philosophy, he had never voiced his reasoning to any other person and was unlikely ever to do so. Whether his argument was genuinely inspired from a deep-seated aspect of his personality or a self-delusory version of his circumstances is impossible to determine, since we can hardly meaningfully isolate a man's opinions from his character. In any case, the argument he made well suited the life he led.

He had no one to confide in. Who would he tell about dreams and sitting alone in the glen and feeling the presence of another whom he had never met or spoken to, and who would he tell that, more and more, he thought about dead ancestors turning mad? Who would he tell such things? Who would suspect him of madness? Maggie Martin was insufficient confidante for any man, and none for him. She gossiped, and ate to excess, and not least was it against her that her involvement in his washing was the reason it was known by acquaintances that, no matter how fatigued he was from the rigours of a working day, he never once wore his daytime clothes in bed. He watched her lift clothes to the clothesline, and saw her fat arms hang down like a web, and her legs thick as tree trunks. All his life he knew Maggie. She loved the mountainy men. They brought her heather from the peatbogs, and rhubarb for jam, and because she did Felix's washing she was not averse to implying in company that there was more to their relationship than met the eye. He knew it and indulged it. If people talked, he dismissed it, knowing people will find any malice to amuse them.

He observed the paradoxical nature of his dilemma. How often the strength and conviction of human feeling stands in sharpest and most painful relief to the ability to act – the perversion of the human condition. Men inclined to great artistry with no talent whatsoever, lovers living in solitude, ugly women whose natures required remarkable beauty; these are the commonplace, the mark of the human spirit that seeks to create in itself conflict and confusion. And Felix Campbell, by nature a bachelor, fulfilling his bachelorhood, had lived alone in the tranquil townland of Ballymully, had been passive in the rural tradition, had scorned the tribulations of high emotion.

When the dreams first started, they ignited an interest in his nature that he had never before dared to indulge. He questioned why, and how, he had come to be alone. He heard, almost for the first time, the silence in his house and in his heart, and remembered, with sadness, the constant sounds and noise of his childhood. There had always been some noise, something to join his senses with the outside world. Now he experienced the world as utterly silent, and was fearful. There was nobody or nothing in life that extended him beyond himself.

Yet he looked the same. When he went to the bridge on the Sunday afternoon – it was his major social engagement – he lay quiet and self-contained by the bridge as he had always done, and made the detached comments he had always made, which were so denigrated by bridgegatherers, who, like Irishmen everywhere, want only to hear and know a man's passion, not his considered opinion, the life taken out of it by consideration.

And when Maggie Martin came to do his washing as she did every Thursday, he sat in the house with her, and talked to her about all the things they had long ago established they would talk about, which were washing and shirts, and farming and weather, and the goings-on of neighbours.

And when he worked on the farm, turning horses and ploughing and tending to cattle, he seemed the same man who had always turned and ploughed and tended.

And when he went to the town, where he went every Monday since the outbreak of war, to collect *The Times*, there was no change in his aspect. He bought *The Times* once a week, and because of this weekly gap in the world's unfolding history of war was required to complete in imagination what he didn't have in newspaper, but this too was the same as before. All outward activity unchanged. Dressed every day with all the care and fastidiousness of a London gentleman getting ready for his club, did his regular daily exercises, and, for the comfort of it, wound up his dead mother's clocks, and, at night, watched the dark descend on the glen and the mountain as it does every night, even long ago when the glen was covered in ice that slid down over the world, and sliced through the world and made Carndaisy Glen the edge of his world.

Felix Campbell grew up in a glen with a glen-shaped soul, and baptism in his heart, and catechism in his mind, and a meeting house, and a Church of Ireland clock striking on the hour, and despite all that would do what he had never learnt from home, or church, or history.

And disrupted everything in and outside him.

4

It wasn't Dolly Birch

*T*he first time they met was at the bridge. Felix was there with the neighbours as he was every Sunday, when the bridgegatherers spotted a figure moving across the brae, nothing more than a dark outline, and they thought it was a boy. As the figure approached, they recognised their mistake. The walker was a woman, most certainly Dolly Birch, out taking the air between her morning and evening praise. Dolly wasn't the type who shouts, but saved her sparse conversation until the last, whereupon she would comment on the weather, good or bad, invariably invoking the Originator of all, 'that our Sovereign Lord gave us, planned and ordained'. Dolly drawled out her words through her tight thin face.

'Sure, it's not Dolly, she's not stopping at the well, there's not a pick on Dolly, she's a sparrow she is, that's a far bigger woman,' scolded Geordie Biggers, indignantly leaning over the bridge, a wooden, shoddy construction, built a couple of years before by the men who now stood on it.

For all their homogeneity, the bridgemen, all Protestants and farmers, could count amongst themselves Anglicans, Presbyterians, Methodists and Baptists. Their disparate souls were widely scattered, and hotly contested, and made for divisions that provoked, at times, their fancy that they could favour the Catholic Church over any of their Protestant rivals. 'Aye, Biggers! You've the eye for a woman's figure!' teased Tommy Boyce, fully attired in the regalia of jacket and trousers that the Ulster Volunteer Force, had issued to him three years before. A farmer more interested in soldiering than farming, Tommy had a way of creating the impression that he lived a more urgent and passionate existence in the far-flung fields of France than in the potato fields of his reality. If it weren't for the farm, he'd be fighting with the boys, said Tommy to a couple dozen men, all farmers like him down from the hills to trade Sunday war stories and gossip and the odd bit of news.

'It wouldn't take much of an eye to make out it's not Dolly,' smarted Biggers, who, resenting all personal comments, however remote from his private life, had himself a way of asking a question as if the whole of a man's life might be exposed by it. Biggers peered from under his cap. Biggers saw a lot more of the world than it ever did of him.

'You'll do with the eye you've got, you'll get no more!' said Stuarty Gibson, chuffed at his own wisdom and chuffed at the others laughing at it. 'That's Dolly surely,' pronounced Stuarty in the direction of the woman disappearing behind the trees.

'Sure, Biggers's got eyes on the back of his head!' parried

Boyce, pulling back and forth on the clasp of his belt. For all his display, Tommy had made no effort to join the Ulster Volunteers, who had long ago signed up for British war.

'Aye, you just keep thinking how you're marching,' snapped Biggers about the militia's former difficulties at distinguishing their left and right feet. Biggers resented Boyce's war pretensions. 'I'll lend you the straw,' he sniped in reference to the army's former custom of stuffing straw in one boot to remind them which foot was which.

'It's when they don't know which foot is the straw!' shrieked Jimmy Smyth, a wizened old man from the top of Tirgan. 'You'd make more use of it feeding it to donkeys than giving it to boys!' Smyth wore patched trousers and a too large jacket, once part of a suit.

'Aul men and war!' snapped young Billy Hutchinson, who sat disconsolate with a group his own age. 'I'll be joining first chance I get!' he boasted, looking around for approval from the Millar boys, Willie Trevors and the Wilsons, who, near enough to be part of the group, were far enough away to experiment with smoking and talking big. None was more than seventeen.

'Aw, the young ones, they think they've seen it all, and they've seen nothing, and know nothing, and there's nobody'd be telling them the difference,' said old Jimmy, making a lot of the ancient wisdom he proffered the world.

'There's nothing new in complaining about the young. Even the Romans complained,' said Felix, who stretched out his legs and felt the faint sun on his face. He felt young.

'Romans! Now there's a thing,' exclaimed Biggers, who in his mind, or heart, or wherever such things exist, believed himself a great orator. It was Campbell's arrogance provoked him. 'Aye, there's a useful thing, all of us talking, and nobody knows a thing!'

'Romans!' repeated Biggers, as if usage would penetrate the word. Lean and wiry like the Biggers always were, he stood with his legs apart and looked Felix Campbell full square in the eye, took him all in, his grey suit and dress watch and the shirt Maggie Martin had laundered. The laugh of it, thought Biggers, the laugh of Felix Campbell thinking he was young.

'That's the perspective history gives us,' said Felix dryly.

'Then maybe it's a Roman coming around!' said Biggers, slapping his leg and jumping back in delight. Biggers could turn a mood any way he liked.

'It's Dolly surely!' tutted Stuarty Gibson, a quiet placid man, his hair, indeterminate between fair and grey, stuck out from under his cap.

'The curiosity'll be what kills him,' said Jimmy, whose old opinion was so badly abused. 'The young have no patience. When they get to my age, they'll find out the only place they're hurrying is the grave.'

'Great gladdings and tidings,' sniggered Willie Trevors from Billy Hutchinson's corner, 'that'll cheer us!'

'It's a serious time with the war,' said Felix, feeling his youthful buoyance deflated before Biggers and the youngsters. Hutchinson was their ringleader.

'Very serious,' said Hutchinson with mock thoughtfulness, and, for an instant, Campbell had the uncomfortable experience of seeing himself as they did. Young pups, he thought, and reflected instead on the great spring it was with his war interest.

'The Germans are at Verdun,' he said.

'At Fenden,' queried young Trevors, deliberately stumbling over the pronunciation, 'where's that?' Hutchinson egging him.

'It's at the French line against Germany,' explained Felix, self-consciously displaying what he'd read in *The Times*. He heard his voice reverberate back, and felt that he hated the words shaped by his own tongue. He saw Hutchinson, Trevors and the Wilsons pull down their faces in a silly impression of studiousness. 'But it's not a geography lesson!' he said smiling. He had a craving for spontaneous gesture, freedom, and suddenly felt no freedom nor lightness, but it rose and fell in an instant, and left only the knowledge that he was ready to go home.

'It's near time for me to be heading,' he said.

'You're not waiting to see whether it's Dolly? Sure she'll be there in five minutes,' queried Biggers, astounded at Felix's indifference to the events he found so intriguing.

'I'll put a shilling on that it's Dolly!' said Hutchinson buoyed up by his fifth cigarette. Billy blew out, and watched the smoke rise and become air.

Biggers looked up, his peak cap tilted to the blue-white sky, and stared like the boy was transparent. 'The young have a lot to learn!' he said with the condescension self-containment makes easy.

Hutchinson smirked, but instead of looking big looked like Biggers could see right through him.

'Whist,' said Tommy Boyce, and everybody listened to pick out Willie on the hill. They picked out Biggers' name, and Boyce's, and Campbell's, and laughed at hearing and recognising their names originated in isolation and madness. Black Willie was their private preacher. His voice was the wind, his chapel the hill, and his congregation goats and God, if he would listen. Each Sunday, fair weather or foul, Willie shouted, and every Sunday he shouted for them. He knew they were there, but all they saw was the hill, and his house half hidden by trees, and all they heard was his voice, which dropped through the wind, like it was part of the wind, with nothing human behind it.

Felix heard his own name, and contemplated the voice, and

the source of the voice, and had no particular thought. 'He's got lungs on him that'd raise a church roof,' said Tommy Boyce.

'It's the only church in him!'

'Making an old cod of himself.'

'I seen him last week, when he seen me, he scuttled off around the back, but I knew he was watching me, so I just shouted until he came out. The sight of him, black and covered in soot!'

'Up there, no wonder. The house always blowing down smoke.'

'He's fell out with the Church.'

'He just wanted to be sermonising himself.'

'Mad as a March hare,' said Biggers to dismiss Willie back to hill and frail humanity.

'Well you're right! It's not Dolly!' exclaimed Boyce, pointing to the brae.

'Aye, she's carrying more beef.'

'I knew it wasn't Dolly, but who on earth is it? There's not many women out,' said Biggers, who knew that their women's strict observance of the day of rest left little time for gallivanting.

'Whoever it is, is a fast walker,' observed Boyce.

'Then it's not Maggie Martin, she's hefty but not a walker.'

'It's some stranger or other,' concluded Biggers, even as he wondered where a stranger could be heading when there was nowhere she could have been heading that he wouldn't have known about. He'd have known if she was making for Allen's or Boyce's, and with being up at the mountain road every morning he'd have known if she was going to Monaghans. He reckoned that whoever it was must be headed for Maggie Martin's, who was a bit of a dark horse, who told nobody all her business. She'd brought strangers before. He turned to Sam Birch, whose intimate relations with Felix's housekeeper Maggie Martin were well known.

'She'll be off to Maggie's?' he asked. 'What do you think, Sam?' Sam blushed with all the hopes and impulses of a schoolgirl, and his eye twitched its lifelong twitch.

'I don't know what Maggie would be up to. I was thatching up there a while ago, but I heard no news of a stranger,' he stuttered in the way the lie spontaneously occurred to him. Maggie was his first experience of women, and Sam believed that his love life was now only starting, when, in truth, it was nearly over.

'She never mentioned a thing?'

'Sure, I never see her,' muttered Sam, who in preparation for her bathed in the river's freezing waters, and had been caught in half undress by the local children, who squealed in horror and delight. Mortified that first time, Sam soon discovered the pleasures of bathing. When next he heard the children's soft steps in the undergrowth, he timed his ablutions accordingly. His washing practices far outlived his relations with Maggie, under whose tutelage he, who had never previously bathed at all, became the most public of bathers. The onset of winter was the death knell to their relationship, just one of the multifarious circumstances that prematurely separated Maggie and her menfolk.

'When you didn't see her, what did she say?' foxed out Biggers, snide and grimacing, but it was Felix who answered.

'He says he didn't see her, and it's none of your business what Maggie says to anybody, or what he knows or doesn't know!' From his prostrate position, Felix rose to his full tall frame, a motion to evoke his small fame for throwing large calves effortlessly. A small fame for a small talent.

'A lot to say when it suits you!' snapped Biggers.

'Not a thing that I heard,' protested Sam, but this time he addressed Felix. The group's focus had turned. 'Not a thing,' he repeated, and his eye twitched.

'Shush, quit your jibbering, nobody's asking your business,

and nobody will,' threatened Felix, making to return to his own company and sanity.

'Would yous wisht! She's coming!'

'Aye, she'll be going to Archie's,' muttered Felix, distracted, and Biggers pounced.

'How do you know?'

'Maggie mentioned something.'

'Well, who is it?'

'I can't remember.'

Biggers rolled his eyes. 'Some use you'd be in the war!'

'Well, if it's a stranger up to Archie's, it'll be some remote relation after the farm,' remarked Boyce, going to relieve himself under the bridge.

'You'll wait till she's away,' barked Stuarty Gibson, but, just as he spoke, and just as Boyce disappeared, the stranger woman appeared. She was all colour and sway, and as far away as imaginable from the puritanical Dolly.

'Afternoon,' greeted Biggers, and the others echoed, and did not take their eyes off her.

'A fine one,' she said, her accent and tone neutral to their ear.

'A great day to be out walking and taking in the air,' called Biggers.

'A grand fine day,' she said, but didn't slow down, just smiled brightly. Right up near them, she had pale skin, and thick dark hair.

'Would it be the same at the town?' enquired Biggers.

'I'm sure it's the same all over the country!' she said, marking geographical distance, when a voice came up from under the bridge. Boyce emerged in all his regalia.

'A leprechaun!' she said gently, almost to herself, but her riposte caused great hilarity and wrongfooted Boyce. The stranger didn't miss a step.

'A troll!' laughed Felix, suddenly caught up in the stranger woman's picture of Boyce. She looked at him then as if she might ask what a troll is, but a youngster asked first, and she nodded, just bobbed her head to acknowledge the speaker and raise up her eyes for a full frank look out of herself at what was before her.

'It'll keep up,' she predicted, meaning the weather. Her chat had already turned full circle, she was already right through them and striding up the lane, leaving them staring at the back of her, the colour and blaze of her, with her long thick auburn hair and her deep purple shawl.

'In a wild hurry,' puffed old Jimmy.

'Aye, leprechaun! She knew how to handle you, anyway!' gloated Biggers at Boyce, exposed in his uniform. 'You'll not live that down in a hurry!'

'Not with yous all to remind me!' replied the soldier, cut down to the size of fairies and leprechauns.

'Teach him to creep under bridges!' rejoined old Jimmy.

'Aw, you're all very clever,' retorted Boyce. 'I didn't see yous finding out where she was going.'

'Aye, she bucked past that fast,' complained Biggers, bringing back to them the bold confident manner in which the stranger woman had moved through them, the swirl and swell of a big woman marching through their dowdy dark dullness. She'd smiled so bright and so sweet to tell them that she was friendly as long as they didn't get in her way. She'd spoken warmly as long as they didn't provoke her, as Boyce had and was relegated then to the status of leprechauns and fairies. In a flash she was through them, standing there with two dozen pairs of eyes unashamedly following the flow of her long floral skirt over her large wide hips, and the flow of her long thick hair cascading down. Her hair fell free, not tied up like Dolly's.

'A fine-looking specimen,' stuttered Sam, 'wouldn't mind her visiting me!'

'A cautious woman in speech,' assessed Biggers, who was confident he'd know her business by the evening's out. With that Felix and Biggers and all the rest of them relaxed into their usual positions. They were sitting on the grass or standing in the middle of the road, or leaning against the bridge, and they were dressed in browns and greys, according to various inter-pretations of Sunday best. Up to forty dogs lay around, and snarled occasionally, and bared their teeth, but were mostly peaceable, and were used to the thud on their back of a black-thorn stick.

5
Properties of passion

After saying he was leaving the bridge, Felix dillied and dallied and felt awkward to leave first after the stranger. He made a spurious arrangement to meet Boyce during the week. This practical matter placed reality and distance between the woman's appearance and his own journey up the lane, but it was still in the atmosphere that he might meet her, maybe even speak to her. He was nervous of strangers. What if he met her? What if she came out when he was on the lane? In some mood of defiance Felix followed the path the stranger had taken. He quickened his pace; the thing to do was to walk past Archie's, his head up, his shoulders back, not so much as a glance, but when he reached the house, its gable on the lane, its yard in full view, he saw there was no sign of her, nothing to see, just hens pecking and smoke rising.

By evening, he was ensconced in his home routine. About half six he had a small feed – just spuds and tea – and then, more habit than need, another cup around bedtime. He went to bed about half past nine, same time as he always went. There was no disruption to his routine; no caller nor animal needing tending. He read for a while in front of the fire, smoked his pipe, and thought how he liked his own company. That was the type of him. Like all the Campbells. The house was clean and tidy, and the dishes stacked. All was in order, and his last impressions before dozing were heat and the hiss of the kettle.

Five minutes later he awoke with a start. He often woke like that, just a sticky fur on the tongue, a creak in the joints, the strangeness of sleeping in the parlour. Ordinarily it was nothing, meaningless. He raised himself in the chair, and rubbed his face, and saw the bright fire, but it was no comfort. A great gaping nothingness tugged at him.

He got up, and heated milk, and went to bed.

And dreamt, that very night, the dream to torment him for a long time after.

He awoke in discomfort, and where he normally sprang out of bed he lay a long while weighing up the benefits of getting up, or staying in bed. Usually it was no transition; the instant he woke, he got up; the instant he lay down, he slept. Now, neither in nor out of bed would please him. Now, he lay discussing. Perhaps it was some sign of getting old. Or illness. Or weariness after Saturday's ploughing. He dismissed his own hypotheses. There was no great urgency. Tomorrow, he'd have his exercises, and reading finished long before the sun rose. Tomorrow, he'd have a day's work done long before the smoke rising from any house around him. He regretted the pleasure of smoke rising. Well, today it'd rise without him. It'd rise while he lay.

Resigned to the consequences of staying in bed – what he would miss, and what he would have to compensate in the future – Felix's mind wandered. It travelled along its well-worn circuits, and, although the mind is no more traceable than invisible threads, his first fleeting impressions forebode a normal Monday. It would be routine chores and going to the town.

The local town was Moneymore. Typical of mid-Ulster plantation towns planned on nineteenth-century drawing boards by London companies making their Ulster investments, it boasted the Drapers Arms Inn, a town hall, a dispensary, schools, churches and shops. The Orange Hall was at the top of Main Street, and in 1833 the London Drapers company had erected a very fine church in the exact model of England's Tewkesbury Cathedral.

To the town, the Campbells had traditionally looked for their practical business – posting a letter, shodding a horse, selling eggs – but it was to the glen they turned their souls. The Campbells were Baptists, and unlike the other Protestant churches, Church of Ireland, Presbyterian and Methodist, who christen their newborn, their spiritual conviction was rooted in the proper age at which a child is baptised and their place of worship a small meeting house in the woods. Each Sunday of youth, Felix, his mother and father washed and dressed, then carrying their good shoes walked one behind the other to the top of the field, descended the steep glen path, crossed over the stile, where, balancing themselves as herons on alternate legs, they changed into their shoes. Once there, Felix learnt by rote great tracts of the Bible and recited Miss Grey's favourite passages. She called it drill.

'In the beginning was the Word, and the Word was with God, and the Word was God.

'The same as in the beginning with God.

'All things were made by him; and without him was not anything made that was made. In him was life; and the life was the light of men.'

Spoken in their flat mid-Ulster monotone, the childish recital was sombre and grave, and, in this long-sustained mood, Miss Grey explained the wickedness and darkness of men and the conniving disguising ways of the Devil, who, not even with children, takes the risk of unmasking himself. To children, Miss Grey denounced him, and was vigilant for young hearts, what she already saw in young hearts, falseness and sin. Felix associated these teachings with the colour and substance of the black treacle of his Sunday treat.

Felix lay back, his eyes open. It was not long to sunrise but the room was pitch dark, and he stared for so long into darkness that there was some inchoate impression of colour. It was purple black or black purple, and the purple became so strong that he imagined that he'd lost the sense of how to see dark. Black is the absence of colour, the total absorption of light, but purple refracts, and sends it back to the world. At school, they'd mixed red and blue, and the science of alchemy rose in his mind, its spirit and mystery. Blue from the sky, red from the sun, himself: these were all connected, and all he understood of it was how separate worlds are brought together, and things random, chaotic are transformed to a whole. For the briefest, fleeting time, Felix lay, saw purple, enjoyed pure free thought. The world is neutral, its light and shade, then colour comes from the sky, and transforms it.

From where had it come? Purple was transported from abstract awareness into the shape of a woman who flashed colour and light and moved free like the world was without boundary, like she was colour's contour. What are the properties of passion? Some men, the world's cleverest, fancy that an object may be no more nor less than its properties, so that not only lit coal always possesses fire, and a clear sky always a rainbow. To extrapolate clever men's fancy, a man may be no more nor less than he was, in which case Felix had always been anxious, he simply hadn't known.

Whatever the cause, his anxiety appeared to derive its source in the external world, and this in the form of a woman, and it was simply a chance encounter that he'd hardly noticed more than his amusement and resentment at neighbours. But she had sneaked in slither-like, and resided in that newly discovered part of him. She turned, and he was enraptured by the beauty of turning, and her rhymic hymn. It was his beautiful dream memory, and what he remembered was the first of what he newly was.

Then the day was breaking, and physical forms, wardrobe, chair, bed, were restored in the half-light. His huge attic room at the top of the house stretched from gable to gable. There was a small window at one end. A bare floor. The roof's beams were exposed. The rest was whitewashed, barely furnished. A large old bed, dresser, wardrobe, and a jug and basin in one corner. In the other corner was a huge wooden travelling trunk stuffed full of papers, deeds, titles, wills and all the documentary paraphernalia not lost by a family.

Felix got up, went out, felt the exigencies of the waking world – hunger in the morning, cold hands in the byre, a cow kicking – then he was only the dream's spectator, and the waking world was more compelling than memory.

6

The great change over him

On Thursday, Maggie came to take over the washing and brought with her Sadie Boyce, who was Tommy Boyce's cousin and Maggie's friend a long time. Because of their ignorance of the events shaping Felix, neither imagined anything untoward. Felix sat in the house a lot longer than he would have normally, and contributed equally.

'You'd have seen her then?' said Sadie, first through the door.

'Who?' asked Felix.

'Sarah-Ann O'Malloran, they think she's from Cookstown.'

'Who's that?'

'She's some woman up after Archie's so the men say, you seen her the Sunday.'

'Never heard of her.'

'Sure you seen her surely, the Catholic they say is after Archie's farm. Archie's supposed to be some friend of her dead husband.'

'Maybe she went on up to the Monaghans,' said Maggie of the only Catholic family around.

'Or up to the mountain road. A right long walk up, it's the hour up to the mountain road,' droned Sadie, who, abrupt as her nature, prided herself on knowing her manners in another man's house and playing her part in another man's house, and today, in Felix Campbell's house, skilfully kept going her conversation to in no way offend by any omission of courtesy, manners, news.

'I heard before about some woman or other up at Monaghans,' mentioned Maggie.

'Well, they never seen her before! That's the first time she came in this way.'

'She must have went the mountain road before.'

'Aye, you could do it in an hour,' said Maggie.

'Naw, an hour would hardly do it,' said Sadie, whose much shorter legs covered distance at the speed proportionate to them.

'And hardly dressed for it,' said Maggie, rubbing her large hands up and down over her large hips. Maggie moved back the kettle steaming up too hot behind her.

'And the dress that tight on her,' tutted Sadie, who had the benefit of Geordie Biggers' vivid first-hand description, 'and a big floppy purple shawl flapping round her, what a sight she must have been.'

'Aye!' said Maggie who knew only what Sam Birch had love-lessly stuttered.

'Would you even think to let yourself out of the house like that on the Sunday!' exclaimed Sadie, her indignation undimmed by the fact she hadn't seen her.

'Or any day never mind the Sunday!' exclaimed Maggie, and the conversation assumed its full rhetoric.

'Sure I told you the other day about the sight of Francis Murphy crawling into the Roman Catholic chapel, and the stink of drink on him, and the slabbers of him, you should have seen him,' said Sadie, and the conversational seam they tapped into, well quarried and marked, was revealed in its familiar pattern.

'Aw, they'll never miss the mass!' screeched Sadie, the crime's full accusation against them. 'Hardly the same on our own side,' she condemned, and Felix grunted. He never went to church.

'I'm only talking about them that's always talking and blowing about godliness,' said Sadie to make her distinction, and Felix's good intentions evaporated. Why had Maggie brought her? What would Sadie be doing when Maggie was cleaning? She'd be nosing about not minding her own business, and collecting facts for her own warped repertoire.

'Sure you were there yourself,' she said, and, worried about the supernatural powers of Sadie, Felix feigned ignorance.

'At the bridge . . . on the Sunday. Sure you seen her yourself,' started Sadie.

'Sam's never stopped talking about her, what's she like?' Maggie knew Felix had left first after the stranger. She was excited.

'I wouldn't know,' he sneered at the conversation beneath him.

'Sure you'd know when you seen her!'

'You've little to interest you,' scoffed Felix, making Maggie wonder what railed him. Sure, it was no skin off his nose, she thought, it's not every day a strange woman comes round the brae.

'The sight of her I wish I'd seen her!' lamented Sadie, blinking too fast to align her worlds, and Felix, who didn't often see her up close, who usually kept his distance, watched her. Here she was. Like some reproduction picture out of *The Times*' section on art, something very odd and bizarre, which he read to understand, and didn't, except the odd moment at night when the world closes down and the mind takes on its own strangeness and pulls you right into the other man's vision and the other man's eye-painting realities. He thought how odd she was, not Irish odd, which requires no thought nor reflection and is only cruel lazy dismissal, but odd in herself, and strange in herself. Sadie was small, extremely small. Took it after her mother, a dwarf proper. The sad fact was that Sadie's mother had suffered terribly at the hands of her insanely jealous husband. His severest abuse was to leave her helplessly stranded on wardrobes when he went out drinking, or working, or for any other purpose. Condemned to spend her life on wardrobes by the pattern of another man's day, Sadie's mother sat passively awaiting his return, and, from maintaining this position, her body grew sore and exhausted, and her mind grew numb. For fear of being found trapped in her dwarfdom, she never called out. Her daughter, Sadie, who had lived a physically comfortable life, in which wardrobes featured only in their clothes-storing capacity, barely recalled these injustices; however, they say that such experiences – unremembered and indirect to one's own person – affect the character, and may well have contributed to her jaundiced view of humanity. It is possible that Sadie didn't so much see it as men, wives and wardrobes but as men, dwarves and wardrobes, and, she being in herself somewhere a dwarf, may well have suffered from that terrible triangular relationship.

'They say she was a sight!' exclaimed Sadie, and Felix took stock. Sadie had a pallid complexion, pure white like she never went out, and yet was out all the time. He saw her walking back and forth to Moneymore, and up and down the hills to Maggie's and all the people Sadie went ceilidhing to. She had a large face with features still too large for it – bulging nose, big eyes, prominent chin. And whilst the eye except the artist's makes no inventory of features, only impression, Felix couldn't help taking stock, and saw that Sadie's features competed for space, and that her dark brown hair was groomed to perfection, and shone with incongruous health. The rest of Sadie was shuffled together with poor diet and neglect.

'A tight wee dress on her!' teased Maggie, winking at Felix, who scowled back. Sadie's influence was always bad on Maggie, and he thought what right she had bringing Sadie. First chance, he'd tell her.

'You'll be needing to get started,' proffered Felix, prudish, and should have got up to go out to his chores but didn't want to leave Sadie behind in the house. That his business was well known on account of Maggie was unfortunate, but to be fodder for Sadie's tongue and wisdom would be intolerable. Once, an unsuspecting stranger, meeting her at a county fair, oh some big occasion up by Omagh, some grand fair, this man thinking he knew her, had in all likelihood seen her before, went up to her, and mentioned he recognised her. 'Of course you do, you idiot, how wouldn't you?!' Sadie had screeched, the obvious but harsh rebuke to the unthinking tactlessness of a man towards a woman sensitive about her appearance. For a moment, the man, neither clever nor sensible, stung with her hardness. But it was only a moment, whilst Sadie remained small all her life.

Sometimes Sadie looked up and saw where the rest of her should have been; all her life she looked up, even when she was old and frail, and smaller than she'd ever been. All her life, the size of the man and woman next to Sadie was sore to her, and all her life she looked up for the rest of her.

'Aw, men and their leching!' snapped Sadie in abrupt assault upon the conversation, and Felix flinched and even his already bad opinion was shocked by her ferocity. 'We don't need that sort of harlot running around the country!'

'Aw, now,' soothed Maggie, 'there's talk about any stranger, sure we didn't see her.'

'Sure what would we need to! Trolloping through the men looking for attention, the air that filthy behind her, Dolly said, and them men all asking her if she'd seen her, and Geordie Biggers' tongue hanging out of him like a dog's leching, sure it would sicken you!' ranted Sadie.

'Naw naw,' said Felix almost imperceptibly, perceptibly shaking his head and trying to defend himself against the lashing Sadie's tongue made, which cut up the world into bits and shreds and made her the hardest person to talk to, harder even than Biggers with his sarcasm, which put down the whole world like it was nothing without him in it.

'Aw, now, naw naw naw,' Felix said, how could Sadie say these things? Felix feared Sadie Boyce suspected his heart.

'Aw, men and their dirty ways, and you sitting there!' she railed at Felix to connect him outwardly innocuous, outwardly passive, with Catholic trollops, and whores, and town bitches on heat.

'Aye, and you sitting there!' she said to inculpate him, in his pipe-smoking existence, with all the sins of man against woman, and all their guilt.

'Hold your tongue, woman, talking like a fool!' he raged, tight-lipped, fearful Sadie suspected the heart his whole life had tried to dissemble. Sadie sat tight, and Maggie, warming her arse at the stove as her own, wondered how she would change the situation if it wouldn't change itself.

'It's either a feast or a famine,' commented Maggie.

'Sure there's no work to hens,' snapped Sadie. 'I could do it with my eyes closed.'

'There's eggs surely, you're just too lazy to look for them,' teased Maggie.

'It's the foolish man who thinks he knows all a hen knows,' countered Sadie, in the manner of all her interests, which were ghosts and tea leaves and fortunes and fates and mishaps.

'Your aul nonsense, what does a hen know?' challenged Maggie. Spud-digging, hen-tending, practical, Maggie would turn them from themselves.

'There's more goes on that people know nothing about,' sparked Sadie, her intense mind scratching and scraping and sparking into fire by any threat to it. Sadie believed in the supernatural powers of hens.

'Maggie doesn't think much of your theory!' said Felix, overseer, far-distanced and remote. As far as Sadie was concerned, there is no unscathed world, and the unscathed world slips by nobody. Felix Campbell was in it as much as anybody.

'Theory, it's no theory,' jeered Sadie. Thinking theories outraged her. She dangled her legs over the done chair.

'Well, idea,' offered Felix conciliatory, thinking the difficulty was pedantry and language.

'Idea!' gibed Sadie. 'I'm talking what hens know! Theory's what a man thinks he knows!'

'You're talking nothing at all!' teased Maggie, to get the heat sliding her petticoats up her legs, which Felix saw, backs of strong legs, firm and supple, and he looked the other way, because he didn't want to think of Maggie like that. 'You don't know what you're talking about,' added Maggie.

Sadie just laughed, would have killed anybody else but Maggie who said it and Felix saw another side of Sadie from the side that was small, even brutal. Sadie was passionate, and even though it was only hens, Sadie had her own knowledge, and kept ten dozen hens, tended and cared and cosseted them, and was maybe closer to them than she ever was to any human being.

'Good fire you've got going,' said Maggie, and a stick, end of the tree, fell in the stove with a thump, and the fire roared with its own action. 'Them roses are growing wild big,' she remarked.

'Wild all right,' answered Felix, and Sadie slapped her leg.

'You must be peeing on them,' she cackled.

'I never go near them.'

'Geordie Barnett peed on his every day.'

'That's a botanist.'

'It's just a story.'

'I thought a poet.'

'Whatever, he's no example for myself,' said Felix, and made to get up.

'Sure he's a bachelor like yourself,' said Sadie.

'Hardly like myself!' answered Felix resenting the comparison.

'Well, I never thought I'd hear you say that you'd be the man for the marriage!' squealed Sadie, happy to distort what he said.

'Sure you'd never marry!' interjected Maggie, glimpsing her own lost world. Felix was nobody's if not hers.

'There's no marrying in you,' said Sadie.

Who, perhaps because of her childhood, had a bitter, one-sided and contradictory view of men. Her rules were simple: Was he married? Was he likely to be? Was marriage remotely possible? In other words, the average sort of criteria applied by women down the ages, and too bad, the very lax sort that results in marriage to wardrobes. Has any woman ever seriously considered the comparative qualities of spinsterdom and wardrobes and perhaps even muttered to herself, 'Better a life on a wardrobe than a spinster'? Perhaps only Sadie herself could have said and truly believed such a sentiment.

'You'd never know what I'd do, I might, I just might,' he said jockily.

'Surely who'd you marry?' Maggie feigned indifference.

'Sure he'd marry anybody, it's different for a man with a farm,' said Sadie, turning it against Maggie.

Sadly for Sadie, subsequent history proved inadequate all once marriageable men. She railed against them. What use to her was an unmarriageable man? What use indeed a big lumpen leaden useless selfish sod of a bastard?! She recognised no incongruities in her situation, and casually deflecting her criticisms from one man to another turned heroes to villains and villains to worse ones. Her men remained innocently unaware of their demise from hero to cad.

'Well, that's a quare change over you,' said Maggie, who had never found him so attractive as at that moment.

'You'd never know what I'd do!' laughed Felix, walking to the door. He wanted to tell his personal affairs, confess, burst out. When he left, Sadie gasped to express herself.

'Flirting away with himself!' scraked Sadie. 'Did you ever hear the like of it! The change over him talking about marriage like that! I never thought I'd live to see the day! Had I not heard it myself, I wouldn't have believed it! I never thought I'd live to see the day!'

'Well, you haven't,' snapped Maggie.

'You'd swear he was drunk!'

'He never touches it.'

'Many's a time he would have went right through you if you'd even so much as mentioned a woman!'

'Shut up and give my head peace!' shouted Maggie.

'What's got into you?!'

'I'm supposed to be getting the bit of work done, God knows that I've not enough to do without you jumping up and down trying to make that big of yourself.'

'Big of myself?!' Almost whispered. To speak in this wee small voice, Sadie must have been cut right down to the bone.

'Aye, egging him on like that, you never give anybody any peace,' moaned Maggie.

'Well, well, well . . .' mumbled Sadie. A few moments later, she stormed out past Felix at the top of the lane, who asked, 'You're away?' and she snapped, 'What do you think, I'm standing on my head?' Then Maggie came tearing out behind her, mumbling something about being busy, and without another word and with the work obviously not done, stomped off down the lane.

'Women!' lamented Felix, past understanding. He looked over the fields where he saw Sadie, small and ardent, heading up the hill, and Maggie, large and languorous, stepping up behind her. Sadie and Maggie'll make up for another day, he thought, philosophically, sanguinely, far away, watching them, not knowing that it was he himself who came between them, not knowing the great change over him that disturbed their world.

7

Protestant, he passed the first hurdle

Mrs Gibson came the next day.

What inspired her was something of a mystery. She had been a distant friend of Felix's mother, and a stalwart of the church, and arranged its flowers, and her husband, Stuarty, made the Campbells the first pitched slate roof in the county, but these temporal and spiritual connections did not explain her sudden and passionate interest in Felix as a husband for her daughter. At twenty-three, Heather Gibson was not suddenly come of age, nor her mother suddenly desperate. No, it was a more subtle wind blew Mrs Stuarty Gibson round the brae, and it was only much later Felix suspected in it the hand of Geordie Biggers.

She and her daughter landed in the yard on some pretext that they were in the area and had just popped in on the chance that Felix wouldn't be over the fields, or up the mountain at turf, or any of the few places he might have been, and thus, finding him in the one place they'd really expected to find him, Mrs Stuarty said how glad she was to see him. She said it all so breathlessly that she was in great danger of running out of things to say before she even got into the house. Not realising that a woman's not comfortable outside like a man is, Felix had to be hinted at until he reluctantly invited them in.

The daughter was Heather. From a big strong girl she'd grown into a big strong woman, who for some reason chose the old Queen Anne with no upholstery. Mrs Stuarty took Felix's own chair. She was all business and polite.

'It's good to see it brightening up,' said Felix flummoxed and uncomfortable.

'There's been showers round our way the day already . . . when you get round the country, it's funny to see it that changeable,' observed Mrs Stuarty.

'Sure it's all the same, it's just the same showers going round,' contradicted her daughter, brave, with the mind of her own.

'Not at all!'

Mrs Stuarty looked about her with the regal dignity of years of looking down on her neighbours. 'I always said this was a fine house, and with a nice big parlour, but it's big up here on your own . . . with only the one of you.'

'I never think of it.'

'Big to keep warm.'

'I never notice.'

'Men don't feel the cold like us,' said Mrs Stuarty, turning to her daughter, who, raising her eyes towards the ceiling, prompted Felix's thought that the ceiling had not been painted for years.

'Stuarty says I'd be cold in a furnace,' chattered Mrs Stuarty, as Felix offered them tea.

Awkwardly bowing to walk back into the room, he saw the girl looking up at him. Dark hair, a strong contemptuous gaze and a passive face – God alone knew what she was thinking.

'You've only the one,' he said, addressing the mother, like the girl wasn't staring at him.

'The one's enough. I see them running around with broods of children after them and I wonder, what in God's name they want them pack of weans for!' said Mrs Stuarty, stretching forwards with genteel gestures for tea. 'There's a respectable number that can be handled. Sure, with just the one, your mother was the same.' All said in a tone of confidence, and approval.

'Sure you'd be handling yourself now,' said Felix initiating chit-chat about the mysterious speed at which young girls grow up. His observation pleased Mrs Stuarty.

'Aye, it's shocking how fast they grow up, one minute they're running round your feet, the next . . . Our Heather was always a big strong girl . . . You never married yourself then,' she puffed out, and the girl shuffled her feet.

'There's no marrying in me,' said Felix, with the mock cantankerousness he'd learnt to defend himself.

'That's what we've come about,' declared Mrs Stuarty, and Felix felt a sudden genuine shock, expressed only in his raised eyebrows. He looked at Mrs Stuarty, who looked back fearlessly with the confidence of possessing privileged information.

'Aw, now, Felix Campbell, people are talking, and saying you're after a woman, that's what they're saying,' she winked knowingly, and nodded at Heather, who sat motionless as stone. Mrs Gibson panted over her great upholstered chest. She nodded again harshly at her daughter, whose proportions were shaping up like her own.

'Who's saying that?' he asked, stricken.

'It's about time a man with a big farm was thinking about the future and settling down. It's a long time since you've seen our Heather here.'

'It's great to see how they grow,' he said in retreat, and turned a polite face towards the girl.

'I wouldn't object,' said Mrs Stuarty, and Felix didn't know whether she was offering herself or her daughter, 'though there's ones that say that you're getting on that bit, and are used to yourself, and your books, and that sort of thing, but I take no notice myself.'

'Books is my interest,' he said objectively.

'Aye, that's what I said, a man needs to widen his interests.'

Mrs Stuarty left first, with the girl, behind her, mortified.

Mrs Stuarty Gibson's interest confirmed that Felix's singular existence was not overlooked, nor despaired of. On the contrary, Mrs Stuarty wanted him for her only daughter.

Protestant, he passed the first hurdle. She knew his parents, his neighbours, he had land. Anglican herself, she didn't mind that he was Baptist since in her experience Baptists changed at the drop of a hat. There was only one difficulty. It was obvious that Felix Campbell was the kind of man who doesn't see what's in front of his nose, and even if he does, phaffs and farts about; in short, would need a bit of help, a gentle push in the right direction, luckily just the thing that she herself knew how to arrange; after all, she'd married Stuarty. With that sturdy and boisterous attitude, Mrs Stuarty got what she wanted, or, if not, dismissed her desire as having no merit, and between these two stratagems had never known a moment's failure. She vowed to herself that, if Felix Campbell rejected her daughter, he would be called upon to explain himself the same as any other man.

Thus the call at the house. Brief, sweet, pointed. That's all it takes. Mrs Stuarty knew that straight talking is worth any amount of pussyfooting about, and that fine ways are all fair, well and dandy, and make people unhappy.

Cheery and plentiful, Mrs Stuarty had remarked to Felix on all his effects, and talked up their good points, and made constructive recommendations, such as turning round the table to make better use of the good big room, and putting his chair nearer the window for reading in the evenings, and the dresser would be better with the books at the bottom and the delph on the top, rather than the other way round, which was just asking for an accident.

'Isn't it?' she'd turned to her daughter.

Nothing. The girl didn't even look up. She may well have observed nothing about the room, she had no interest in it, nor its owner. It was the worst moment, and Mrs Stuarty stormed on over it until Felix's whole familiar world had been fully turned on its head. He explained that he never changed anything, he just kept the layout his mother had, which, after all her criticisms, Mrs Stuarty agreed, was as good as any.

But the point had been made. Through the avaricious eyes of Mrs Stuarty, Felix had seen that his room had other possibilities, and that what was permanent and unchangeable could be reconstituted quite as if it had no historic precedent. What he saw was himself sitting in the midst of the house filled with men's things, bits of farming implements, and pipes in the corner, and a hoe propped at the door; which he knew where they were, each of them extensions of himself or farflung limbs. All that mattered was utility and practicality. He nearly opened his mouth to say he was unused to company, never had visitors, but Mrs Stuarty saved him, steered the talk around her well-known territories. She had her own vision of who he was, what he was for, and upon all this she made her own judgement, which she called taking people as she found them, and rode roughshod over them.

'Aye, ever been up this far?' he'd asked, conscious of being so far located up that long long lane, and then made it a talking point, and half apologised as if he had made them walk it. It was nothing, said Mrs Stuarty, who did all the talking, and the girl sat mostly dumb in the hard chair, and only interrupted to contradict her mother. To see himself through others' eyes was a new curse.

It would have been different if he was affable, and open, and used to saying the things women expect to hear. Instead he'd sat in his mother's old chair, and looked at Mrs Stuarty's authority in his own chair, and couldn't bring himself to look at the girl, whom he knew by other senses was perched on the edge of hers.

He vaguely remembered his mother's pearls of wisdom, contradictory in advice, but uniform in the message that Campbell men had no time for women. Nor was the irony lost on him that, even though he was lonely, he didn't want Heather Gibson who was young and healthy, and not bad-looking. Taken logically, there was no logic. Beggars can't be choosers, and he wanted nothing to do with her.

Geordie Biggers would have known that.

The history and family of Felix Campbell were of great interest to Mrs Stuarty.

Felix's father John always knew he would call a son Felix. His own father and grandfather were Felix, and the name evoked the family's unusual origin. Like his forebears before him, he believed the first Felix was a Scottish Protestant lay preacher persecuted under Queen Mary. The name then fixed him as a Ballymully Campbell, and commemorated the martyr.

His full name was Felix William Thomas Campbell. Just as Felix was rare – unlikely he shared it with any other boy in the country – William was ubiquitous amongst Protestant Ireland. Thomas was for his maternal grandfather.

Pious and self-righteous, the father John was a bully who effortlessly and silently directed his wife's every thought, action, movement, and she spoke always in a low dead whisper. When her husband was hungry, she jumped to feed him, and when he was thirsty, ran to get him drink, and when he needed anything at all, deliberately and immediately set off to fetch it. At meal-times, Martha Campbell stood by the hearth in silent attendance, the rest of the time she rarely raised her head from her work, and then only to look through the window at the back of the house where, by the tops of the trees, she saw the colours and the passing of the seasons, and on the other side, the view over the brae, which she watched to see anyone coming.

Her son she fed, washed and clothed beyond all reproach. All she asked in return was that he sit good and quiet, and that, when his father came into the room, he got out of the way. These ways, his life was regular, and each day of his boyhood Felix woke, ate, played, slept at the times measured out by his mother's clocks, which, like his mother, valued nothing but routine.

Felix was the last of his line. The marriage of impotent Campbell men to weak-natured women was part the cause of it, so too was their religious fervour, which, denouncing fornica-tion as the greatest evil, proved a powerful impediment to family reproduction. The Campbells' crusade against sin was unrelenting; the holy spirit held them rapturous, they prayed in the morning, in the afternoon, and at night. When an ill thought crossed their minds, they prostrated themselves to beg forgiveness. A timely ideological conflict with Methodists dis-rupted their efforts by causing a wave of defections from Baptism to Methodism, and from Methodism to Baptism. The bitter feud interrupted the family's sexual abstinence.

Too, an ageing aunt coming late into farmland – an event that overnight transformed to beauty her plainness and relieved her social charms – fortuitously rescued them. In possession of her newfound lands, she immediately found a husband, and conceived the very next year, demonstrating that a suitor's unscrupulous motive may produce some good.

The rapacious ambitions of Methodists, the slow-blossoming beauty of a blighted maid; to such incidental interventions did the Campbells submit their destiny. They may somehow have been supremely assured that they were invincible.

But they were ill suited to recreate themselves in perpetuity. Life was too harsh, and the wrath of God a daily reminder of the temporal nature of being, causing them, a family whose chance of birth was so unfavourably stacked, to take their lives excessively. By rough calculation, a member of the family committed suicide every thirty years. Sufficient proof that man's appreciation of life barely reflects the improbability of his existence.

The first suicide was Felix's namesake, a first-generation Ulster planter who'd arrived from Scotland with his uncles. He took his life in 1642, one year after surviving an attack by Catholic marauders. The attack, part of a wider revolt of natives rising up against the settlers, was recorded in the *Dispositions of 1641*, a litany of allegations by landowners and farmers of theft, pillage and violence. The first Felix Campbell's account of the heinous crimes perpetrated against him was amongst them.

His report commences with his first sighting of a gang of men coming over the top of the glen. They arrived at dusk with sticks and cudgels, and stood for a moment at the top of the scarp as if drawing their breath, before overpowering the terrified Felix and stealing his livestock.

In detail, Felix noted the colour, value and age of each stolen head of cattle. His sheep he noted according to the year of their birth, and their location 'on that terrible night when neither man nor beast was safe'. He speculated that his attackers 'were from out of the county, most likely Tyrone where they are wilder than any part of Ireland, our misfortune to be so proximate'. His pen steadfastly testified terror for all the generations, and was ubiquitously cited in pamphlets and circulars, which, designed to stir up the plantation population, were widely distributed, and read aloud, by the educated to the uneducated, or their contents passed, by word of mouth, one man to the other, all over Ireland, the means by which a large population came to sympathise with Felix Campbell's sufferings at the hands of rebels.

His report, in a level of detail far in excess of the authority's requirements, consisted of thirty-seven pages written in the beautiful large bold letters of a confident man. There was not a single ink blot, nor spelling mistake, nor written error of any kind. Without obvious writing resource nor schooling, Felix Campbell, living on a remote farm in the heart of mid-Ulster in the 1640s, had presented a perfectly pristine testimony of the fears and trepidations of his fellow Protestant settlers and countrymen. There was no mention in it that Felix, whilst still alive and suffering, was summonsed to the county court in Omagh. Nor that the summons, arriving on a morning, interrupted his wife's announcement of her worries about a baby. With no interest in her news, and unperturbed by the procreative evidence of his fornication, the seventeenth-century Felix was calmly digesting his very large breakfast when the town clerk rode up the lane carrying the summons that would change his life entirely. As the first Felix read, his heart palpitated with the knowledge that his future was set, and the breakfast his last sensory pleasure. Never again would he see beyond the fear which settled in him that day. It contaminated every bone and sinew, organ and limb. His wife, a tough Scottish lass confirmed in her pregnancy, ridiculed his despair. He had the constitution of a gnat, she taunted, driving him further to despair.

The first Felix took his life by hanging, a method perennially popular amongst the suicidally inclined. The rope he used was made from flax from the lint pond. He stood on an old wooden stool in the barn, and tied the rope to a beam. As he arranged the angle of the stool, he said his regular daily prayer, then walked out the door to see, for the last time, the glen and the brae, and the farm. Everything was how it should be. The cattle and goats were grazing at the gable, the hens were clucking round the door. There was nothing else to stir the eye, and he re-entered into darkness, and stood on the stool to feel ordinary in the last few moments of his physical existence. The rope, strong enough to hang a man, was later tied around hay.

Poor Felix had simply behaved as many had seen fit during that turbulent year – he had exaggerated immodestly his claim of damages by twenty-four cattle and six hundred sheep. The local recorder, a farmer's son, quickly calculated that his farmholding could not have sustained a herd and flock even half this size.

In the final analysis, the recorder dropped the case because of the lack of concrete evidence and an influx of even more grandiose claims by more vigorous individuals. But Felix was already dead, and his insect constitution could never be reprieved. The pamphleteers exonerated and venerated him, creating in the early days one of the most disturbing Ulster pamphlets ever written. The first Felix's small story, elaborated and expanded, fed the fears of many, confirming what they knew.

So Felix's namesake took his life by hanging, and was placed by his wife in a box and stored in a box, man's last box, man's last bed. What point brought him? Rebels over a hill? Some horror beyond him?

On the night of Mrs Stuarty's visit, the present-day Felix opened the family trunk and pored over the unsorted dusty papers. On the top were his parents' death certificates, dated the same day and stating that they died from natural causes.

Felix then smoothed out papers, deciphered dates and names, but could find no document that bore relation to any other. A map was for the purchase of fields he still possessed, and there were deeds of his grandfather's sale to Archie's family. A pamphlet, dated from the 1750s, was entitled *Property and Security*, and referred to his suicidal namesake, and Felix thought how, one day, he too would go into the trunk and turn into dusty paper.

Then, tired, with his research of family history exhausted, Felix rolled up the maps, slid them into the corner of the trunk, and went downstairs, where he lit the paraffin lamp and stoked the fire. The house was utterly empty. His actions didn't fill it. Restless and dissatisfied, he pulled a chair up to the fire, and with his long legs wide apart and his body stretched forward had the appearance of a man who, at any moment, would commit to the full movement required to rise. There was nothing to do. No book remotely tempted him, no war paper interested him, he looked at nothing, and the weight of nothing roused in him an urgent need for escape. The slightest provocation might propel him. He would get up, close the door – close it carefully and finally – and without future plan, decision, step out the door, hear it click behind him, and at the top of the lane would pause and look back, and from that new perspective, see the house only as object, bricks and mortar and clay. He went over the motions, and was at the brink of movement when again he went over the steps of getting up, walking, closing the door. Simple and impossible. Conflicting forces rooted him.

8

Journey into the world

On Saturday Felix decided to go to Cookstown. Last time he'd been in Cookstown, two years ago, there had been no war in Europe. Still he didn't imagine Cookstown would be any different. Even that minute people would be milling about, young girls walking and gossiping, wizened men standing at street corners. Saturday was market day. Farmers from all parts would bring in cattle and sheep and stand around anxiously chewing tobacco, and comparing their fattened stock, and guarding against false expectation by remembering that, in the past, they had been pleasantly surprised, and bitterly disappointed.

Getting ready took a long time.

He stretched out his body, his arms and legs and his stomach, grown slacker in his forties, then he went downstairs where he filled up a basin, and carried it back up, and undressed, and scrubbed his whole body, his face, and arms, and legs almost to red, then dried himself with an old towel.

Standing up close to the mirror he opened his mouth wide as he could, and inspected his tongue, which he saw was covered in fur. With the end of the towel, he rubbed his tongue back and forth like a housemaid polishing furniture, then examined with pleasure the towel's residue, a thick yellow stain, and the evidence that his hygiene routine was truly a cleansing experience.

He dressed in a heavy white shirt, his checked suit and a tie, and admired himself in the mirror. He was smart and tidy, his face was clean and fresh, and his hair was thick and shiny. He could find no fault with his grooming.

Except he noticed his reflection was ageing. His black hair was flecking grey, his eyes were lined and dark and, when he turned his profile, there were traces of a double chin, which he felt and pushed up. He smoothed down his hair, but it was no good. The grey was uniform, and the lines on his face indelible, and the neck's cragginess irreversible, all of which he saw with a critical eye, which pitied him, and the damage to him, and the time that ran ahead of him. He restored his hair to its normal parting.

Stepping back, he saw from a distance that the mirror was cracked and dull and, half aware that he fooled himself, he smiled and imagined that his reflection was the fault of the mirror, which was dusty and old, and had lost its ability to accurately record the world.

Careful not to crease his clothing, he went downstairs, where he lifted his hat and coat and admired the room which he had put straight that morning.

The journey was outwardly uneventful – he walked eight miles and spoke to three people – but he had a heightened awareness. Colours were vivid, light was luminous. He saw the white and black clouds cover and uncover the sun, and their shadows play over the lanes and hedges, and the sun all over the mountain. He passed houses with hens and geese and ducks outside scraping and barefoot children playing. He bypassed Moneymore along the Minister's Way. The road from Moneymore to Cookstown was busy with people walking and riding bicycles, and there was the occasional pony and trap. At the approach to Cookstown, the noise grew of people calling and talking, of horses clipping over loose stones and pavings, and the phut-phutting one time of a tractor.

His eye was fresh and open and hungry. Nothing was familiar. Men, women and children came out of nowhere to play their bit part in the world. All sizes and shapes, ages and religions, country folk and town folk, some well dressed and some in rags, they were happy and contented and sad and depressed, and in a hurry or not, and each in oblivion was making his own journey for his own purpose, and crisscrossed the other, and didn't see him. They were all the same, interest or none, hope or none, and they walked in pairs, and in families or alone.

The street was a hive of activity. Dull and lively farmers herded their cattle and sheep along the Main Street. They were mostly windbeaten and lean, and each, following his own need, made his way to the market, and each stoical face revealed nothing, and the cattle roared, unused to the town.

Men outside doors leading to dark pub interiors were having their chat, and other men, with no use for the sun, squinted when they came out, and nodded solemnly to their fellow cap-wearing customers. Of their own accord, the doors of dark pubs opened and closed to shy farmers slipping in and out.

Felix looked up Main Street, longest and straightest in Ireland, stretching up the hill with the day's brightness at the end of it, and the small tight horizon of terraced houses at the other end. Businessmen were coming out of Orritor Street. Ponies and traps turned into Molesworth Street. A drunk fell out on the street at the feet of his wife, waiting in all weathers, and she looked at him and admonished him, and he snarled at her. Even for all her vitriol, she still looked weary and helpless, and then a posse of raggedy children came running up to their quarrelling parents, and the saying crossed Felix's mind. 'Him drunk, and the weans drinking water.' Then they turned into Oldtown out of sight.

Farming girls in from the country for the day were large and plump, with big wide faces and big wide eyes, and they carried packages and parcels and baskets, and talked to each other loudly or in whispers, and walked brusquely and roughly as if walking was no matter of grace. They heard the car approach, and looked up, and stared in at the lady and gentleman looking out on Cookstown Main Street, and Felix stared too at the new-fangled machine owned by the Greers of the Sandholes. The excitement over, he walked on down Main Street, past the farm girls walking in the opposite direction, and one of them with auburn hair and large dark eyes stood out as bearing more than a passing resemblance to the stranger woman, but younger and not so large, and he thought to look again, then kept on down Main Street, past the pharmacy and hardware stores, the draper's and grocer's and blacksmith's. He was satisfied with ordinary things.

A couple of mongrel dogs, thin and nervous, ran at each other, and sniffed and licked and panted, and he wondered what they recognised, when his eye was attracted by the improbably large load of hay carried by a passing trailer. As it wobbled uncertainly, Felix was watching to see it capsize when he spied a boy's feet, bare and small, protruding out the top of the hay. Seemingly unconcerned by his precarious position in the world, the boy woke to sit upright and stare down at Felix from his freckled unformed face.

As he walked, Felix looked for Sarah-Ann. He glanced in and out of shops, he stood at the corner of Molesworth Street, he said her name softly. The day was still young. He had a sense of the great plan of the world, and that she would come.

At the top of the street, the Catholic church was filling up for afternoon mass, and others passed and made a sign. A dead cat lay on the kerb and he thought to lift it, but turned instead and walked back to the middle of town where he stopped to light up his pipe and to watch the flat-capped men stream out of the market. Their main business done, they filed out in groups and pairs or alone, and each, pleased or not with the day's perform- ance, made gruff practical conversation, and conceded no more than he had to. 'A good day' or 'A quiet day' was the only clue to the outcomes of personal ambition.

They scattered up Main Street, into Molesworth Street, across Orritor Street in the tribal dance of the market men. Felix watched their different purpose as half went home, and the other half, happy for their day's excuse, went to the pub. He searched for their moral laxity, but they all looked the same, same worn dress, heavy posture, sallow skin. Everywhere was their tempta- tion, dozens of anonymous pubs – without sign, nor name – spaced out along Main Street, their doors dark and ajar to absorb the newcomers who disappeared with a shifty glance and quick shuffle of feet. Others descended into ponderous silence as they crossed over the door, and some, in groups, talked and laughed and made a loud entrance to the pubs owned by Catholics and frequented by Protestants prevented by religion from the trade.

But all sins, pleasures, justifications have their scale, and since the sin is less to drink in the pub than own it and the pleasure greater, the publican happily catered to his mixed custom.

Felix had never been in a pub. As if all his life accustomed, he entered the first he came to. He stooped under its small door and stood aside for two large farmers, smelling of alcohol and tobacco smoke, but their passing didn't change it, it was the pub's smell, and for the second time he lowered his head under the inner doorway. Up to twenty free men, without conscience, sat on small benches, or stood at the bar, or leant against the wall. The bar was no bigger than his own front room, yet there was space enough for each man and his thought, and the atmosphere adjusted imperceptibly to accommodate him. He hesitated about whether to sit on a bench or at the bar, and nodded to pretend he was used to pubs, an old hand, and sat down at the bar. He fixed his eye on the bottles and glasses and mugs stacked up on the shelf, and wondered what to drink, and how to ask for it, but the publican, courteously appreciative of his custom, asked if it's a whiskey, easy as that. The publican pushed across a glass, and mumbled something cheerful to his health. Felix drank, but the first sip, being fire, he had to stop himself screwing up his face, then saw that the procedure was mixing it with water. There was nothing to it, nothing at all, uninitiated to initiated. He had done nothing to draw attention. Drink followed drink, and a man came up behind him.

'Deep in thought?' Felix jumped, he knew the voice. Boyce, windbeaten and sharp-featured, and decked out in his ordinary clothes. Some confused greeting.

'You're out of your normal pastures!'

'Two years since I was in Cookstown.'

'What brings you up? You're not one to change your routine.'

'A bit of business,' said Felix.

'I only called in for the one myself,' said Boyce, whose public persona was brash, but with Boyce there was a private man. No older than himself, Boyce was exhausted, and far away from his moments of high comedy.

'You'd do with getting out of the house more,' he said, and from his vantage point at the bar Felix watched him walk out the pub, and turn at the door, and ask when Felix was going home. Felix nodded and smiled and said he was sorted. That moment Felix felt great warmth for him. After the war, strange things would happen to Boyce. Boyce, who would never set foot outside Mid-Ulster, became the same as war veterans. Their nightmares were his, their horror was his, and he was sick in his heart, like real war veterans, and recorded as one of the last survivors of the Battle of the Somme. In the middle of the night he had fevers and nightmares, and got up to crawl and creep around lanes and hedges, and go on drinking binges in country shabeens where his only companions were true war veterans. That was Tommy boyce who never left Mid-Ulster.

Felix ordered another drink, and fingered his pipe, and filled it up, and thought of his small contracted world, which was only the size of the bridge, and the lane, and the house, and he was glad to be away from it. The drinks were flowing into each other, but his mind's eye was detached from the pub and drifted off in a million directions. What he had imagined is what he had seen – composed and strong at the bridge, but at the other side no one really existed.

He had seen her once, and knew her name second-hand, but he had loved her spirited performance – how she thought nothing of the bridgegatherers, not even them weighing her up like a pig, but had walked her separate way, and had twenty strong men suddenly fixing at their collars and hair and shuffling their legs all as if they could see themselves through her eyes and saw that they needed adjustment. He had loved the spectacle of Biggers plastering down to his head the last fine hair left to him! He rehearsed in his mind her looking at him, all visual and heady and his stomach turned at his heart's memory of it.

And then she had turned and looked him straight and hard in the eye. He almost thought he could see what she saw. A man standing at the bridge same as all the bridgegatherers, all farmers dressed in their Sunday best for the purpose of begrudgingly enjoying the only relaxation and pleasure not prohibited that day. Was that all he was? Lived all his life in the same place, serious as a boy, serious as a man, and with only the bridgemen for company. Was he no different? He was the last of his line, and he read a bit, and at thirty gave up the church for theological reasons, but even that was quiet, modest and ashamed, and he could never have suspected the talk that said that his parents died from the heartbreak of it.

Tired of the barstool, he sat in the empty corner from where he could see the whole bar, and listen, and observe, each time the door opened, the momentary silence, the resumption of talk. After a time, the pub grew darker, and he watched its shadows, and the light his pipe made in it, his dark sanctuary, and he felt the luxurious movement of the pipe, lifting it, and resting it, lifting it, and resting it, and lifting his drink, and the drink's effect.

People walked in and out, and some tried to engage him, but he didn't rise beyond the basic civilities, he ordered more drinks until the pub was a suffused blur, a haze of smoke, and warmth, and comfort, and he knew he showed no sign of the secret that he had never before sat in a pub.

Another whiskey, must have been the eighth, he poured in some water, and was now used to pouring, and had a momentary awareness of his pouring arm, and the body, which was his, sitting solitary and distant in the corner, and the mind, which was his, thinking but detached and separate. But it was his mind and the cynicism was his. It was his cynicism that said thinking all adds up to nothing. That was the voice that rattled over him, and heard thinking rattling on and on, then his head was spinning, turning, he might throw up. He had to summon up all his powers against it, and didn't risk movement for fear of falling down, spinning, like two spinning bodies, the one his father staring up at the ceiling, the other his mother pressing down on the floor, the apron beside her.

A man helped him up, and he stood at the door, and tried hard to think, and some men pointed right, and he started to walk, but remembered and came straight back where he saw a man tall as himself, but his face was a blur, and his face was in the air and sick. 'Where are the men now who answered advertisements in the *News Letter*?' he asked. 'Where are they now?'

Mumblings, that's all he heard, or they said nothing, or some other sombre noise, and then his own voice reverberating like it was someone else's.

'Or the *Irish News*.'

'The Kaiser . . .' he said . . . and saw more faces in the dark, and voices, but they couldn't stop him, he was too lucid.

'War in Europe, and Cookstown exactly the same,' he said, then stumbled up Main Street, and because he was too clear in his mind, he shouted behind him, 'Where are the absent men? War in Europe and Cookstown exactly the same.' He caught the rhythm of words tapping out in his mind, 'War in Cookstown and everything looks exactly the same, and everything happens under the surface, below the level of the eye, out of the way of normality, where normality is the foil for war and men who leave their families to follow advertisements in the *Irish News* and the *News Letter*.' All under the bustle of Cookstown. And under the bustle is the timid whisper of people, who ask where France is, and pronounce Kaiser the way they read it.

And, under the bustle, men sit in dark pubs to change themselves.

Then Heather Gibson stepped up behind him.

'The *Mid*, the *Mid*'s got it all, anything you could want,' he said wantonly, recklessly, chewing up his own small world; here the bridgemen, here the soldiers, here the churchmen, every Wednesday, the local newspaper, the *Mid Ulster Mail* recorded them all. 'Oh I'd never miss it, do you read it yourself? All them advertisements in big writing and joining up?'

'Are you all right?'

'Your country needs you!'

'You're drunk! You great big eejit!'

'Heather Gibson, that's right, it's Heather Gibson.' Out of the whirling world of Cookstown spun the great big girl like a shilling on a table.

'Well, at least you know something!'

'Oh, I know nothing at all! Not a thing! I was just sitting there in the corner minding my own business, and thinking I know nothing at all,' tossed out Felix out of his small world, and out of Heather's, and Tommy's too, when, out of nowhere, in purple, whirled Sarah-Ann O'Malloran.

Felix caught his breath, for there not being enough air in the world for his emotion's great and sudden need and his body's great stored-up soreness. There was only the one breath rooting him to the single spot. 'A right gypsy!' murmured Heather, but he barely heard, he was right up close to Sarah-Ann, with her wide large eyes, startled like a young girl's, and her sensuous mouth, he might have grabbed her. In the tumultuous turmoil of the world, she was perfectly still.

'I'm sorry . . . at the bridge in the purple shawl . . .' He spilled words, he realised he had touched her.

'Town was busy today,' she said, as she'd say to any stranger. Confusion, part disdain. She was trying to cross the road.

'And no rain,' he said, but too fast, like it was only a greeting, or some offhand pleasantry moving by, and insufficient to detain her from the world's greater flow, 'but we need a drop more, rain's what's needed for grass.' He said this half turning to face her, and her still walking. She stopped and turned, and because they blocked the pavement, people had to step into the road. He saw her large face open to the world.

'This time last year . . .' he mumbled, not knowing what he was saying. Anyway, she showed not the slightest feminine interest in the influence of weather on grass, nor the effect she'd had on him randomly. 'I met you before . . . the purple shawl . . .'

'I had to wonder, just a minute, I thought that there was something wrong, like my skirt was on fire, or the wrong way round,' she laughed, thinking he was a bit of a madman. He'd stepped without warning straight out of the corner into her path, then he stopped dead, and she'd made to step into the road, but the road was obstructed, and in the lapse between turning and stopping he was upon her. An odd man. Neither market man, nor gentleman. From his dress you might have thought he fancied himself a cut above the rest, but even that was unsure. Old-fashioned and perfectly pressed, his three-piece suit was from another age, she couldn't put her finger on it. Maybe the cut, maybe the style. The check itself was familiar, but not the Prince of Wales, the only one she knew. Even the shirt. No doubt that it was gleaming white, and perfectly pressed, and starched, but cut so far into his neck she couldn't help noticing his discomfort and the intimate effort behind it. It made her uneasy. Then the bridge dawned on her. Nobody for

miles, then turning the corner, the middle of nowhere, there
they were, a couple dozen men, all she thought of them was that
she had to step through them, no way round them. Apart from
that, nothing else struck her. Dogs barked, a soldier jumped,
men guffawed.

'Does he often jump out from under the bridge?'

'He's restless since the war, and can't settle his head to anything,' said Felix in perfect clarity.

'Except hiding under bridges,' she said sharply, and saw him
cynically. Within the blink of an eye, briefest of timespans, his
face was so accurately reflected upon the contours of her mind
that were she to stare for another hundred years she would learn
no more. His face, unique as every face, the same as every face,
moved a millimetre in the jaw, a fraction in the hairline, instan-
taneously transforming Felix Campbell into the archetypal
Protestant face: the strong jaw and cheekbone, the wide eyes and
high-bridged nose. Her prejudice was devastatingly precise. 'He
gave me a right fright,' she said, and her scathing eye watched
him, and was a scalpel over him. His long wide forehead was
lined and dark from the weather, and stretched up in search of
his hairline; it was big, bare and exposed, and his skin's dry
tautness and dearth of flesh gave his cheeks a sculpted appearance. Two short parallel creases ran deep from the base of his
earlobe.

'Well, you had the make of him on Sunday,' he said, and
Sarah-Ann softened.

'There was some crowd of you. All locals I take it?' she fished
amidst the subtext of men meeting for politics and war all over
the land.

'All locals, we've been meeting there for years . . .'

'And who are you amongst them?'

'Felix Campbell, I suppose that's who I am, I suppose,' he

scoffed, and Sarah-Ann laughed at that rueful construction. 'That day I met you, you had your hair long . . .' he slurred.

'It's still long, I'm just wearing it up,' she laughed, and tossed her head. She had her admirers. Her dark hair fell long to her hips. She knew the effect of a sleight of hand to pile it up, a seductive toss to tumble it. That was her style. She had willed it, crafted it careful as any old master at his self-portrait, or fooling himself, in any case she was aware of her feminine charms.

'I didn't mean you . . .'

'Ah . . .' laughed Sarah-Ann.

'All down your back . . . it comes down all as a piece,' he said, transfixed, and Sarah-Ann smoothed it. As a child, she had watched her grandmother unravel her luxurious long grey hair from under her bonnet, shake it loose, and let it roll down gently, then her grandmother cupped it up and swept it back, transformation in gesture.

'They talked about it at the bridge . . . your hair and they were wondering where you were going, they wanted to know, it's not often a woman on her own walks through.'

'But not you, you weren't interested?'

'I dreamt about you in your purple shawl,' he stuttered.

He's drunk, she thought. 'You've been to the market,' she said.

'I just wanted to talk to you, that was all, I just wanted to say . . .'

'Well, it's great to meet you and talk to you, I'd better get going,' she said. On parting, she noticed he was hiding *The Times*.

Felix watched where she left him. Then he dandered up Main Street, and with all the time in the world glanced in and out of the tradesmen's shops shutting up for the day, and curious about the dirty industry of the blacksmith's trade and his day's work, repeated daily a lifetime, stopped to watch him, and idly wonder what happened to Heather Gibson.

At dusk, and half drunk, he stood at the back of the house, and looked towards the glen, and watched the sky translucent white and the mountain a bold black line running along the full scope of the sky. During the day he mapped out this world, every step, every landmark, but when night fell he saw that the mountain defined in black, and coloured in black, was not so much a mountain, only a large flat hill. The map of the world was lost.

9

Main Street, Cookstown

*I*rish history is always the same. Two sides, one Protestant, one Catholic, fearing defeat in the other's advancement. All the rest, for those who have lived it, for those who have not, the military tactics, battles, wars, the plethora of a nation's history, is mere detail converging to this one point of a religious assimilation that never took hold. To be born Protestant or Catholic in Ireland, almost always, with the rare relevant statistic, sets the course of a man's political identity.

In 1916, and for their own reasons, both sides had sent volunteers to the war; Ulster Protestants because they wished to morally oblige the British government to withdraw its plans for Home Rule; Nationalists because they wished to secure the opposite.

Frank Duffy joined. Why he did was more out of economic necessity than political motivation, of which he could be justly accused of possessing none, or almost none. With a wife and fourteen children, Frank had sufficient to occupy him, and reason enough to conscribe, and opportunity, like everyone else, to die as soon as he reached the fields of France. That is promptly what he did. So Frank had a short war, and unlike Tommy Boyce, Geordie Biggers and Felix Campbell, didn't live long enough to know of its long prosecution or his Catholic community's increasing hostility to it.

He left behind a wife, Sarah-Ann, who, when he left, was not so much the stripling lass he had married but more a mother and wife borne down by fourteen children and tied to the domestic roles she sometimes whimsically and pointlessly rebelled against, since there was no escaping them. Looking over his shoulder, the departing soldier could feel content that the situation he left behind would be much the same as the one to which he returned.

For Frank was not a jealous man. He was steady, and slow to anger, and calm in a crisis. That his wife was thought by some a silly frippery creature only made him laugh. As far as he was concerned, her reputation, built on flimsy grounds, was nothing more than that she walked in winter without a coat. But perhaps her neighbours had a point. To see a bare pair of legs on a bleak winter's day in Cookstown is indeed a spectacle. For those who don't know, Cookstown is like this. The longest barest widest street runs down the hill from Moneymore Road to the Fair Hill without shelter anywhere. If you stand on one end, you can see straight a half a mile in front of you and know there's another half-mile over the brow of the hill. When the wind blows, it whistles straight down it, and those in winter who venture along it are sensibly dressed in coats and boots and hats, and the children you meet are attired in various layers that they never take off. This is how it should be. Anything else, for the sensible person, wrapped against the elements, sliding along on the Main Street snow, or bearing against the lashing rain, is an affront. So to Sarah-Ann. It seemed the worse the day, the less she wore; on cold wintry days, she dressed in skimpy dresses, and on wet blustery days, she wore too long skirts, which dragged along in the puddles, and for working around the house, tending hens and geese, she wore her best finery. She was never what is called appropriately dressed. Not even for church. 'What the hell's she wearing now?' was the common refrain when, for mass, she turned up in some devil's mad outfit, or something tight-fitting, or some big hat. It didn't change as she grew older. If anything, as the winters marched on, and the children came, one after the other, Sarah-Ann's hems grew shorter, and her legs got barer. Each and every Saturday, snow or shine, attired in the outfit she had put together the hour before, Sarah-Ann walked Main Street as others walk the grand boulevards of Paris. She had everything to see, and everything to savour, and everything to hope for. She was blessed that way. Her father too. When he was living, he relished the street. Dressed in flamboyant clothes, he cut a fantastical sight, with his waistcoats adorned with colourful flowers off women's aprons, and patches of coloured quilt, and bright bold buttons. He was an incurable exhibitionist, in contrast to his wife, who, as staid in dress as he was eccentric, as inward in character as he was outward, was in every way conceived for his opposite. This shadow of a husband's dress might have been a gloomy place, but Sarah-Ann's mother, during the time that she loved him, was happy to hide behind him, and during the time that she didn't, didn't care. Theresa O'Malloran had her religion, and from her superior vantage point viewed with equanimity her husband's preposterous figure.

But her daughter sorely tested her. Even when widowed, Sarah-Ann wouldn't don the traditional mourning dress or experiment with any possibility of black. Where black was concerned, she wouldn't be seen dead in it.

Theresa could have blamed herself. Somewhere, here and there, came creeping in the doubt. How could she have encouraged, or discouraged, her daughter's spiritual poverty?

10

The secret life of a bigamist

On the Sunday, Felix leant against the bridge, and squinted up his eyes, and tried to concentrate on the banter between Biggers and Boyce and old Jimmy, who were outwitting each other on the subject of Creation.

'Sure if we came from monkeys, we'd all look like Jimmy!' said Boyce, gesturing towards the old man.

'Aye, see what you'll look like at my age, if you ever make it!' snarled Jimmy out of his scraggy sloppy face and thick hanging skin, and not one of them, no matter how old he lived, could ever imagine he would look remotely like Jimmy.

'Aye, started out as monkeys, and then over a long, long time turned into the likes of us,' said Biggers restating the fairytale, and Felix smiled, and said nothing. His mouth was dry as a fig, his head hollow, and his stomach in distant motion.

'I hate that aul talk about monkeys and men,' snapped Jimmy, unaware that his pockmarked warted appearance took him beyond the normal human empathies.

'It happened very, very slowly, like nothing you could see over a thousand years,' lectured Biggers, who seemed to believe they would grasp the idea by their senses.

'It was 'specially slow here!'

'Old Geordie had a monkey, and I swear it looked like him.'

'That proves it!'

'And a horse that looked like his wife,' fired Boyce deadpan.

'There'll never be a science clever enough for wives,' retorted Biggers, comfortable with the inconsistencies of evolution and women.

'Monkeys'd well explain the wickedness of Sadie Boyce, the old witch, there's no God in her,' slurred Boyce.

'Monkeys don't kill each other!' observed Biggers to distinguish the viciousness of the cousins' feud.

'I haven't killed her yet!' trumped Boyce. Longstanding and vitriolic, the feud would last as long as they lived, and no one remembered how it started.

'Well, you're well met,' said Biggers, and everyone laughed and knew that in any struggle for survival Sadie, small and frail, would win against the big strong Boyce. 'Aye, there's no fitter than Sadie, and none fitter than you to handle her,' teased Biggers.

'Huh, you're the wise 'un,' shrugged Boyce, 'who doesn't live beside her.'

'I hate that aul talk about men and monkeys,' complained Jimmy who knew about monkeys and a spherical world, but his belief was in the flat ground beneath him.

'It's scientific,' said Biggers, enjoying the commotion he caused.

'Dolly'd better not hear you! She'll have you for blasphemy,' said the young cub Hutchinson, too timid to make his own point.

'And blasphemy it is!' shouted Jimmy, and Felix speculated idly.

'To believe in monkeys would take a far greater act of faith than believing in God,' he mused, and there was a moment's awkwardness when he wished he wasn't so earnest.

'You're wild tired-looking,' remarked Biggers, looking at Felix.

'Aye.'

'The eyes are standing out of your head.'

'You'd flatter a man.'

'And the colour of you!'

'I'm bright enough.'

'You look like a puff would blow right through you.'

'I'm secure on the ground.'

'Aye, well watch what you're eating when you're run down like that,' said Biggers.

'The feeds men used to eat after a day's ploughing, they couldn't eat them now,' lamented Jimmy, for whom everything good had occurred fifty years before. Biggers ignored him.

'The Gibsons were up,' he said. Statement. Cross-examination. Accusation.

'She was a friend to my mother,' deflected Felix, and wondered what Biggers knew.

'That Heather's a big strapping girl.'

'I hadn't seen her in years but she's grown up a nice girl,' said Felix, more than Biggers expected, and went on. 'Aye, Heather Gibson's a lovely girl, a handsome good-looking girl,' said Felix, so unexpectedly saying it, smiling so knowingly open towards him that had Biggers not had all his armour he would have quickened at Felix's spinning him along.

'Aye, she's grew up a right nice girl, but not the swell of the O'Malloran woman who came through,' smirked Biggers, who normally played a subtler game.

'Who?' asked Felix, but his question admitted only weakness.

'Aye, you know her surely,' accused Biggers, and Felix nodded his head to deny wanting anything in a place where wanting anything was a sin.

'Aye, we thought you'd have seen her on the glen road last Sunday,' taunted Biggers, whose impressions were fast fluid as quicksilver, and fixed stubborn as any great stone.

'The water's high,' said Felix, turning brusquely and looking over the bridge. He had never known Biggers so blatant or rash.

'Aye, high,' grunted Biggers.

'A right gypsy . . . All them earrings and fancy clothes dressed up like a gypsy,' sneered Jimmy Smyth.

'Any more word what she was up for?' asked Boyce, mock innocent of the contest between Felix and Biggers.

'After Archie's, no doubt about it,' speculated Boyce.

'Looking over the place before she goes to see it.'

'Aye, she'll be back up to see Archie,' said Boyce, and Felix pictured it clearly . . . Archie – old, housebound, a man who'd never done anything he'd not always done, seated in his own chair, directing her to the guest chair to tell her about the farm, how there'd be no selling it, nor splitting it, nor any Boyce ever allowed on it. So that's what drew her, he thought. She appeared out of nowhere, knew no one, no one knew her. Guest and host were worlds apart, seemed what brought them together was a small bit of land.

'Or Sean Boyd?' mocked Biggers.

'Him who's married all them women all over the country and has houses all round the place, and was always going round pretending he was somebody, and saying he was from Portrush when really he was from Fermanagh?'

'If he'd married my wife, he'd have been keener to stick with the law!' quipped Stuarty Gibson.

'One's a just punishment, but six wives is a self-immolisation.'

'Immolation,' corrected Biggers.

'Them Catholics have all the big words.'

'They've bigger sins,' smiled Biggers, pleased with his wit.

'To marry the once should tell any man.'

'He kept women all over the country.'

'He'll plead insanity.'

'Hiding that you're from Fermanagh'll stand against him.'

'They'd think only a sane man would cover it.'

'I never met anybody good that came out of it.'

'Sure, you never met anybody.'

'Now when I think of it, I seen him flirting around,'

'And to think that she was on the way to see him!' threw in Biggers.

'Aye, and her a good-looking girl!' said another unable to fathom the motives and fortunes of good-looking girls.

'That's the one that'll fall for a rogue,' said Jimmy wisely, and Felix, who had never much thought about the tastes and fates of good-looking women, wondered if it was true.

'A real dark horse always moving around and looking suspicious, and I always said all that moving around was suspicious, but I still can't think that he had it in him,' said Biggers but Boyce interrupted him, 'He was the most goddamned useless trumped-up dealer that God ever put amongst cattle, and always bragging and boasting and blowing about going here and there, and all over the other place, and all the amount of money he was making, when you'd know for a fact that there's no money with a man that talks that much and that long, and that blows his own trumpet,' poured out Boyce, who must have been left with some sort of debt.

'Sure you were the greatest of friends, and always doing business,' corrected Biggers.

'No more than the rest of you, anyway, sure, who else was there?'

'He owes him money,' sniped Jimmy.

'He owes me no money!' snapped Boyce.

'You didn't know you were funding a harem!' Jimmy slapped his leg.

'And always wearing that same suit,' added Boyce accusingly, which prompted Biggers' prolific knowledge of Sean Boyd's wardrobe, how he'd organised and maintained it, how he'd located and replicated it, and how his wives had lived in continual and happy marvel at the meticulous and apparently effortless manner in which Sean Boyd presented himself. Sean Boyd's wardrobe was the symptom of strange and extreme character. It was the key to his philandering. Only one among them worried about clothes.

'Only Campbell would have given him a run for his money,' laughed Biggers, and Felix looked at him, and saw the pitted Biggers eyes, and the Biggers snout drawn out and curved, and thought how the Biggers were a bad-looking sort with their long thin foreheads, and cheeks squared out into jutting wide jaws, and their thick short necks. Their only fineness was their eyes, which looked out wistfully from pugilistic faces. The Biggers aged young.

'Aye, we'll be looking out for signs!'

'That'll soon wear you down,' snapped Felix.

'A walk to Moneymore's a lonely walk with no woman at the end of it.'

'A lonely walk!'

'A nice comely woman would brighten up Ballymully.'

'Books is no use in the bed.'

'Aye, all them reading of books was what has you putting it off this long.'

'Johnny Kelly went for years and years protesting that he'd never have a woman around him, and outlived the two wives.'

'I always said all that moving about was odd,' pondered old Jimmy.

'Aye, kept them all over the country,' intoned Boyce, the seventh time he said it for the great satisfaction he derived from it.

'The meek will inherit the earth,' said Stuarty Gibson piously but in a low voice, sensitive to the fact that nobody listened.

'Well, she'll not be around today, it was Sean Boyd she was after,' concluded Biggers, satisfied to revive into imagination the flagging story of Sean Boyd.

'You mean Sarah-Ann O'Malloran?'

Felix had only now connected the two.

'Aye, the very one we were talking about,' said Biggers, in quiet celebration of his own mysterious mastery of fact.

'How do you know?' asked Felix.

'Aw now, no sources,' said Biggers, who believed himself possessed of some latent unworldly wisdom, and Felix shuddered at the lack of grace startling even for Biggers.

'Aye, her that walked through us?!' said Boyce intrigued by his own role in the affair.

'Just the last week!'

'With the skirt and the shawl.'

'Swanking through like a gypsy!'

'And me thinking she'd be back today!'

'Aye, up to Monaghans!'

'You'd never know what's going on under your very nose.'

'Well, we know now what she was getting at Monaghans!'

'She's seen him every Sunday the last year, but only now at Monaghans,' revealed Biggers, who had long observed the all too human instinct to blurt out. He had no such inclination; he only looked like a pig tossing truffles carelessly over its head, in truth he plotted out every effect, timing and delivery, and had carefully timed his revelation about Sarah-Ann O'Malloran.

'Well, you'd never know what you're looking at!' said Jimmy Smyth, who had no advantage to look at himself.

'The one woman in Ireland he wasn't married to!' exclaimed Biggers, who knew the storyteller is more than spectator.

'And her walking through us on the way to him! Who'd have believed it?' they asked. The sexual way she walked through them connected them directly.

'How do you know?' asked Felix, his dissembled heart quickening.

'Even that day when she came round I knew she was after him, and her the only woman in the country not married to him!' declared Biggers, who knew time would cast his shadow forever. Felix Campbell would never escape. 'Bigamy, they call it. Aye, that's what it's called. Bigamy!' he said, and the word's drama echoed round the bridge. Felix couldn't bring himself to say it was polygamy.

'A secret life,' pronounced Biggers. The bridgegatherers listened in awe.

With his parallel lives, Sean Boyd had rarely had time to be bored or sad or desperate. He had moved constantly, worked constantly, and loved constantly, all according to a well-orchestrated routine that had him in a different destination each day of the week,

Omagh on Monday, Pomeroy on Tuesday, etc., and in a different abode each day of the week; on Wednesdays it was the strong arms of Martha, and on Thursdays the gentler touch of Annie. Sophie's embrace got him through Fridays. His day off was Sunday, but since he spent it with his mistress, this, the most obvious day for boredom and depression, was filled up.

The constant in his life had been cattle, which he'd transported in trains all over the country or shipped to England and made money at it. When he'd had time to think, it was about the condition, markets and prices of cattle, but men have expended their life's thought on much less, and worried about much less than the progress of bovine creatures on ships bound for Liverpool. He spoke with a soft-drawl accent that he said was Portrush but sounded southern, and because he was different women found him attractive. Whether or not he'd chosen it deliberately, the peripatetic lifestyle was the perfect foil.

His tall rangy body was weathered and hardened, and his eyes squinted narrowly from being all his life outdoors, and his exoticism was the aura of a man who moves through places where people stay still. No one travelled more than ten miles. The land bound them, the work bound them, and the need for security held them in its grip and liberated them from the need to be anywhere other than where God put them. Not Sean Boyd. He was restless, and could happily pass a night out of his own bed and rise in the morning to unfamiliar noises, smells, impressions and not be oppressed by their strangeness. Ordinary life stood still, and he passed through. With his wry independent eye and easy unobtrusive manner, he gained the trust of farmers who sold him their cattle and waited for him to falter from the unnatural life he led.

His only baggage was the story of his life, which he had long ago contrived and at times believed, a trick of the mind that had helped him to relate with conviction that he'd been born in Portrush, and that soon after his birth his mother and father had died from typhoid (he sometimes said tuberculosis). He'd been raised by a neighbour, but at the age of fourteen had run away and found work on a beef farm at Bangor.

Upon these bare facts he had built his life of duplicity, and over the years had honed them into a fascinating pattern of wit, wonder and pathos, in short, into a tale to satisfy the indomitable curiosity of women for whom no aspect of his life was considered sacred once he professed his love. With the full guile of an Irish lover and liar, he had made a response appropriate to all sorts of proposition, theory, scenario, and out of improvised response had spun a cohesive story to oblige beyond duty his wives' feminine curiosity. That was his story's great success – it was transferable between wives.

He had travelled light. Everywhere he had kept a wardrobe, and everywhere his wardrobe was an exact replica of all his other wardrobes, the same shirts, the same trousers, the same waistcoats. With two of each of these items in each wardrobe, and carrying nothing, he had moved freely around the country, and, after long absences, had returned to his homes in much the same respectable condition in which he had left them. To his neat and fastidious character his wives attributed the smoothness of collars that had supposedly been to England and back without the attentions of an iron.

At the beginning of his trial, he had hinted that he sometimes confused his real life (born in Fermanagh, his parents still living, his elder brother got the farm) with his fabricated story, but cross-examination revealed that Sean Boyd had no certainty of mind. He was convinced of everything, sure of nothing, and the simplest question flummoxed him. The story that had for so long held together diverse women and cattle deals all over the country could stand no light, the first flicker of which reduced him to terror. For foolishly imagining it to be nothing, Sean Boyd had lost his own history.

Craving more and more love had been Sean Boyd's antidote to ageing, to the slow drip of life that dripped, dripped even when he was frantically busy. In the arms of different lovers he had clung to the moment, cherished it because soon it would be over, and consoled himself with the knowledge that he would soon be in the arms of another. He was found out, and by the time he made his claim in court that a man's life story is of no importance it was only empty rhetoric, a futile clutching after straws. The ordinary pains were his after all, the shame and the anguish.

When Sarah-Ann met him, she'd had an inkling that Sean Boyd lived a secret life, but she couldn't have imagined, no one did, that his secret was living over the same dead life. Sean Boyd had seemed composed and assured, intelligent and expressive, but personality is a dull barometer of the spirit and Sean's was merely the flicker of dead emotions with only repetition for depth and ceaseless situation for spectrum. His secret life did not transcend life's ordinary sorrows and despairs. He was in continual flux, and six women away from mortality.

'That's the rain on,' said Biggers, and Felix left without another word.

11

A small wrist

Sarah-Ann's friend Rosey Bradley said that it must have been greed for Sean Boyd to have wanted that many wives. Because he could deny himself nothing, and admit himself nothing, he'd sought out woman after woman, cattle deal after deal. This explanation, sound as it was, was no comfort to Sarah-Ann, who had to disintegrate in her heart the exotic impression he had made there. When the story first broke, she'd pretended she'd never met him, and heard him described as that tall sly lanky cattle dealer who went around the country inflating prices. He'd been everywhere, doing everything to everybody, and none of it was good, and she'd listened with an ironic smile, and tried to reconcile what she heard with what she felt.

She had met him at Monaghan's, and their friendship had grown out of his intense manner and her longing to do something different. Sean Boyd had fitted that bill. She couldn't have known his intensity was the effort of co-ordinating diverse wives with lucrative cattle deals. That was his intensity, a man who had married six times because it seemed the transaction's natural conclusion.

Now every night she dreamt for what seemed like a lifetime. Frank, her husband, came back from the war, he came marching up the hill, and was huge against it. Next thing he was in the room saying about the long bloody war, and it wasn't clear whether it was the war in Europe, or to do with just the two of them. Then he saw Sean Boyd, and the shock on his face, and the dream went on and on, every feeling and nuance like a whole bloody life had to be lived every time she went to bed.

Her involvement in life's ebb and flow had left little time for the sort of quiet contemplation that gives great weight to deliberation and choice; the death of Frank and the fast demise of Sean Boyd were the first times she took stock, and she was angry. All the fault and hurt and pain in the world lay tightly within the frame of Sean Boyd.

But it didn't last. She talked too much to Rosey Bradley, and lay in bed, and argued and fought with her mother, and got over it. The exigencies of her physical world – work, Cookstown, children – were already settled, they mapped out the day in tending and minding and caring, and so she satisfied herself to say that she never foresaw a mistake until it was made. She was so funny to herself being so much in the whirl of the world, spinning and tossing and whirling, and coming here and there undone by its traps and guises.

Rosey came every week, and said how easy it would have been if he'd never gone away, and Sarah-Ann agreed. It should have been easier. It shouldn't have been Sean Boyd and Frank marching on hills.

'I've made my bed, I'll have to lie in it.'

'And a bawdy bed it is!' thumped Rosey.

'You're one to talk.'

'A big bawdy bed.'

'You'll give yourself a rupture by your amusement at everybody else's misfortune.'

'What else do I have to cheer myself up?' said Rosey. 'You look like you haven't slept for weeks.'

'I've done nothing but,' said Sarah-Ann, who lay in bed with the curtains open to the daylight, and looked out the window past the curtains, which were old and faded from the imperceptible influence of light that had taken away their colour wherever colour goes, and she fancied light faded her too, slow, slow, imperceptible. No one sees the plough rusting, nor the picture fading, only the result, but Sarah-Ann could feel the process, and remembered old Meta Bell, who kept her curtains drawn against light's pernicious damage on her small prized furniture, and once held Sarah-Ann's wrist up to the oil lamp to measure it, and didn't know what to make of such a small wrist on such a large girl.

Sarah-Ann had always been big. As a girl, she had looked far bigger than children her own age, but as the years progressed, the differential narrowed; she looked thirteen years to their ten, and she began to lose her rabbit proportions. Her large cubic head ceased growing whilst everything else moved on apace, her legs and arms lengthened, and her ludicrously tiny hands filled out.

From no age, she told stories. In the Irish tradition, she confused the past with the present, the dead with the living, and worse, her stories had only one ending. That was the fault of Sarah-Ann's stories; bogged down in detail, then everybody died.

At five, she expressed her sympathies on account of black Ned's mother just dead.

'She's better where she is,' she said.

'Out of the mouths of babes,' said Ned. Black after his hair, he patted her head.

'Better where she is,' she said, and pranced across the bare earthen floor. She was heavily dressed in a ragged assortment of clothes.

'Jigging and prancing,' mimicked Sarah-Ann as her mother and father jumped up, ill tempered at their disturbance. 'There she's crying,' said black Ned half an hour later.

Next door, Sarah-Ann lay at the bottom of the bed with her feet touching her brothers and sisters, and her head half out, and her body swathed in thick heavy clothes, and she felt the comfort and rhythm of crying, which was her sole singular activity; huge solitary tears, red-faced and sobbing, and she cried effortlessly over two or three hours. Who knew why she cried? Who would reduce the infinite intricacies of childhood? Her mother and father did not. From children they only expected survival.

But from the perspective of childhood, adults are giants; they control certainties and proofs, turn the day and the night, check atmospheres and tensions. Sarah-Ann knew her father was the strongest, tallest man in the country, and his hay the finest and best, and she knew her mother was the greatest of walkers. Only in fiction and childhood is life assured.

When she started school, she was more in step with the world, which is just as well for there's no end to the cruelty for a girl with a very large head. Her huge body, and large undeveloped mind, sat in a very small room in a very small town in the centre of a very small country, and she was surrounded by a thick brooding body of children, each equidistantly spaced one from the other behind ink wells and desks. She stuck up her hand,

God knows where her hand came from, and spoke, God knows where her voice came from, and accused the teacher, God knows of what she accused her, after which she said she had no more use for schooling and the teacher said the same thing.

By the time of her confirmation she had straightened out, and, big as she was, she looked normal, and didn't talk so much. The Irish love talkers as long as they say what they want to hear, and over time Sarah-Ann mastered this well. As she grew up, less what she said was her own, and more was what they wanted to hear. Anyway she had nothing new to say about religion, she knew you're just born with it; it's like skin.

At the age of thirteen, she went into service in the big house in Cookstown, and was placed under the direction of the house-keeper Mrs Kennedy, a distant and vague woman to whom you had to speak three times: the first to attract her attention, the second to convey the general meaning, and the third to com-municate. Via this convoluted process, Sarah-Ann learnt her trade and the benefit of rising at a certain hour, and its boredom and emptiness.

In the family tradition, she walked each Saturday to her mother's. She brought money, and relaxed with her family, who were increasingly receptive to her stories now that she was out in the world and no longer just plain Sarah-Ann chittering and chat-tering. They thrived and trilled on her tales, especially those of Dorothea Antonia Cunyingham, who was Sarah-Ann's mistress and possessed of a dozen white poodles all curly and groomed, and cuddled up to their lady, and yapping round gardens. Sarah-Ann imitated their owner squeaking along beside them. 'Yes, Dorothea, I would have thought so,' squealed her friend and, 'No, Lady Edith, the dogs and sun will weaken us.' Sarah-Ann mim-icked well, and left the impression that ladies of fine houses spend their days walking poodles back and forth over lawns, but Sarah-

Ann couldn't have sworn it. During her days as a laundry maid, she only ever saw poodles the once, and those two grey sickly specimens clung timidly to their owners, yelping and crying, but who knows, there weren't more that were soft and beautiful and white? Certainly Sarah-Ann didn't; she had no view from the basement where laundries are so often located.

Whatever the case, poodles and their uselessness became the O'Mallorans' deepest association with big houses, and were so confused down the generations that the gravest injustice was at times absurdly located in those most innocuous creatures.

At fifteen, Sarah-Ann met Frank Duffy at the market. He was around twenty, and noticed her by her intense dark concentration and her large firm size. He sidled up and asked if she was well, and she said she was, and looked him up and down, at his bicycle clips at his ankles and arms. Looking costs nothing.

'You're well clipped up,' she said, and his metal clips glinted. He took one off and gave it to her.

'I've no bicycle,' she said, but he offered her his.

'I don't know how to work it.'

'I'll show you.'

'Suppose there's no harm.'

'You've good-looking hair,' said Frank with his newfound ability to flatter. It was easy standing in Cookstown with a summer breeze blowing against his neck and legs.

'Milk,' she replied, and touched her long thick auburn hair shining thirty shades in the sun.

'What has that to do with it?' he asked with his eye's practised twinkle.

'Makes it grow,' said Sarah-Ann, 'and brushing.'

'What a notion,' laughed Frank, who was small, and pale, and lively, and came from the townland of Plumbridge.

'I know nothing about the place, or anybody in it,' she said, but Frank didn't care. His taste was large women. Distance didn't worry him, he had a bicycle.

'You're fearless,' she laughed.

Sarah-Ann had the common dream: to love and be loved. Imagining this to be simple, she'd married Frank as the conclusion to whatever small struggle had marked her first fifteen years. There is always some struggle into identity, and Sarah-Ann's choice was the entirely ordinary one. And perfectly natural. More so, it was a triumph. Many who viewed the comparatively normal-looking fifteen-year-old searched in her for the trace of the child with the very large head, or even the Sarah-Ann of ten years old, who was so gangly awkward she stood amongst all the confirmation children as a duck amongst swans. She wore a white dress that split up her legs into stumps so thick their appearance disturbed her mother, who experimented with raising and lowering her hem to disguise them. For all her efforts, hems could achieve nothing nature had not intended. So even a woman equipped with a good eye and a keen thread may be overwhelmed, so the overwhelming defeat by nature, too bad. Sarah-Ann's mother was not the type to lie down and accept what came her way; she was a fighter and turned her efforts to the practical. Sarah-Ann would learn her confirmation better than any other girl; when she spoke she would shine. Who knows but this may have been the starting point for the young girl's burgeoning confidence? Who knows what small drop of water on the head of a ten-year-old girl may bring to life? There, that day, standing amongst all the other girls Sarah-Ann had a sense that she was distinct from everyone around her. She was not Frances Murphy standing behind her, nor Bernie beside her, nor Philomena in front. She was Sarah-Ann O'Malloran. That was who she was. The transformation happened so imperceptibly no one could have said one day she was like this, one day like that, but perhaps one of her acquaintances, someone who lived alongside her, one of the neighbours, a casual observer, remarked secretly into themselves the change that had occurred in her. That SOMEONE notices is an abiding need. Perhaps then with our audience, imaginary or real, we can bear anything.

True, Sarah-Ann, like many young girls, played out in her head a series of dramas and fantasies with her at their centre. For love, nothing less, she married Frank. The marriage took place in a parish church just outside Cookstown. In just ten minutes she was bound to Frank Duffy. He was a good lad. He had a bike, and on the day of the wedding they cycled for miles with Sarah-Ann on the handlebars and Frank pedalling along carefree and happy. That was a great day and a wonderful start. Oh, for a wonderful wedding when you're free, happy and beautiful. Sarah-Ann wore a pale pink dress with flowers pinned on to the neckline and more flowers pinned at the hemline. She held tight on to Frank. She lifted her head high then threw it back into the soft gentle air of an August afternoon with its rarefied atmosphere of a wedding and the start of all dreams. They picked dog daisies at the side of the road. They stopped the bike at the side of the river in the meadow, they lay down at its banks and dipped their hands in the water and felt it flow through their fingers. The day showed no sign of its end. Perhaps it had none. The day would go on and on, the sun would shine forever, the birds would sing, the trees would move gently, the river waters would flow constantly. As Sarah-Ann and Frank frolicked carefree by the banks of the river, they believed the day would never end, it would live in them forever. It would live forever in Frank, who died anonymous somewhere in France, and it lived forever in Sarah-Ann. On their wedding day without end Frank said that the purpose of life was to be good. Sarah-Ann realised that this too was her dearest wish. What better than to try to be something bigger than herself, what better than to escape from her small enclosed shell? So she and Frank cycled in harmony. The day was already chilling, the sun descending, the air sharpening. She and Frank leant against a gate to watch its demise. 'Everything you said about your bike was right,' sighed Sarah-Ann. At his parents' they ate some bread and bacon and cheese quietly at a dark corner of the table. They ate everything his mother had laid out for them. 'If I'd known I'd have made you more,' she said before retiring, her husband shuffling behind her. 'That was embarrassing,' said Sarah-Ann. 'You'll get used to it,' teased Frank. It had been the most perfect wedding day. The girl with the too large arms and the too large legs trussed up in her confirmation dress receded from view. How big she had been, how ungainly. Perhaps her wedding day was a day to put it behind her. The arms she glimpsed in confirmation swathed in white, the legs she glimpsed in confirmation hemmed in white, these were her arms, these were her legs, she felt the power roused in her.

She and Frank had fourteen children.

The first eight were boys, a coincidence of gender that caused the young parents to believe they'd no talent for girls. The birth of Mary confounded their wonder, and the soon soft complacency of adults set in. Within days of her birth, Frank and Sarah-Ann ridiculed themselves for believing there was anything to girls. By dint of her sex, timing – eight boys before and five girls after – Mary was the biggest Duffy girl, and was destined to seventy years of rearing and weaning, tending and nursing, and no children herself. Only once did she plan her escape. One time she thought she'd go to America.

By the time the last girls were born, the older children were leaving home, and said they hardly knew the younger ones, and the younger ones said the same thing, and that they were really two families.

Whatever anyone says, fourteen is a litter, a pack. Everything is collective, each experience shared. All emotion is compressed, distorted. Anger reverberates, jealousy smoulders, temper ricochets. This can't be exaggerated. The physicality, noise, fighting, screaming, crying, laughing, talking, defecating, pissing, eating, farting, burping, beating, drinking, hating are boundless. The first family lived without precedent, model, rule, etiquette, standard. The trauma of the first relationship between the first mother and father, the first daughter and mother, the first father and son, the first brother and sister. These were the first siblings.

Patrick was the eldest. He became a labourer and never learnt reading. Young, he always walked the lane sidestepping the puddles, his toes on the pebbles and his mother beside him telling him about her own mother walking.

Connaill was born a year later. He left Ireland at eighteen, the last that was heard of him.

Brian was the third. He became a Donegal fisherman, and also his sons, but not their sons. During this pregnancy, Sarah-Ann positively bloomed; her pale childhood skin turned translucent white, and her black, black hair fell majestically down her long straight back, and her very large head assumed the most delicate proportions. By the age of nineteen, and a mother of three, she was considered a magnificent woman, especially when pregnant.

Sean was the fourth. He went to labour for a farmer in Moneyneena, and married Cherry, the farmer's lovely daughter. They had three boys called Pat. No matter their christening, Moneyneena men answer to Pat.

Francis was the fifth son. He became a cattle dealer like his grandfather and great-grandfather before him.

The sixth was Joe, who was ill all his life from unspecified sicknesses.

The seventh was Johnny. He left young for America.

Seamus was the youngest son. At nineteen, he married Molly Devlin.

Mary was the eldest girl. She lived to over a hundred.

Annie was the second.

Katie, the third, married a Methodist pastor from Dublin. She had three sons and a daughter.

Josie married a wealthy man and left her family behind her.

Betty and Therese were the youngest.

Within all that chaos and motherhood, Sarah-Ann had turned her flaws to advantage, had skilfully willed herself to beauty. Her dark eyes transformed to black diamonds, and her huge graceless body turned to strength and form and beauty. Sarah-Ann was that hungrily ambitious.

Over time the flow of children dried up.

How else to mark time?

How to measure out the dull minute with nothing to do, the slow minute slowly accumulating itself to an hour and a day, a birth and a death? If we could at some single moment experience the full chain of human existence, birth unto birth, child unto child, mother unto mother, might our separation dissolve, our boundary fade, our divide disintegrate?

Time is free; neither birth nor death distracts it, neither action nor stillness moves it, shadow and light do not form it. If we could experience the full chain of human existence, might we confound and deny it?

Sarah-Ann felt time once, measured it on a waterwheel, turning in the one time the one place.

At thirty-seven she imagined she'd never again get involved in life, and never again with a man.

12

Mad black darkness

The next week on the Sunday Felix got ready for the bridge. Biggers pronouncing, Boyce boasting, the bridge was always the same. Felix walked out the door, and over the yard, and opened the gate into the field where the cattle stood lethargically watching. The field was hard and dry and good for walking, and too hard for grass. He walked to the top, where he sat down and looked over the glen.

Right until that point he had intended to go to the bridge, but in the simplest of movements, the single step, he slid over the top, and disappeared into the undergrowth, and was sliding, sliding all the way to the bottom, and over the stile. The glen was dark and heavy, its gradient was steep, he slipped controlled to the bottom, and made across the meadow, then clambered up through the bank's ferns, bracken and grasses. He was there. On the glen road. Trees grew up the sides of it, and grass up the middle of it, it was gravel and muck, it was bending and winding along the contours of the glen. Felix's aspect changed utterly. With time to appreciate everything, he at once focused on the ground and all its minutiae, and on the glen and all its expanse, and nothing, big nor small, escaped him. He relished light and air, and the faint sun on his face, and at the waterfall stopped and admired its great volume of water cascading forever, tumbling and turning over the high rock, and made his observations of rainfall, and the erosion of rocks. From these brief unstructured reflections he moved along the glen road. At Williams' he turned up the steep path until, apparently satisfied with his location, he placed a foot on Williams' gate and hung his arms nonchalantly over it. The cows came up to the gate, and nuzzled it, and blew warm visible breath into the fresh spring air.

To warm himself, he rubbed his hands, and flailed his arms, and paced back and forth over a small space, no waste or extravagance of movement. A big man, he moved small, measuring out space as the precious thing it is.

The glen road was empty. The glen church, the Baptist church of his childhood, was over. Unlikely there'd be anybody, he thought, sure there'd be nobody at this time, and it near dark. He became used to staring at the trees, and the empty road, and the stream trickling silently. He became used to staring at nothing, and he was thinking about nothing, except maybe justifying with the inbred detachment of Campbells, the unusual circumstance in which he found himself. There he was sitting waiting for her to come, and her not coming at all! This was the essence of his thought, although in his mind its configuration was different: not that likely she'd be coming, he thought, not that likely, sure it didn't matter, he thought, for all else he'd be doing, for all else he'd be doing, he was as well sitting around doing nothing.

Each line of his internal argument was rooted with the long accumulation of pessimism, so acute it was beyond hope and despair. He didn't blink when she came round the corner, a sole figure on the road, just watched her, his eyes transfixed at the motion of her. After staring so long at the bare road – so strange for something to be on it – he half wondered for a second if he'd imagined her. Before when he saw her, she was large and bright and colourful, but from this height she was small and drably dressed, and walked so purposefully he had no time to study her. He sat for a few minutes staring at where she'd been, and where she'd gone, just a transitory image, a memory as vague as watching a cloud forming and dissipating, and then he got up, and saw that all the light in the world was sheltering on the glen's small horizon, and all the mad black darkness covered the rest of it.

He walked home at breakneck speed, and where possible took short cuts, but these physical exertions were in vain. He could not put distance between himself and his actions. He could not suppress the images of his own pathetic figure setting off for the bridge then making the frantic and urgent descent into the glen. He could see the whole skulking movement, all of a piece, underhand and disgusting, then the journey had its own momentum, and he the fool blithely following it. Halfwit. She was making for Sean Boyd. He could see that now. He tried to recapture the sequence of events, what he'd intended and what had happened, but it was the mental equivalent of vigorously shaking one's head to get in wisdom. How he wished he'd dallied the day away in the comfort and safety of the bridgegatherers.

Too late he realised she was just an ordinary woman, a

shadow on the glen road, a speck of humanity as much cursed and blessed as the rest of them. Too late he regained his senses. He was forty-three. An Ulsterman. His background was discipline and hard work. He hankered after nothing, asked for nothing, and the lesson was long imprinted upon him that he who expects little will not be disappointed, and he who damns himself is no more to be pitied than stone.

But even in anguish the mind receives other impressions, and as he approached the house he was angered to find the gable gate open, swinging back and forth, creaking in the wind. He couldn't imagine that he would have left it untied, yet there it was perfectly open, and with a great sense of weariness Felix pulled it behind him, tied it up, and wondered who had been to the house, which one of them, Biggers or Boyce. He thought of them coming up to the house, and noseying around the back, and poking themselves in where they weren't wanted.

He hated anyone around the house. Maggie coming up to launder he felt as an invasion, but the bridgemen made him shudder. The house had been empty, he had been nowhere to be seen. At the intruder's arrival, the dogs would have rushed down the lane, but their bark was bigger than their bite, and when Felix didn't call them back, Biggers or Boyce or whoever it was would have known there was nobody about. Then, with the dogs all agitated and yapping, the trespasser would have boldly made his way to the door, no doubt rapped it, an unusual occurrence in itself, and performed only because he would have had little expectation of answer. Presumably, then, to further legitimise his presence, he called out Felix's name, or shouted hello, until, fully assured there was no one there, he scurried round the back, peered through the scullery window, then all the other windows, and no doubt about it could not have failed to notice the awful state of the place. Full of debris and stale food. Any of the bridgemen, even the least sophisticated to know the cleanliness of a house, would have noticed. It was awful to contemplate. It was evidence of his demise. That's how they would interpret it, and privately deduce that all was not well, and would call, to their argument, the history of a family prone to mysterious and sudden disappearance. Deep down he knew what they thought of the Campbells, that history would not have escaped them. With him absent, and the stranger woman passing through, they'd have said that there was no smoke without fire. That's how irrational they were, how they would sooner disregard the thirty years he'd shown not the slightest interest in women than yield up their wicked suspicion that, at bottom, Felix Campbell was distrustful and sneaky, for which proof, always anticipated, had now been uncovered. Unmarried, odd and superior, he had run straight after her, and hadn't turned up the next week, and had displayed in her presence an uncharacteristic spontaneity by shouting out 'troll' or some other obscurity. That's what he had to swallow, their tut-tutting and categorising him in with Sam Birch.

Opening the front door into the dark porch, a single peg for a coat, a tiny nine-paned window, his Wellingtons in the corner, the expanse of the glen contracted to the small size of the hallway, and to the size of the room, where every physical object, table, dresser and chair was laid out in its original comforting pattern. He lit candles and pulled over the curtains to keep in the heat, and started to tidy; carried scraps of food and dirty crockery and cutlery out to the cold scullery, scrubbed the table. Then, to keep his Sunday clothes good, he folded and placed them in the wardrobe, and with a precise tidy finality shut the door behind him.

With palpitating heart, he opened the Bible. Randomly, it said, 'And I saw an angel coming down out of heaven, having the key to the Abyss and holding in his hand a great chain. He seized the dragon, that ancient serpent, who is the Devil, or Satan, and bound him for a thousand years.' Long ago he had laid down the Bible for the temporal life of sensation and thought, but now sensation and thought offered up nothing, yielded nothing, made no peace. The certainties of childhood had gone. Even the glen house. Only bricks and mortar and stone, and men raising up their voices above the trees of the glen. There Miss Grey instilled in him catechism and God's purpose, there he sang psalms, verses, catechisms with boys, whose whole world was mapped out in psalm and verse and catechism. Gone forever. Giants no longer walked over the earth. Not even Miss Grey. Once she had, in the one small Sunday school, garnered all the world's faith, roused up all its passion and fear to exercise over children powers – of life and death, good and evil, heaven and hell – limitless to infinity, where God is. Children small and receptive. Not a movement Miss Grey didn't orchestrate, not a word she didn't call forth from them. How they'd trembled before her. How they'd memorised by heart, fear, terror every word. They were silent on hard benches. Pliant in rows. The Boyces sat in a tidy row where Miss Grey addressed them collectively. The Martins sat at the front where she could watch them, and Willie Thompson sang loud to make up for sitting alone, with only Sadie, her mother the dwarf, behind him. All wore their Sunday best. All faced the one disciplined direction. Miss Grey, the guardian of young unformed souls, all stretched up to meet her. Now extinct. Her mammoth form no longer walked over the earth. Even then she was an old woman, small and decrepit, a hunchbacked Sunday school mistress. But what a voice! Strung together with faith, fortitude, God, a voice to deny for a psalm the hunchbacked struggle of her existence. Now nothing remained, only waiting and watching, which never yielded any childhood certainty.

His mother, in her pale faded paisleys, small worn clothes, well cared for and tended, had stood in front of the fire then suddenly gasped, convulsed and fell down, with him clinging to keep her in the world. But she was already dead. What part of him was the speechless man witnessing death? Felix watched crows fly and turn in the air, the lightness and freedom of birds, like his body descending into the glen, and he thought then of Maggie cleaning the house, lifting her large thick arms up to the mantelpiece, turning over the heavy porcelain dogs, and her flesh, all the great mass of her absorbed in a porcelain dog, turning it over, cleaning it, and walking slowly back across the room to the grate. The strength and solidity of that large, large female body. Man is not bird, he is bound to the earth.

At night he hardly slept, and in the morning woke up wondering what it was he hoped to forget, and then he remembered.

The defeat of colour, the defeat of hope, Sean Boyd was in the neighbourhood.

He set about brushing up dead ashes and burnt-out coals, which were scattered in front of the hearth, and lifted them into a bucket and brought them outside, and as he swept and stooped and lifted he couldn't ignore his doubts. What was sweeping and stooping and lifting to do with his feeling? What were his practical activities to the day's events? He continued lifting and stooping and cleaning, and as he did his mind wandered back and forth over the glen, and the serenity of walking down the glen road on the bright afternoon, and the anxiety of waiting, and the shame when he saw her. Over and over he retraced the same moments and motions, and in reliving the day's events came the doubts that momentarily but recurringly jabbed at him. What was this world to his despair? What was stooping and lifting and sweeping? He only went through the motions because action was better than no action, and to brush up dead ashes was better than not, and he took the dead ashes to the front door for taking out to the yard the next time he went out. Then he set about lighting the fire, which he built with sticks and turf and coal, and when the fire had conquered air, he went into the pantry where he got bread and milk and cheese, and as he did all these things his mind again re-enacted what devastated it. The sight of her. Sean Boyd. His own degradation.

Each slow minute ticked away, and then the next, and the one after, until Felix imagined that time had caught him up in a snare, bound and gagged him, condemned him to feel all its shades and sicknesses and heavinesses. Time went on and on, there was no stopping it, nor breaking it, and the only relief from it was sleep, when he could achieve it, but even over this he had no resolve. Time directed sleep, chose to keep him awake until four in the morning, and wake him at six, and so exhausted and awake he witnessed time in its laborious journey, sun up, sun down, light, dark, sitting in front of the fire, not reading, nor sleeping, only time beating itself out to the sound of his mother's clocks, ticking away in the corner, without end and without purpose, thinking themselves to be time's witness, but it was him, he knew it was him, not clocks, which tick, tick, tick as if they have never ticked before, and will never tick again, without memory, nor thought for the future, like the very essence of time itself, tick, tick, tick, which does not witness nor fret for itself. He was not so fortunate. Time was piled up in the past, and stacked up for the future.

The next morning he made tea and bread but was too light-headed for the physicality of eating. The weeklong change of his routine had taken its toll, he was almost devoid of the awareness that is part of our every waking moment: the backside on the seat's hardness, the draught at the knees, the face too hot in front of the fire, all the myriad contacts by which we know our body so that even the man most involved in emotion, mind, spirit will stop to scratch the nose's itch, will feel his head sore, his tongue dry. Felix moved slowly. He wasn't one of those people constantly moving themselves, shuffling their feet, agitated with their hands, wringing and cracking and moving their fingers like Biggers cross-examining. He could sit perfectly still for long periods of time, and now sat in his own chair, hard wooden, high back, and ran his hand through his hair, felt it sticky and tight on his scalp. He pushed back the food, leant forward, got up again, and looked through the window. Looking out over the fields and the lane, he thought of sitting waiting for hours, and hoping and arguing against hoping, and how useless it was that the disappointment crashed in when he saw her.

Never before had he imagined himself a companion, nor sat in the glen with the sun shining and the glen road empty and a rush of warmth so strong that he imagined that if he were to go there he'd find her in the glen near the waterfall, dressed in browns and greens, waiting for him coming, and looking up smiling happy at his arrival. He could see the sparse spring sunlight squinting lazily across the glen, and the streaks of light breaking before nightfall. Even then he had felt the air on his face and the stillness of her presence as if they were the same bright presence with no ripple between them.

That night he didn't sleep at all. About half past four in the morning he wrapped up like an old man and took a chair out to the step. He had on no light in the house, so behind was complete darkness, and in the distance were small isolated lights, from small isolated houses, right up to the hilly horizon. The night was quiet and cool, and the moon was a small curved sliver. The sky, unevenly shaded in its various darkness, was here and there relieved by a single star, or a cluster, and the atmosphere was still. He sat in his chair, and looked out blankly, and wondered why he didn't come out more in the night.

When he first noticed the cold, it was just a slight tingling in his hands and toes, barely perceptible, then he began to feel his backside cold on the chair, and his hands growing numb, and his feet chilly, and, almost resentful that he had to move, he started rubbing and squeezing his hands together, and pulling his jacket more tightly around him. Now that he had noticed it, he realised that he could just feel colder and colder. The cold would spread into his arms and legs and body, until any indulgence that he could sit forever was gone, and he would accept that all positions are temporary, and all concerns, getting in heat, doing the next thing. He sat out much longer and experimented with his body's endurance, felt each stage of cold and discomfort, his feet painful, his toes numb and his face as if the top layer of skin had been flayed. He was back in himself, and out of the picture of himself sitting on the chair on the step in front of the house, looking into darkness. In the world's picture, he couldn't be ignored.

Finally, reluctantly, he got up out of the chair, carried it into the house, and stood by the table and cried, which he never remembered, how it felt, what it was for, but the tears streamed down his face unbidden, unbridled.

13

Whatever had happened him ?

In Cookstown, Rosey Bradley wondered what on earth Sarah-Ann had seen in Sean Boyd in the first place. 'I never seen what you seen in him.'

'You never saw him,' Sarah-Ann reminded her.

'I know enough without having to see him. He's married every woman in the country and I'll never know how he did it . . . and they say now they've found another in Omagh. Anyway, where were you on Sunday?'

'Nowhere,' muttered Sarah-Ann sitting on the step in front of her own house, where the girls were running riot.

'You weren't here when I came.'

'No,' said Sarah-Ann, who wore an apron tied up round her neck, a thick woollen cardigan and a knitted purple shawl. She hadn't even bothered to take off the hat she'd worn that morning to town. In every way incongruous, it was the hat of a lady, large red and flamboyant, with a long steel pin protruding dangerously out of one side, and its brim dropping down. It was badly squashed from her sleeping on it.

'I thought that, for all your talk, you might have been up after him again.'

'Sure isn't he in prison?' countered Sarah-Ann. Last thing she wanted Rosey to know was that she had walked up towards Monaghan's last Sunday. She couldn't have explained, not even to herself, why she'd gone. She knew it was madness, yet she resented Rosey's insinuation of her lack of control.

'Marrying women all over the country! Sure you'd know there was something wrong with a man travelling all round the place!' pontificated Rosey, who, in this hour of her glory, found herself possessed of all the infinite serene wisdom of one friend to another. Rosey jumped up on the step. At just under six feet, Rosey's standing figure leant strangely forward as if she might fall over at any moment.

'Aye, cattle was a good excuse to take him anywhere! There's a lot looking at their husbands now and wondering where he is really when he's trapping rabbits.' Rosey had wild wiry hair, and her tiny eyes were far spaced. She had a great expanse of forehead and a thin wide mouth. She looked like one of Henry VIII's unfortunate wives. Warming to her theme of her motivation and execution, she continued.

'There are indeed!' muttered Sarah-Ann, trying to stop her.

'To think if Frank were still here!' exclaimed Rosey, and Sarah-Ann wondered wearily why she put up with her.

'That's enough of Sean Boyd,' said Sarah-Ann.

'Well, well!' tutted Rosey, turning her attentions to the activities of the yard. Katie hit Betty, Josie and Theresa were fighting over something or other. Sarah-Ann moved not a muscle to intervene.

'Them weans are wild,' criticised Rosey.

'As hares!' laughed Sarah-Ann, simultaneously aware and oblivious to the criticism. 'They're as wild as hares!'

'Well! If mine were tearing around like that . . .' sniffed Rosey. The condemnation fell away on her tongue. 'You're just that reckless!' burst out Rosey, who couldn't help herself. Sarah-Ann shrugged her shoulders as if to say, 'This is how I am, take me, or leave me.'

Sarah-Ann might, like a magpie, draw to her with magnetic power the stories of other men's lives, but this was a passive quality and, in her day-to-day existence and in the manner with which she lived her own life, she was motivated largely by what was in front of her. First it was Frank Duffy, next it was Sean Boyd. The characteristics that led her to each were not so much intrinsic to the men but to the situation. It was then opportunity and circumstance that impelled her. At fifteen, when she met and married Frank Duffy, he might have been anyone. She would, it seems, have been every bit as happy. The same went for the children. Without forethought or planning came one after the other. In her chaotic and undisciplined fashion, she loved and cared for them. She did not, like her own mother, harbour for them the slightest ambition. When Frank died, she determined to make the best of it. Because he was there, or because he was travelling, or because he was not scared by a war widow, the best, it seemed, was Sean Boyd. This, depending on the way you look at it, is a simple way of living, or an open-minded impulsiveness that may lead you anywhere. In reality, with Sean Boyd there was little foundation for love.

As Rosey criticised Sarah-Ann's wayward, fickle nature, as the noise of Rosey washed over her, Sarah-Ann diverted herself with recollections of the tall thin Ballymully man who had admired her on Main Street. She recalled his flattering attentions, and strong workman's hands, cupping with an untapped power the English newspaper. She had felt then a sudden sympathy, almost a tenderness for him hiding it. Whatever had happened to Felix Campbell, wondered Sarah-Ann.

14

Benweed amongst corn

The bridgegatherers met in full formation all through the spring, slow days for men tired from ploughing fields, and planting spuds, and farming industry. There was no more sign of Sarah-Ann, but Dolly still came regular as clockwork, and by her piety and frigidity comforted them, and by her constancy assured them the world was a pattern and moved in circular ways. Even Willie, shouting down the hill, was regular and appreciated; it was his habit and amused them. The war had gone to his head. With his old obsessions he had mixed in his new obsessions, Home or 'Rome' Rulers, and Carson and Asquith, and from Willie no one received a favourable review. About all things Willie was equally afrenzy, and the fierceness of his fury made the bridgegatherers laugh. They themselves talked about the Ulster Volunteers, and Redmond, and the most respected amongst them spoke sombrely and pithily about these things in their serious mid-Ulster tones, and even amongst themselves were careful with words not to say too much, and knew that if hotheaded fools wanted to be talking then that was up to themselves, and when they spoke they shushed them. Bridgemen know that things can get out of hand, things can go too far.

Ulster bridgemen had hoped and prayed that the Great War and their support for it would put behind them forever the scourge of Irish Home Rule, which sickened and embittered them and which they no more understood than a man who would pull out his own heart. Ireland was the heart of the British Empire, more British than the British, more proud and fierce and loyal, and their blood ran warm with this British pride and was chilled by the threat to it. Plenty and vociferous, the Home Rulers cropped up in Ireland like benweed amongst corn, which disguises its poison in golden summer colours, and is enticing, romantic and beautiful, but when cut, kills cattle, and would in turn be killed by men whose names they knew, and whose motives they understood for eliminating without qualm what threatened them. That war intervened was miracle enough, ordained and predestined, and it uplifted every believer by the new future it offered, and by the thought of this future. The union with Britain was safe another day.

But by 1916 even war seemed no sure intervention. The rumblings were as before, the unrest was deep and sick and sore, and Irishmen went behind backs to enter pacts with Germany, and run guns from Germany, and thought they'd make war in Ireland whilst loyal bridgemen were otherwise occupied. The rising rose in April, and hatred covered the country in a thick fog. Even an enlightened man struggles in fog.

Mid-Ulster, garrisoned and barricaded, knew the events of the Easter Rising. The Fenians had risen, had stormed public and government office and, after harsh response, after pummelling by a British gunboat, had surrendered. Now a post office, the scene of rebellion, was a new monument to fear. Boosted up by moral outrage, bridgegatherers drew strength and reserves of old, and cheered that the veil of Fenianism had been pulled back to reveal a more vile and poisonous darkness. It was strangely comforting.

On a late Saturday afternoon, Felix sat idly in his Cookstown pub drinking a whiskey and sipping a pint, now all part of his well-established routine. He had made the long journey by foot and had spent an hour dandering the town observing the townspeople and all other distractions to detain him from entering the pub before the self-appointed hour. That was his rule. However he contrived it, he had never broken it. In anticipation, he woke early every Saturday and, after doing his work, tidied up and got ready for Cookstown. All along the way he observed the progress and quality of corn, the growth of potatoes, the grass growing slow or fast dependent upon weather and lime and drainage. At the town, he strolled up the Fair Hill, or made some small purchase, or called in on the market. At five, he called casually in on Pat's like he was in town anyway, but if it weren't for Pat's he wouldn't even have contemplated the long weekly journey, the walk there, the walk back.

Pat's was at the head of the town. A small dark smoky cupboard, too hot on a hot day, but great on a cold wintry day with no heat anywhere. Felix never went anywhere else. After that first random stumbling upon it, he was a regular, as comfortable there as at home, and never tempted by any other anonymous door leading on to Main Street.

He sat in the darkest corner, and drank Guinness and a chaser slowly to savour them. He liked to feel the heat of the whiskey on his tongue, and the smoothness of the Guinness, and the contrast. The expense was only secondary. Even so, he'd looked at it all ways, from thinking that the afternoon in Pat's was pure unadulterated decadence, to its being his only weekly diversion, to how it was as natural as Sunday amongst the bridgegatherers. Whichever way, there was no getting away from the one bare economic fact. This. An afternoon's drinking was very dear. A stout on its own wasn't cheap but, with the chaser on top of it, it soon mounted up, and when he had a few rounds it was far more money than he'd ever thought he'd spend in an afternoon. Far more than a whole week's tobacco, or a pound of tea, which, sparing all visitors, could be drunk every day and made to last the month. To make a drink last all night is a skill in itself. Felix had tried everything, all methods of drinking, all dilutions of whiskey, and all types of it, but the whiskey on its own was far too dry, too strong and quickly drunk, and the stout by itself too filling and heavy. In sum, he had acquired the old taste, and, after all experimental variation, discovered that the traditional, tried, tested properties of whiskey and stout cannot be improved upon. They must be drunk together, as they always have been. Felix drank slowly to savour them. He strung out his drink, which, if not for the cost, he might not have strung out in such exaggerated manner.

Felix cast a weary eye over the fire. It was getting down. Just a crude stick blackened out at the front of the grate, a dull redness, a warm glow at the back. Seated by the fire in the Cookstown pub, he didn't need a fire at home, nor the cost of the fire, nor the handling lighting carrying to a fire, with only himself to sit at it. In Pat's the fire warmed more than himself, and with no need for a fire at home he saved the cost of the turf and sticks and bit of coal, which he wryly offset against the day's drinking. That was a canny calculation as reflexive as blinking, and whatever the cost he'd still have drunk his whiskey just as slowly and placed his Guinness just as preciously. Good. The cost changed nothing. Good. He calculated from habit, and, from lifelong conditioning, offset the cost of the low dying fire, and experimented with alternatives to whiskey and stout, none of which worked. He enjoyed his whiskey and stout, he enjoyed the fire and its mitigation of flagrant luxury. He was master of his own deliberate pleasure.

He pushed back the Guinness to the exact spot where the Guinness should be. He moved the whiskey a fraction to the right, then poured the smallest drop of water. He slowly lifted and set down his pipe. The pipe was perfectly placed at an aesthetic timing between drinks slowed down by smoking, and economics, and discipline. In the corner's dim darkness, Felix felt the warmth of the fire direct on his legs, and felt the whiskey trickle down his throat. He sipped slowly. Neither cost nor nature detracted from his skill. The warmth of the fire was suffused along his body.

There was a stillness in the corner.

Pat, wherever he was, would soon be back to fix up the fire.

Whatever market men to come in hadn't yet come; there were still less than a handful. When they arrived, he would see them talking their prices, and he, an observer of life. But happy, aye, happy just to watch them, what would he want to say to them that he couldn't say at the bridge? He made only the barest acknowledgements, and when, for familiarity's attractions – a friendly face, or manner, or sense of something, anything, in common – he had made the easy acknowledgement, gone the step further, it almost always ended in awkwardness. Today, thank God, there was no one even vaguely familiar. Felix hated anyone else in his corner, or the odd day without a fire, or Pat away stone-cold drunk wherever he was not stone-cold drunk at home. Fortunately Pat rarely ventured abroad. Pat's own custom was his greatest recommendation. Today, no doubt, he was out the back sipping himself, his ghost tinkling coins at the drawer, counting them out with all the nervous mannerisms of Pat shaking his head, steadying his hand, nimble with coppers. However he saw them, his sight skewed by drink, however he held them, his fingers tremulous with drink, Pat counted out coins in an eye-blink. Poor Pat. In Felix's eyes he was the perfect host, who said no more than he needed to, hardly said anything at all. Any minute, he'd be back out stoking the fire, tending the bar, looking out down over Main Street, waiting for the market men, who'd come or not as they pleased. That was the pub trade, and this was the Saturday, which was supposed to be the good day to tide him over the rest of the week.

Pat came out. In his dull, drink-dimmed way he performed the bare necessities of publican life. He spat into the fire, nodded at Felix. Felix was a regular. As Tommy Boyce once had been. Tommy had been there that first time, but Tommy came no more. Up all night at shabeens, there wasn't much drinking left to do in the daytime. Tommy was more for the war. He was all for it. He was away to the dogs. He was . . . Felix didn't like to think . . . just one of those things he didn't like to think about . . . like Sarah-Ann. It was a lifetime ago, that long ago he could hardly remember, yet every day she flashed into his mind, and he tried to suppress her. Once, a long time, a lifetime ago, he'd thought she was in it the same as himself. What a fool! In reality she was out in the sophisticated world of Sean Boyd. Felix sipped his whiskey, held it in his mouth, felt it waste, and pursed his lips to retain it, then his mouth was empty, just an aftertaste of Bushmills.

A newcomer appeared at the doorway. He pushed the door, half shut to keep in the heat, half open to invite. He was no market man but some sort of gentleman, tall, drawn, elegant, with a gentleman's face and gentleman's clothes, but cautious as a market man. He stood at the doorway, squinting to make up his mind on the inward scene; three farmers, their profiles; a fire; no barman. He came in. His overcoat was too much for the weather. Gloomy and tired, he walked past Felix; he was a man used to make heed of no one. Up close, Felix saw his stranger's gaze, practised, weary, averted, and saw he was young. He had the bold, daring confidence of a man who knows his life a mission where others are simply biding time.

Felix had no shyness studying him.

He asked for a drink in a low hushed voice, then took from a worn leather bag a small book that he placed on the table, and that he must have been well practised to read in the darkness. Many's a time Felix himself had thought to bring a book, but he knew how odd he would have looked, every bit as odd as the stranger himself who didn't seem to care what the world or its pub made of him. The most Felix ever brought was a newspaper, the *Mid Ulster Mail*, or *The Times*, but he knew for certain that anyone who saw him fully suspected that he didn't read it at all or read *The Times* only for show, or, like the newsagent who supplied him, believed that he had neither enough to do, nor enough to interest him and that there was far too much news. The stranger propped his book against a glass. He seemed the sort of lazy reader who'd skip pages, read the last page first, or only what interested him. His book was well fingered, and he held it away from his face, then propped it up again, and was obviously straining to see in the darkness. He was very tired as if any comfort of fire, and stout, and quiet cosiness, would put him to sleep. He slumped his head back against the wall. His small round glasses slid down his nose. His hair was dishevelled, and his jaw loose, and his mouth half open. A sleeping man looks vulnerable. Suddenly, he spoke.

'The heat gets you,' he smiled to explain his weakness, and raised up his book, and resumed reading, and Felix remained at the bar.

Some minutes later the stranger spoke again. 'It's a nice quiet area,' he said clearly, precisely.

'It is quiet with little to do,' said Felix. 'You're English?'

'I'm from Dublin, Irish,' he said and whatever way he said it, Felix felt some lack of respect for himself.

'What brings you here?'

'Curiosity,' said the stranger, ironically lifting up his eyes to query Felix.

'There is nothing interesting here.'

'Nothing?' The stranger looked as if he had seen him for the first time.

'It's quiet,' said Felix. Irony is a double-edged sword, and he was not so easily flattered.

'There's nowhere without interest.'

'People here keep their own business,' said Felix and heard the room quiet with farmers who had nothing to say to each other.

'As many places.' Smug in himself, he laid down his book as if for the first time taking interest in the conversation and knew exactly where Felix stood. The couple of sparse farmers at the other side of the bar looked flat into the distance.

'If you're looking for adventure here, you will be disappointed,' said Felix, and Pat, the barman, mysteriously returned, made his barman moves as if he cared nothing for his clientele's business.

'These are exciting times everywhere. In Dublin people have fought for what they believe in,' said the stranger.

'Feelings are running high.'

'Passions are aroused where they should be.'

'And defeated,' Felix said almost peevishly.

'People smell freedom and are heady with freedom.'

'And what do you make of that?'

Silence. Felix suddenly felt he had some language to match him.

'You have spoken like only a fool talks, and now all of a sudden coy as a girl,' challenged Felix, and Pat, washing glasses, did it more slowly and carefully as if glass was suddenly more fragile.

The stranger said nothing, looked Felix straight in the eye, bold and open, and Felix didn't know if his recklessness was the consequence of some recent adventure or intrinsic to the man. What was certain was he cared for nothing, only his passion.

'You're as obvious here as a crow amongst doves,' said Felix.

The stranger smirked, and Felix got up to walk out the door, past the farmers and Pat. He caught the stranger's eye, and was going to say something, but said nothing, he was back on the street leaving his drink behind. What was right? What was wrong? We only fight for what is right, the stranger had said, with a manic look in his eye. Was that proof of right? My conscience, he had said, and Felix had nodded.

Back on Main Street, Felix wondered if the fabric of himself was only random chance.

Sarah-Ann recognised him instantly. Indistinguishably him. He stood fragile on Main Street, looking up Main Street. That's him, she thought, standing where she left him. The same stilted bearing, the hands behind the back, and all he was straining to while away time with no talent for. He wore the same clothes as when she last saw him, the same formal suit inappropriate for market day and the white highnecked shirt. She had every opportunity to turn. Or cross to the other side. Main Street is wide, built on grand proportions, but no features at all, nothing designed, just a market street with only width and breadth to distinguish it and Saturday crowds to enliven it. But she was lonely, and had no notion of turning. She watched as he looked one way, then the other, like any moment he suspected someone to sneak up his unguarded side and ask what he was doing, why he was there?

'In for some shopping?' she said, and recalled his impression of her. A woman in a purple shawl. Simple, easy, happy. She knew she could be these things, and if she had somehow lost sight of them it was only temporary, her buoyant spirits would return. 'And still reading *The Times*?' she asked, as he stood formally erect with his full faculties about him, and his fear of losing them. He didn't know what to do with his hands, he held one behind him in the market man's gesture for studying form, or the cleric's for solicitous sincerity. 'I thought it was *The Times* the last time I saw you,' she said.

'The last time . . .' stalled Felix, confused after his bar-room confrontation, and unused too to Cookstown flirting, and flirting of every sort. Coming to town, he'd had no expectation, nor thought of her; any thought was of the freedom of Cookstown on Saturday, and the pleasure of town to walk into, and the familiar sense of Saturday anticipation.

'Aye, sure I saw you,' teased Sarah-Ann, who nodded quick-witted with the superior insight she had into him. 'It's not that many that read *The Times*.'

'I get it in Moneymore . . . for the war . . . but not every day, it's got good coverage of the war . . .' said Felix, trailing off thinking what another man would say, but he couldn't, he'd never be another, and he stood suddenly taciturn. Already the market town waned, it made him wistful, the first traders packing up their market stalls and winding down the day. He preferred the afternoon when the crowd was at its height, and traders, shouting their wares, had everything to shout for. Livelihoods turned on the day and made everyone receptive.

'The war, I'll have to start reading it then,' she said. 'Can't you get too much of war?'

'I suppose you could, but they don't report it all anyway, they can't report it all,' he said, thinking of Sean Boyd and the taint of Sean Boyd. She had been most starkly, and improbably, revealed to him by Biggers, orator of bigamists, and the shock had penetrated his imaginings as deeply and painfully as the fantasies had transformed what had been dark, dour and ascetic.

'I've often thought of you and your *Times*,' she said, and he tried to recall his impression of her before Sean Boyd, but this exercise in mental purity was useless. He couldn't help compare the man who had married women all over the country with himself, so lonely he imagined he was loved by a woman who didn't even know he existed.

'Aye, I brought it a couple of times to see what it was about, and what was in it. I think I bought the Friday copies because they were the fattest and you got your money's worth, but I never heard of half the places,' she enthused far too passionate like a child, fired one moment, distracted the next. 'That day I met you before in Cookstown, and you were excited about reading, and I thought it's great to meet somebody happy about something and interested. I have often thought of it.'

'Well, it's easy to buy,' said Felix, tentatively trying to understand who she was, this woman who, from the most fantastical colourful creature as a figment of his mind had faded over the days and weeks and months to stand before him, an ordinary woman, good-looking, yes, bold, yes, the same woman as at the bridge, but up close now, looking in at him, far too interested in his readership of *The Times*, which told her something of politics and prejudices he preferred to keep hidden. His indeterminate hope, fuelled by some whimsy that she had looked at him, or recalled him, or spoken to him, was all in the abstract. In reality there was no one to love him.

'You should get it yourself,' he said. 'It's only a few pennies.'

'We haven't seen you at the bridge again,' he vocalised against the backdrop in his own mind of her on the glen road, and her at the bridge with twenty bridgemen turning this way, then the other, himself amongst them. 'You never came back. They talked about you week in week out,' he said. 'It was to do with Sean Boyd, and what happened with him, but they would have remembered you anyhow. They miss nothing, you see.'

'You could come to Cookstown.'

'They see that too, they see living in them big towns with not a blade of grass between them, they wonder what takes me!'

Sarah-Ann laughed. Was he attractive? With his tight-fitted suit and starched-down shirt and well-polished shoes?

'After that I started to come. I come every Saturday, week in, week out; before I hadn't been for years, I hadn't been from long before the war and I thought it'd be changed, but it's no different at all, everything's the same as it was.'

'And what do you do?'

'I walk up and down Main Street, I look in at the market, I look in at Pat's, do you know Pat?'

'I don't know Pat.'

'I thought everybody knew Pat.'

'Not everybody.'

'You'd see him on the street . . . Tinkling his change.'

'She nodded her head, she shook her lovely head, this way and that.

'And drinking his drink . . . And stacking his bottles . . . And smoking his pipe out on the Main Street.'

'I never see him. There's other things in Cookstown,' she said, 'And other people . . . and places to go.'

He nodded his big, big head.

'And things to do.'

'There is?'

'Aye,' she said, 'I'll show you my town.'

'Any time you like,' she said, 'any time.'

15

Mary Duffy

When Felix first came to the house, Mary was the only one in. She came to the door, which was always left open, to find him, a tall, awkward stranger, standing some distance from the house like he was reticent of houses and pretending that he hadn't knocked. He wore stuffy clothes, a dark grey suit, on the warm day, and carried a pipe, and when he turned and asked if it was the right place, she said it was, and he asked for her mother. For a moment she thought she'd tell him that her mother had gone, maybe over to Kelly's or some other place further away, but when she opened her mouth, it was to tell the truth.

'She's here,' she said, already afraid he was no ordinary caller. His largeness and darkness estranged her.

'Thank you,' he said, and she just stood there looking at him with her head halfway round the doorpost and the rest of her somewhere hidden inside the house, and as she watched him from this half-hidden vantage point she thought he was shy for a grown-up. He didn't speak for ages.

'Will you tell her I'm here?'

'She's not in the house.'

'I thought you said . . .'

'Naw, she's doing things out the back,' she said, and wondered afterwards if a lie would have made any difference.

'Is it better that I get her myself?'

'I don't know.'

'Maybe I should go round there.'

He moved. Maybe to go round the back, maybe to go home. He regretted being overdressed or inappropriately dressed, or too old or stuffy, or any other criticism and fault she might see in him.

'I'll run and get her,' she said, and came back five minutes later.

'She'll be round in a minute.'

He took off his hat. 'A very hot day,' he said.

'She said for you to come on into the house,' she said, and he said, 'Thank you, and I'm Felix,' as he stepped in, but he was as uncomfortable in as out, and too tall for the beams. He didn't sit down.

'I never heard it before.'

'What?'

'That name.'

'Aye, it's after my great-uncle. What's your name?'

'Mary,' she said, but he didn't ask her who it was after, just took out his pipe and, as he worked absorbed at it, she went into the bedroom and closed the door enough that the stranger man

121

wouldn't see the clothes strewn all around the place but she would still be able to watch him. He walked across the room to the fireplace, and stood there, almost stone still, then lifted up his pipe again and stretched over the fireplace to look at the photographs on top of the mantelpiece. She watched him and assessed him, and perhaps had some strong sense of the moment. Her world was already full. She had her mother, her siblings, and her father, Frank Duffy, whose memory lived on, and didn't need Felix Campbell's large, imposing figure taking up the whole room. What right did he have to stare at their photographs, or stand in their room, or wait for their mother? She felt sorry for herself at the tall dark stranger man who had come to turn Ma's head. Even then Mary knew that she was to blame, and even before her mother came in was filled with guilt for passing on the message that she'd had in her power to make disappear as if it had never existed. Felix felt her bad feeling against him, and searched about to avoid it by fixing his gaze upon the photographs on top of the mantelpiece. The concentration steadied his nerves, and blocked out the girl, and temporarily diverted him from the reason why he was standing in the room at all. In one of the photographs Sarah-Ann wore a large soft hat, and small glasses rested perkily on her nose, and her eyes looked out as if challenging some great imaginary audience. He couldn't help wondering how on earth she had managed to dress up in such finery, and why.

Mary heard Ma walk past the window and turned to see her fix her hair quickly, the way Ma did, then she walked in the door, and Mary heard their first muttered greetings.

'You found it,' said Ma, and he said it was no trouble, and said something else about knowing where the Kellys lived, and Mary thought how he lied. Then Ma said it was a wild long walk, and she heard the stranger huffing and puffing some longwinded answer. They left a short time later. Hadn't she told him, thought Mary, he would never have waited, and her mother would never have known.

Felix heard Mary's door click and thought no more of it.

16

Baptism by water ~ early spring. 1977

Six months later, they walked the brae for the first time. He was awkward and tall beside her. She felt his shame like the heat of a fire.

He wore the shirt she'd made. I stitched the clothes on his back, she thought.

'The shirt suits you well,' she said.

Not a word from his shame, not a word from his vast shamed world from the top of the mountain and the brae before and behind them. The brae ran along Willie Thompson's and Tommy Boyce's fields. Those of the Martins and the Biggers adjoined them. He felt his shame before the trees and the hills, the bridge where he'd first laid eyes on her. What will they make of me, he thought, what do I make of myself?

She saw the shame-shape of his head lowered as if to reduce himself. There was shame in his feet lifting over the ground, and in his arms and the space where his heart should have been. She thought of the shirt she had made and the shape, of sadness and strength, his back made of it, and where anyone else might have felt shamed by his shame she felt love.

He was peremptory with the neighbours they met, and didn't introduce her. None of them greeted her but they looked at her and said nothing. They knew who she was, a backdrop of rumour and innuendo; they knew her all right, but she didn't know them. They should have been the same as the people she came from, farmers and labourers and people from hills. 'They'll be wondering about me,' she said, imagining what they saw, some vixen vision of her prancing and flouncing along with the big dour Campbell tramping beside her. He didn't reply, walked stiff and slow and carried her bag out from himself like it was on fire.

'I know fine well what they're saying,' she rejoined with final-ity, and between her words and the meaning of them lay their common understanding, the nearest expression yet accorded it. The Biggers and the Martins and the rest of them would be saying to anyone who would listen how Campbell and the O'Malloran woman came waltzing round the brae as bold as brass, and her up to move in with him! The right neck on her! they'd say.

'They can think what they like,' he said. He'd heard them before about other people and places, but never before on their doorstep. The mix and the match of it. Her the Catholic, married with weans, and him at the age of him and the cut of him and the dry odd type of him. What did they say about him, what must they say? What has come over him? What has befallen him? Rhetorical questions asked rhetorically by neighbour to neighbour like some riddle they knew. Some riddle of hatred, riddle of doom, asked without expectation of answer because there is no answer nor surprise in the question, nor question in the question, only the dark dead beat of neighbour talking to neighbour, only the familiar riddle practised and pattered and perfected down the generations. Ah, scant small explanation, his dryness and oddness! His dryness and oddness, scant small explanation for him chasing after the Fenian from Cookstown.

'Who are they?' Maggie was on the outside, and Sadie was on the inside.

'Neighbours.'

'Who?'

'Maggie and Sadie.' They made their inexorable approach.

'Maggie Martin? The Maggie does your washing?' she hesitatingly asked.

He nodded, and she scanned their absurd spectacle. Soon they would pass, Felix and she in the one direction, Maggie and Sadie in the other.

'As big as the other's small.'

'That's the comicness of them,' he said, and she thought how his mind worked inscrutable, and revealed itself idiosyncratically as a faraway mystery.

'I thought she'd be older . . . from the sound of her,' she said, and wondered if he had something to do with the large one more than a neighbour. She never even thought of the small one.

'No more than thirty-five if even that,' he said, inadvertently catching Maggie's eye and turning away.

'I can hardly believe it . . . from the sound of her . . .'

'Aye . . ' he said, distracted, and she contrived to cure the intolerable silence.

'A quare pair,' she said as Maggie and Sadie approached. Their full force almost upon them, she and Felix walked on.

'Not a bad day if it keeps dry,' said Sadie, wearing a dress over trousers and a man's belt over that. Her small squat face was scrubbed carbolic clean, and her hair was pinched up tight in a thin hairnet, and from somewhere, wherever she'd acquired it, she had a cigarette behind her ear. Maggie, with her dark curly hair, a scarf around her neck, had made her own effort for going to town.

'Hardly a spittle all day,' said Sadie, her small vigorous face struck up to them.

'You're late on the road today,' he said sharply.

'Not that late. Sure we go down to the town all times,' said Sadie so glibly he almost blushed at her cheek.

'Sure Molly's shop will be closed, she was closing up when I went through the town,' said Felix, and felt Sarah-Ann to the right of him one step behind.

'Naw, Molly'll not be closed,' said Maggie.

'Do you need anything out of the town?' asked Sadie in the most unusual form of question from her.

'I was in,' he said, walking on, and Sarah-Ann following, and everything in the situation incriminating him.

'It'd be handy with the morrow the day for your clothes,' said Maggie.

'Leave it th'morrow,' he shouted behind him.

'The man for fanciness that gets his clothes done,' muttered Sarah-Ann.

'Whatever you like, you'll suit yourself,' said Maggie.

'Who else would I suit?' retorted Felix.

'Not a soul else,' answered Maggie.

'Not a soul else,' tittered Sadie. There was no point shouting after Sadie. She always got the last word.

Out of earshot, Sarah-Ann said, 'They'll be wondering about me,' but Felix didn't answer, and she grew ever less certain, and smarted at Maggie and Sadie's reaction to her. 'Wondering who I am and what I'm doing,' she imagined out loud. 'I'd be wondering myself,' she said almost to herself. If there had been no overt confession that their relationship was anything more than friendship, the signs were all there, which she had read as clear as day, to convince her that he was romancing her in the most delicate slow way, so slow, so gentlemanly she hardly noticed being wooed and romanced. So long as he came every week, she had never doubted him, but had made all her excuses about his shyness, and her own circumstances, then came the invitation to his house; she had read it as nothing short of portentous.

'They'll not be wondering anything,' he said sharply. He might criticise them but nobody else could, and she thought whoever they were to him they were more to him than she was.

'They're not the worst,' he said, and each drifted off into their separate worlds to experience there, in isolation, the disturbing and powerful feelings that Maggie and Sadie had unwittingly brought to the surface.

They passed the Martins', nobody in the yard, nobody in the field, they passed Desertlyn graveyard, they walked up Wilson's hill. Felix, who had just moments before congratulated himself on the smooth and enjoyable walk from Moneymore without incident, was morose and gloomy, and Sarah-Ann, far from being a woman slowly imagining herself seduced by the man she loved, was nervous and agitated. Every step was a long one. Powerful as a magnifying mirror, Maggie and Sadie reflected back all they had seen: Felix's shame, Sarah-Ann's uncertainty, their illicit relationship. What preyed most on Felix's mind was that Maggie and Sadie had timed their walk to coincide with his and Sarah-Ann's, a suspicion not dulled by its unlikelihood since Maggie and Sadie couldn't have known Sarah-Ann was coming. But Felix ignored this inconsistency. For Maggie and Sadie to be on the road the same time as he and Sarah-Ann seemed to him too much of a coincidence. Their demeanour told him as much. Maggie and Sadie were coy and conspiratorial, and searched out all the evidence. It was all there. The weeks and weeks of Maggie cleaning the house, the mystery of where he went on Saturdays and Sundays, not to mention that, in the last six months, he had been conspicuously happy. His weeks were spent in anticipation of seeing Sarah-Ann. Eight miles away, she lived in another part of the country; he had re-orientated his world; his private compass now stretched far beyond Ballymully, geographical distance added to the pleasure of delicate romance and escape from the ordinary travails. In contrast to the slow uneventful pace of former life, Saturdays and Sundays were now frantic. In the mornings, he rushed through his work, then there was the walk, he relished it, and the first rush of seeing her again. He loved her open frank face, and gentle manner, and as the weeks progressed felt relaxed and joyful in her presence. He had envisaged that they would meander along this continuum of happiness. The matter of her visiting had arisen naturally. Talking about his life – the farm, the house, the daily routine – it had emerged that something was missing. She had never visited. Seemingly of their own accord, arrangements took shape. He dismissed any anxiety he may have had about it. She was a friend, as a friend she would come to his house. Now meeting Maggie and Sadie had blown away that pretence, now all the ambiguity, confusion and terror of their relationship had been brought to bear on the present. Fifteen minutes from the house, he could withstand no imprecise word, and so said nothing.

'Wondering who I am and what I'm doing,' she said as if to herself, and thought self-pityingly how she could so much more easily have borne Maggie and Sadie's scrutiny if she had had any intimation of love. Sarah-Ann recalled with contempt the excuses she'd made: that he was shy with no experience of women, that he was an incurable romantic who preferred her in the ideal rather than the domestic, or he was biding his time. But Sadie's bunched-up swaddled appearance told her brutally what excuses avoided; far from being in love with her, Felix Campbell was ashamed.

'They needn't be wondering,' he said more gently. 'We'd more readily wonder about them.'

'They'll have read it different than you think.'

'That's maybe the way they'd have read it,' he said slowly, unsure of the words to admit that Sadie and Maggie had read that he was running after Sarah-Ann O'Malloran. That was the only sign she needed. She stretched to take his hand.

'Big, big hands,' she laughed, getting used to the warm masculine feel of his hand in hers, of his clasped round hers, of hers clasped round his.

At the bridge she recalled their first meeting.

'That's where you were,' she pointed.

'It was the other side of the bridge,' he laughed. It had meant more to him. She had been making her way to Sean Boyd. She had been dressed for him foolishly and colourfully. It had been almost the year ago to the day.

Sarah-Ann turned the corners round in her mind. She'd always imagined that he'd been standing near the place where Tommy Boyce had come out from under the bridge. Geordie and Tommy, and Felix, the dark shadow between them.

Her first sighting of the house was a grey blur through trees. Even from there it looked dilapidated. The two or three times she'd seen it before it had meant nothing to her, only some strange curiosity why it was so big and neglected.

'We're nearly there,' he said, looking back and seeing, through the trees, the distant figures of Maggie and Sadie. Maybe they were going to the town after all, he thought.

The lane became rougher and narrower ad the hedges higher

and thicker. Indifferent to its function as bearer of traffic, long green grasses grew up the middle and, near the house, they met hens and ducks and geese. Sarah-Ann stood passively waiting as he shushed them out of the way.

A glance across the house told her everything. Grey, large, damp. She entered the small narrow doorway straight after him.

'Not much room in the doorway,' she laughed, a squeeze on top of him as he opened the door into a large bare room. There was only a table and three or four scattered chairs. The only effects were two white porcelain dogs on the mantelpiece and a grocery calendar on the wall.

She warmed her legs in front of the fire.

'There's a parlour at the other side of the hall,' he said.

'I never had a parlour,' she answered. The lack of a parlour hung in the air as real as the black pot over the hearth and exposed the greater difficulty. How would Sarah-Ann and Felix make a parloured home? To break the momentary tension, Felix told her something he hadn't meant to.

'I tidied up for you coming,' he said and instantly regretted sacrificing his small prides.

'You didn't need to do that,' she laughed, noting his pipes, which lay in a hole high up in the wall. The familiarity of his pipes was a comforting sight.

'When do you smoke the different ones?'

'According to a pattern.'

'What pattern?'

'I couldn't tell you, I'd just know if I got it wrong.'

'It goes by the days?'

'By the days and what I would be doing. A different one for a wet Sunday from a dry Sunday,' he laughed, making rules out of his head.

'Do some light better than others in the rain?' she teased.

'That's a bit of it but it depends what you're doing.'

'What might you be doing that would change it?'

'I never think about it.' Perplexed. Looked at her. 'Well, maybe I'll study it for you, but I'm just worried that I'll forget it if I study it or get mixed up in my mind.'

'Well then, you better leave it alone, and I'll observe for myself.'

He went to the pantry to bring out sugar and bread, then lifted the tea caddy off the mantelpiece. Sarah-Ann filled her tea with sugar, and thought how contented she was to be in this secret place where time stood still.

But as the afternoon progressed, and tea followed tea – they must have had four fresh brews – she felt Felix's discomfort at playing host. He manoeuvred awkwardly about the room, placing wood on the fire, asking if she was too warm or too cold, or if she wanted more tea. It seemed that Felix didn't know how to conduct himself in his own house. It seemed too that the visit passed beyond some natural point of behaviour, and neither knew what to say. Sarah-Ann felt it was up to him, and thought that if he was so uncomfortable he should offer to walk her home. All he'd have to say, she thought, was, 'It'll be time to be on the road.' That was all. He might almost have said it involuntarily.

'The silence here you could really get used to it,' she said, then suggested he show her the farm. This was supposed to be why she was here. By the time they looked round the yard, and the immediate fields, the dusk was upon them. They returned to the house.

'There's no point making off this late,' said Felix, showing her the ladder.

'I never slept upstairs,' she said. His bedroom was big and dark, with a large wooden bed.

She orientated herself in the half-light, and took from her bag a long thick nightdress, which she examined and held against herself, and asked to herself the most embarrassing questions. Should she go to bed naked? Should she wear only her bloomers? Or wear both bloomers and nightdress? She thought of what he would think. No principle or experience to guide her the first time. What would happen if she wore nothing? Would he find her naked and warm, no need for fussing and pulling at knickers and nightdresses? Or be shocked and rebuff her? Would she wear the gown and discard the knickers? She took off her dress, and looked around the room, and thought, 'Where will I put it?' There was the bed, a wardrobe, a dresser covered, it seemed, with old things of his mother's. She couldn't lay her dress over his dead mother's clutter. What about hanging it over his wardrobe? But his ties were there. He would blame her for crumpling them. Or leave her dress on the floor? And have him think her slovenly? She settled on hanging it over a chair, then, for the first time, got into his bed, and lay waiting.

Felix sat downstairs smoking his pipe and drinking the whiskey he'd bought for the house. He drank until his senses were dull and his bladder was full. When he opened the door, his dogs darted past. He slabbered incoherently at them and patted them, and called out their names, which he hadn't done since the whole thing started.

Upstairs Sarah-Ann felt the room warm and foreign; the bed-clothes were heavy and musty and sweet, and there was a strong strange smell she thought was some smell of the house, of the furniture, or the musty old things of his mother. It never occurred to her that it was Felix's odour pervading the house, extinguishing hers like she had none.

She thought about why she was there, and why he didn't come up. Random sounds rose from the vast featureless world beyond and entered the house. A plaintive muted call of a cow echoed from some distant mountain recess. It touched the house and her ear for the briefest second like the smallest living thing turning silence to sadness. She sat up and stared through the window at a section of the dark, impregnable mountain, and the smaller section of the luminous, darkening sky.

She wondered what he could be doing down there muttering and humming to himself, sitting in the dark when she was up there on her own. Then it fell silent, and for the first time it occurred to her, how could she have missed it, that Felix was a virgin, him a terrified virgin, and her terrified herself, without half the need to be! She sprang out of bed chuckling, what Felix called a cackle, and pulled up her elasticated knickers to her waist and climbed down the ladder, anxious how she would find him.

He was slouched over the table, a bottle and mug before him. The newspaper, covered in dirt where the dogs had lain on it, was at his feet. Oh, her big clean man, lying over the table in a stupor, and the dogs growling at her like the stranger she was to them. She shook him, but he didn't stir, so she went out to the pantry to fetch a bucket of water, then facing him like one dumb animal facing another she lifted her hand, strong and steady as any man's, and threw it over his head. Every drop. Baptism by water.

Full proof of his constitution, he stood bolt upright, and shook his head like a dog drying itself out of a river.

'My God, what's happening, what's wrong?' shouted Felix, seeing before him the knickered, white-robed vision of Sarah-Ann.

'I tried to rouse you.'

'You didn't have to drench me, I'm soaking, I could have died with the shock of it.'

'We'll light the fire, and make some tea,' she said, walking to the hearth and poking it.

She dumped the tea out of the caddy and poured the water in and banged it down. 'The Campbells weren't used to the women,' he said.

'I'm surprised there are any of you left, even yourself,' she snapped. She went to the cupboard, there was nothing to stop her, he watched helplessly as she ransacked him.

They both sat supping and watching the fire until daybreak, when Sarah-Ann led him by the hand up the ladder.

She took the shirt off his back. 'You looked fine in the shirt,' she said.

'So fine you've took it off me.'

Sarah-Ann stood up, and slid off her knickers, and in a single swift movement pulled up her gown. She was as white as the snow she'd been born in, and her hair was as black as a raven's, and her shape was as curved and carved and full as the mountain behind them.

Felix's knowledge of flesh's beauty was the soft dewy down on a day-old calf, or Maggie Martin's sturdy arms masinating butter. He'd never seen flesh in its completeness.

'We'll have white children,' she said.

'The great light this morning, I will never forget it.'

17

Sadie who was very small and Maggie who was much much larger

Felix had been wrong to suspect Maggie and Sadie. Their errand to town was entirely innocent, and no different from countless other joint excursions entirely frivolous in intent and serious to pass the long time of a spring afternoon with no man nor diversion. It was then no fault of theirs, only timing, that they met Felix coming along, a woman beside him. All they knew about her was that she was Sarah-Ann O'Malloran on the periphery of every story they ever heard about the infamous Sean Boyd and his women. She was good-looking, as they said; apart from that there was hardly another solitary fact they could have hung to her, yet in the few moments they met her they knew everything about her. She stood demure and reserved behind Felix, but there was no hiding she was bold and brash with a great flopping hat on her head and a sash or some shiny blue belt around her waist. She was trussed up proud as punch at the feather in her cap. Some feather! Felix Campbell was the oddest loneliest of creatures. His attractions to women – single, tall, a bit of money – were no antidote. Of this, both Maggie and Sadie were certain; Maggie did his washing, and cleaned his house, and Sadie knew his family, and their demise, and all demises. And what both knew for certain was that Felix might well be with a woman today but wouldn't tomorrow. And the other certainty. Before they'd even get to the top of the lane, news of their liaison would be out and spread like wildfire. Sadie herself was torn between telling what she knew first, and keeping it to herself.

Maggie was in shock. She'd always had a notion of him. More than that, was in love with him. More than that. She knew herself what it was. She had disguised her love behind washing. She had grown used to the slow dull longing for a man who looked to her only for the small domestic function he could have looked for to anybody. From time to time, now and then, rarely, when he was lonely, her lonely too, he'd looked for more. He'd look for a chat. She'd settled for that, the something better than nothing. Now Sarah-Ann O'Malloran had come to usurp her from even the smallest satisfaction of her smallest need, and she, in the presence of Sadie, in the presence of anyone, even herself, could not afford to let out any single sigh, gasp, breath of her heartache. If she needed to sigh, she'd sigh inwards; if she needed to gasp, she'd gasp inwards; if she needed to breathe, she'd need to breathe, she'd breathe inwards. Sadie wouldn't help. No way would she. She would rattle any word, breath, sigh of it. Only mercy was Sadie's talking herself into the ground. The minute they passed she broke out in a rash of exaggerated conversation, and Maggie breathed inwards. First on the scene, Sadie was rushing on headwards like nothing better had ever happened to her. Which maybe it hadn't. Sadie was the first witness, and thus an authority on the affair and all its subsequent event. She talked and talked. Reworded herself. The sight of Felix, the sight of Sarah-Ann, she repeated it all self-sufficiently and breathlessly. What had happened was that, out walking to town, she and Maggie had met Felix Campbell coming with his woman, Sarah-Ann O'Malloran, and, without stopping, only slowing, had bid each other time of day. Unaware of the protocol, Sarah-Ann had made some point out of turn. A bit of bitterness over his washing was inconclusive.

As Sadie spoke, Maggie speeded up her pace. Every step she took, Sadie took two. Maggie marched to the town, and every step Maggie took Sadie took three. Maggie walked even faster. Sadie's short legs were no match for her long ones. Her short legs worked faster and faster. Sadie would rather fall, collapse, die than for one instant request Maggie to slow down, even though Maggie was the first and only person she'd ever have asked; she'd never ask Maggie.

Breathlessly, Sadie kept up her conversation about what she had seen. Bare fodder for less agile minds was for Sadie a feast, and she zealously applied herself, gabbled and laughed, mimicked and mocked. 'Who else would I suit?' she said, every nuance and innuendo, the look of him, the change in him, the look of her. It was entertainment and critique, and the most exciting thing that had happened Sadie in a long time. Maggie gave no sign of her heartache.

Sadie even talked about the talk there would be.

'There'll be some talking about the country,' said Sadie,

fascinated at the talk that would be going on without her active participation.

'Aye, girning and gossiping and going on if they stick it,' answered Maggie, striding out.

'He'll maybe up and marry her,' said Sadie proudly, as if she herself were to marry.

'Up and marry her? Sure there'd be some outcry if that happened! Sure the Catholic Church wouldn't even allow it!' argued Maggie, clutching for straws. 'Apart from Felix himself, sure they'd never allow it!' This fact of her Catholicism was Maggie's only comfort.

'He's the quare odd one these days, you wouldn't know what direction he would take,' Sadie replied, half for her own titillation, half to goad Maggie. 'What I wouldn't have minded,' said Sadie, 'is if he'd been that way before but I never seen him after a woman. Did you ever see him after a woman?' she pointedly asked. As she spoke, her face possessed all the supreme concentration God ever bestowed on a man, which isn't to say He bestowed it for such a purpose as Sadie's.

Sadie's remark was deceptively simple. Despite its dogmatic tone it courted all views without admitting any. It was exploratory. It required a delicacy of mind to assimilate for which Maggie felt herself experienced. In the instance of Sadie speaking, Maggie understood that Sadie wouldn't have minded Felix's behaviour if in the past there had been some hint of it. But there was none. He was forty-four, and there had never been a woman. Thus what Sadie so eloquently highlighted was the inconsistency and the late revelation of his character. She was ambiguous too about the woman involved. On the one hand, who she was didn't matter, not even that she was Catholic and had been married with weans, yet who she was, was of the utmost importance so that Sadie was affronted that he had chosen her.

Overriding all, Maggie appreciated that Sadie welcomed the turn of events. Hadn't it, in Sadie's eyes, transformed what would otherwise have been an ordinary dander to the town? And wouldn't it transform many's a conversation thereafter?

'Did you ever see him after a woman?' she asked again, stressing in the question's direction to Maggie that perhaps Maggie, with all her experience of Felix Campbell, was not so shocked as she herself was, and this for the very good reason that in the past Felix had pursued Maggie, which, if he had, no doubt that he caught her. So sneekedy and sly that Maggie hadn't let on. Final vindication of Sadie's long-held feeling that there was more to Maggie's washing than met the eye.

For all its opacity, Sadie's question was fully transparent.

'I never heard tell of him after a woman, and I would have been the first from being round him so much,' said Maggie, attuned to all Sadie's motivations.

'I was around him at all times of the day and night, what with doing his washing.'

'I thought you'd've been in a better position,' cajoled Sadie with purposeful flattery.

'I would have been in the best position.'

'Well, what would you have said after knowing him so well?'

Maggie paused before she spoke.

'I would have thought, and more so I knew, that he would never have laid a hand on a woman, and what his intention is for that O'Malloran woman is more than I know.'

This remark was the conversation's high point, superior even to Sadie's initial joy at reliving in words their experience of this their first sighting. Sadie instantly recognised that what Maggie said was excellent, reflecting as it did her innermost appreciation and ambition for the situation. It was clear now to Sadie that she and Maggie, and all the townland, had not so much been duped by Felix Campbell as he himself had been duped by Sarah-Ann O'Malloran. Simultaneous to her recognition that external influences had acted upon Campbell, she loosened her garter and sighed in relief.

'That's what I thought,' mused Sadie, absentmindedly pulling at the garter digging into her flesh. 'I thought that,' she said gravely. 'Them garters of Stewarts are fit for nothing,' she muttered.

'You're not wearing them right.'

Maggie and Sadie's first call was at the draper's. The draper was standing behind her big wooden counter, with her big leaden bosom protruding over the top of it. Her small sour face peaked out, hungry for gossip.

'There's been talk round the town about Felix Campbell, is there anything in it?' she asked.

'Oul' town gossip, you wouldn't believe the half of it,' said Sadie to affront her. The colour rose on the draper's cheek.

'I thought that myself,' said the draper in a vain effort to regain her composure. She started to fold handkerchiefs on the counter.

'I wouldn't give her the pleasure,' said Sadie as they left. 'I had half a mind to mention her old done garters.'

On their return journey, they met Tommy Boyce.

'A woman's tongue never stops,' he teased.

'He's the one who would know,' they muttered.

18

Maggie came on the Thursday

*T*he next day Felix and Sarah-Ann rose in the middle of the morning. A long day lay luxuriously ahead of them. They went out to the yard and watered the calves and she was glad that the house was remote and high on the hill, no neighbours to look down on them or peer out of windows at her kissing him whenever she wanted. He showed her a map of his fields, the ones that were original and those his grandfather bought. He showed her the farm improvements out of journals he'd made. She saw he was progressive and a practitioner of knowledge. They looked through his records of calves and sheep that had been born, the dates and the sizes, diseases and worming and when they had died. She saw the lands to the south hidden and quiet stretching down to the river and the lands to the north stepping up to the mountain, and she thought not for the first time if he was wealthy with money. She basked for a while at the prospect of it, and wondered half idly what difference it would make. Not a bit, emphatically no, never preened herself except for red rouge on her cheeks and lipstick when she got it. For the fat lot of good it'd do me. I'll have what'll do me, she thought. He showed her the apple trees and the big stones set into the house gables to stop it sliding. He pointed out the gap in the hedge where scoundrels had come down over the hill to rob and pillage his ancestral namesake. 'Terrible,' she said then went back into the house, and the quiet atmosphere compared with home. The house stretched away in its cavernous unlived-in distance. She felt the peace and calm of the empty countryside before her. She watched the brae. Only yesterday she and Felix had walked along it innocent of what would happen, only yesterday she'd told her daughters she was off to see a friend and they'd questioned her and she said that even if she told them they'd have been none the wiser, she was none the wiser herself. She smiled how it happened. She thought of Maggie and Sadie. There was no mistaking their interest, they made no effort to disguise it, she could almost see what they were thinking. She didn't care. From the happy perspective of the new day, future hurdles of children and neighbours presented themselves neither urgently nor consistently.

She set about making tea, opening cupboards and drawers. Nothing was where she expected it; she opened cutlery drawers and found bits and pieces for horses and cattle, and a cupboard full to the brim with pots and pots of jam; she made a quick count, over fifty pots, and she wondered why he was stockpiling jam. All plum. What a luxury, she thought, Maggie must have made it. She wondered where he'd got sugar during the war, it must have been a great season for plums. She investigated the larder. A large tin can of milk, potatoes at the bottom, some tins and candles. She peeped into the wash basket in the corner. The wash basket was empty. She returned to the room. Each utensil had its space, the poker, the crockery, his papers stacked in the corner. In her fantasy she'd arrived at the uninhabitable house of a bachelor everything in ruin, all tending to decay, but everything had been done, and she felt the ghost hand of his mother still placing and moving and stacking, and for an instant she thought where would she clear a space for herself, where would there be a space? She sat down in the black wooden armchair and ate bread and plum jam and drank strong, sweet tea.

In the afternoon, Sarah-Ann stood amongst the parlour's chairs and rotting sofas and imagined what it must have been like when Felix was young. He had no sisters nor brothers, and his mother had been some sort of recluse, so he must have run alone through the house's old nooks and crannies, and the house must have been quiet as it was now, and it must have been lonely. Martha's parlour had a strange quality, dark and peaceful and a calm repository for all its things. In contrast to the rest of the house, it was full of ornaments, Sarah-Ann wondered if she'd ever seen such a collection. She didn't see the point of them. When she saw someone dedicating time and effort in restoring some small thing of their possession, or taking great lengths to preserve it, or becoming unbearably distraught at its loss, she felt bewilderment. If she needed a thing, she used it, discarded it, simple. Martha's room recalled her days as a laundry maid glimpsing through into a drawing room to see some maid placing flowers, taking care to arrange them then stepping back, and readjusting a flower first one way then another until it was perfect. She'd hated that devotion to the inanimate object, to the cut dead flower, to the satisfaction of some small need somewhere for someone to gaze upon a table and view what had been set perfect after the fashion of flowers. Who set such standards? Who devoted their life's heart to the table in the drawing room? Then she was young and could be stirred by such things. She was more used to living from moment to moment, to taking the bread direct from her hand to her mouth, to haphazardly and chaotically feeding and clothing her children. She'd honed no talent for housekeeping. She set no store by it and gave it no value.

She watched him shave in the evening. He shaved carefully and precisely. He lathered his face, swished and swirled the bristle brush, lathered, soaped and slapped, and stretched down his jaw tight as goatskin. He craned up his neck darkened by sun and wind, and hardened by rain, then ran the blade down his face. He shaved almost to the bone. When Felix was happy, he put all his care into the world, and set out tangible worlds – soap, razor, basin – in order and discipline and form, and performed action like it meant something. She thought then that he thought about nothing only razor and blade, basin and motion, only smooth shaving, whilst the dusk had unsettled her. All her boys had left home but the girls were still there, and between them made as much noise shouting and playing and fighting as ever the boys had.

She dressed the next morning in the only clothes she had. She put on her dress, and favourite pink cardigan, then stood up to pull up her stockings, and put on her shoes. She sat down in front of the dresser and rubbed ruby-red rouge into her cheeks, which she dulled down with saliva, and cleaned her finger on her petticoats. She thought then that she would talk to him about the children, but no words came, and the moment passed.

With long, mannered strokes, she swept her hands down over her hair, and cupped it up in her hands and piled it up on top of her head, held it there loose, dropped it down, her hands wanton, and all the thick thick hair dropped down over her shoulders and over her back. She closed her eyes. Moved loose fluid hands over her.

Her movement and reflection of movement was captured in two places, in physical space in front of the wardrobe and in the mirror. His presence was dark strength emanating from a dark corner. His eyes were perfectly still. Only once she gave sign that he watched her, held his eyes in the mirror, and saw him waver by his lips, which turned in the faintest darkest smile to acknowledge the mystery of her performance. He was the man.

She walked across the room and turned at the top of the stairs, and there smoothed down her petticoats and dress. Movement was slowed down to the one unified pace. His chair scraped out, and she waited motionless.

They spent two days sleeping and eating. Felix rose early to set the fire and do the things – feeding cattle, cleaning byres, fetching water – that needed doing every day, and with all these done by eight o'clock was little inclined to do anything else. The rest of the morning they spent lying around drinking tea and smoking and chatting. Afternoons they went for a leisurely walk over the farm, where they hoped to see no one. They went to bed late afternoon, and in the evening drank whiskey.

She slept more easily than he did. Felix woke up in the night feeling hot and cramped and having to go to the toilet. He went outside and stood at the gable getting cold, and when he had finished tiptoed back in up the ladder, to lie still in the bed not to touch her. She never stirred. Sleeping deep and faraway beside him, he worried in the night how long she would stay. She could be gone by the morning.

She slept on her back, her face up to the world and the blankets tucked under her chin.

Sometimes he watched her.

She was as still as the moon all night, as dark as the night, she was lost to his world.

All those months he'd dreamt of bringing her to see what he saw. The beauty under the mountains, and the hidden lanes, and the meadows, and around every corner something unexpected and more beautiful. At the deepest parts of the glen he showed her the waterfalls and their wet darkness. And the surprise of a sheep looking down curious into the ravine and you looking back. No one else ever to see it.

But in the event he was reluctant to walk past Shaw's or Martin's, and was afraid if he brought her to the glen, he'd meet Biggers or Boyce, and that fear outweighed the joy he'd managed. He still worried about Maggie. Sarah-Ann had said she'd stay a couple of days but he didn't know if she might not still be there on Thursday when Maggie came. He well imagined the stories Maggie and Sadie propagated but the thought of face-to-face in the house with Maggie filled him with dread.

Tuesday passed and Wednesday, Sarah-Ann was still there on Thursday morning. As they dressed he saw Sarah-Ann set the dressing table back the way it was, and make the bed more carefully, and perform other subtle preparations for leaving. He had his own interest in her not being there when Maggie came so said nothing when he saw her small bag ready at the door. He washed out the teapot, Sarah-Ann laid the table, soon breakfast was ready. They ate eggs and bread and plum jam, washed down with tea. They talked about what Felix would do after walking her to Cookstown, how on the way back he would stop to collect his paper and pass the time of day with Gibbons the newsagent, who sold no other *Times* and seemed genuinely bemused to sell the one. Felix told the sly pointed way Gibbons handed it over, which he did disdainfully to repress any doubt what he thought of the paper he wouldn't thank you for. Sarah-Ann got a distinct impression of Gibbons, smallminded and petty just like the shopkeepers at Scotts, who looked her up and down for all the clothes she never bought, and she laughed at the thought of him, but despite that laughing and that vivid impression of Gibbons, her overwhelming image was Felix waiting in the dusty quiet Moneymore shop for the London paper no one else ordered, no one else read, just Felix standing there shy struggling for identity with his tuppence ready in his hand or nervous in and out of his pocket like a child thinking he's different not wanting to be. Unfortunately the paper made him more so. Difference was he was a grown-up man. He claimed he never opened the paper before he got home, only time he did was the Somme, which like the battle was the exception and hardly worth it. She saw him out of the shop savouring the paper one way towards the post office, the other towards the Orange Hall.

She told him how upon arrival home the children would all be clambering all over her, and her mother no doubt scolding her, and the house filled with things to do so that after an hour it might well seem she'd never been away. The children, you see, she said would miss her over the few days, and she missed them too. Mary, thirteen, was the eldest at home, and the saving grace of the family who helped look after the younger ones, and the house, and even Sarah-Ann's own mother Therese who lived with them getting old herself, and not so much of a hand as she used to be. The younger ones were Annie and Katie, Josie and Betty, and Theresa, who was five. She said about her sons. The boys were married and in the army or living in Moneyneena and Donegal and all over the country, that was boys for you, she said. Johnny was thinking of America. Felix who didn't like to admit what it meant changed the subject back to his newspaper, the highlight of his week, which he read pipe in hand, in front of the fire; *The Times* took up most of his day, that's how he absorbed the shape and horror of war.

But Sarah-Ann had no inclination to leave and was still there when Maggie came late that evening. She and Felix were sitting in front of the fire when they heard the dogs barking over the field, followed by the gable gate opening and shutting. Felix rose up jumpy and went out shutting the hall door tight behind him. Sensing the visit unwelcome, Sarah-Ann pressed together her lips and smoothed down her hair, and weighed up the sway of what she should do. There was little she could do, stay where she was or go to the pantry, she had an urge to run into the pantry, but she might get trapped there. She heard the front door open, and Felix speak to the visitor. A woman's voice, a female visitor. The hallway door opened, the big woman was Maggie, hello said Sarah-Ann before she entered, but said it too quick, too anxious, Maggie was still in the hallway taking off her cardigan, hanging up her cardigan, maybe, she hoped, she wouldn't stay long.

'This is Sarah-Ann,' said Felix, and Sarah-Ann stepped forward to shake her hand. Either Maggie didn't see it, or pretended she didn't; she made for the seat at the window.

'Maggie that does the washing,' said Felix with bluntest explanation.

'Aye, I do the washing,' said Maggie perfunctorily and sat down. She seemed bare, her light summer dress draped over her incidentally as ship's tarpaulin, her large bulging calves ballasted her one end, her thick naked neck the other, and the impression was of large dimpled flesh exposed without relief. She crossed over her thick legs like stacked tree trunks.

'Aye, the washing,' mimicked Sarah-Ann. Felix stood at the door neither in nor out the room waiting. It was up to him to speak.

'Aye, I met you the other day,' said Maggie, thick naked skin folding round her neck and thick ankles poking out of tight black shoes.

'That's right,' said Sarah-Ann, 'we met the other day.' For two days she had come across traces of Maggie, the curtains Maggie had hung, the cupboards she'd sorted, and for two days she had wondered about Felix's relation with Maggie. She looked at Felix. 'You'd maybe sit down', she said cross to him, and Felix hesitated like he might make his excuses and leave, 'I'll shut that door,' she said brusquely to trap him, and Felix had no choice to sit down. Sarah-Ann was the only one standing.

'A good enough day for the time of year,' she said busily.

'Aye,' muttered Felix, knew weather better than anyone, and Maggie said nothing. Sarah-Ann tried to smile. 'Good enough,' she muttered, and felt the effort of conversation's custodian. She directed herself at Maggie, up close she was even bigger but prettier, there was a girlish freshness in her round, full face. 'You live across the fields?'

'Just over the fields, the lane to the right, but over the fields, it's not that far away,' said Maggie, whose full flesh kept her out of breath.

'You'd take a cup of tea,' said Felix, and Maggie said aye, and Sarah-Ann expected Felix would offer her too. Felix didn't rise.

'I'll make it,' said Maggie, and Sarah-Ann smarted at the unnatural intimacy of Felix's guest suddenly assuming the status of hostess.

'Not a bit of you, I wouldn't hear of it, a nice pot of tea,' said Sarah-Ann, self-consciously polite to take the sting out of rejecting Maggie's role in it. She couldn't stand by whilst Maggie walked past to the pantry to make noisy activity whilst Maggie and Felix sat helpless in the room.

'It's no bother,' said Maggie.

'No, I'll make it.' Sarah-Ann felt the weight of all the compromises the situation demanded of her. To go to the pantry confirmed in action what Maggie obviously assumed: that she was Felix's woman. To let Maggie make the tea was to yield too far in the other direction. Neutrality was impossible; go to the pantry or not, Maggie would draw her conclusion.

'I'll not be a minute,' she said and as she got up to go to the pantry she had an acute sense of herself as if omnipotently perceived by some eye detached from herself. It was an external vision of herself, not necessarily the combined perception of Felix and Maggie, not necessarily informed by them. The vision was at once fleeting of everything outward in the flesh, her body, her limbs, her body moving, her limbs moving, her gestures, even her clothes, which were one and the same time impressionistic and complete in every detail like her dress, which was a flash of red in motion and a study in minuscule of every white daisy represented upon it. Whatever it was, once in the pantry that self-view, flawed as any, disintegrated with a violent resistance against Felix, morose and useless, and Maggie's importunate imposition, and Sarah-Ann herself having to make the compromises she shouldn't have had to. Inside she raged. That she would prop up Felix's world for him was more than she could bear. In one spasm of response she tore through the strain of genteel gesture, her fists clenched, her arms forced rigid, her face contorted hard tight against its bones, then she pushed out her arms behind her as if to hit something nothing but air. She damaged nothing but herself. Smoothly she recovered, the inner eye observing and controlling the outer gesture, she lifted down the cups, and set them down, and arranged them on saucers, and thought then that she was thinking only about tea. Her rebellion had been shortlived. She called in needless from the pantry.

'There's no sugar,' she called highpitched, affected, about a provision no one had in the war. 'We'll just have to do without sugar,' she chirped as if improvising, used to better things. Even to her, it sounded put-on. She pulled down the tray and placing things on it couldn't push back the foreignness that engulfed her. For all the response back from the room, they might as well have been dead.

Felix sat glum at the table, and Maggie shifted in her seat. Any other day she would have gone to the fire, slid the skirt up the back of her legs. 'There'll be no more washing,' thought Maggie.

'There'll be no more washing,' said Maggie. The only noise was clocks ticking and Sarah-Ann moving muffled in the pantry.

'The day's never cleared,' said Felix, who didn't want to think about washing and vexing Maggie.

'Wild bad for the time of year,' answered Maggie, who had expected some change in him, but nothing was different; if anything, he was more subdued. Weather was all he had to say to her.

'Aye,' said Felix, 'you're well enough.'

'Why wouldn't I be?' snapped Maggie. She had waited all day. She had dragged out all morning looking at the clock and drinking tea, and she had dragged out the whole afternoon thinking about whether she should go and consoling herself that she hadn't, and she'd dragged out the early evening . . . until she could drag out no longer . . . The day was a lifetime. Underneath, Felix Campbell must have known she loved him.

Felix curled down his lip, and said nothing.

'Aw, well enough,' said Maggie ungraciously, and felt the indignity of tea she didn't want. She knew her face looked dead, felt it from the inside. She should have stayed away but the day for staying away was too long.

'Right,' said Sarah-Ann and pushed the door open with her foot. There they were same as she left them.

'Can I give you a hand?' asked Maggie, seeing good-looking as they said, but not that good-looking. If you saw her up close, you'd see she was ageing that bit around the neck, and was tired around the eyes from better days, and her mouth was maybe sad, or big, and her eyes too far apart further than they should be . . . Not that a man would notice, thought Maggie. All he'd see was the thick dark hair falling down her back, and the fair skin fairer against the darker hair, and the ruby-red lips, most likely all he'd see was the tight pink cardigan and the laced-up shoes . . . most likely . . .

'I've got it all here,' said Sarah-Ann and went back to the pantry to return with another cup and saucer.

'They've let them out,' said Maggie, as if continuing some conversation that Sarah-Ann, occupied with tea, had no part in. She thought she was glad they'd started conversation, but at Maggie's remark Felix looked up, furtive, to see his responses in the old oval mirror ahead of him, and his jaw prominent holding tension.

'The tae's out,' said Felix but didn't divert her. From the moment she spoke the atmosphere, already oppressive with strained relations, tautened.

'I wouldn't have let them out, I can tell you that,' said Maggie, and it was clear she meant the Republican prisoners from the Easter Rising, released last month by Lloyd George, trying to encourage America into war and Republicans into negotiation. Even sympathetic with everything Maggie condemned, he raged at the affront of her timing. 'They'll soon learn there's no pleasing them,' she said with all the bluster the subject demands, and all the cant. 'And Carson huffing and puffing away useless as ever,' added Maggie of the man who once talked them into war, now talking them into partition of Ulster. Carson was the undisputed leader of Ulster Unionism. 'Useless,' said Maggie, damning Carson the lawyer, their only defence.

Felix was horrified at Maggie raising these politics before Sarah-Ann, whom she must have known was Catholic. Her motive could only have been bitter distinction.

'That's a sudden new interest in politics,' he said to abuse her credentials.

'I always keep up with what's going on,' answered Maggie, outside confident but inside befuddled with no interest in politics or talk about politics. Pressed to name who had been released from where by whom, she would have struggled, and inside she stung at Felix unmasking it.

'Naw, Maggie, you never took any interest in politics,' he said to neutralise all she had said so that the conversation, ostensibly opened on Maggie's substantive issue, was now embroiled on the matter of whether she was qualified to speak at all. Seemed she wasn't.

'Sure I've always been interested.'

'Not a bit of you,' he said to establish the underlying principle he was driving for, which is that politics doesn't matter even when they do. He was helped in this by his conviction that Maggie had not a scrap of interest in the negotiations he thought the war had put an end to.

'Well . . .' faltered Maggie, and Sarah-Ann, who until then had sat red-dressed, inscrutable, spoke for the first time.

'I've no interest myself,' she said lightly with deadly accuracy to smother with empathetic flattery any comeback Maggie might make. 'Would you like more tea?' asked Sarah-Ann, already out of her chair, and Maggie with no interest in politics changed the conversation.

'You've turned round the room,' said Maggie, and they talked

about the room and the space in the room, and the table nearer
the window for light, and Maggie mentioned Martha.

'For years, even when Martha was here, I used to come and
help with the big jobs,' said Maggie, who recalled Felix's mother
and her way of doing things, and Martha's routine, and her own
critical involvement in Martha stitching sheets, and baking
bread, and bedding roses, and as Maggie talked on Sarah-Ann
felt the point Maggie was making, that Martha Campbell would
never have let her over the doorstep. Sarah-Ann felt herself hot
near the fire, and Felix cold at the table.

Maggie left straight after tea.

On the way home the next morning, Sarah-Ann met children
at the bridge. They stood deferentially before her, and waited for
her to pass, and she said hello, and they sniggered.

'I'm Sarah-Ann,' she said, 'who are you?'

They giggled the five of them, four scruffy boys and a girl
with thin stick legs and a round fat face and rabbit teeth same as
her brothers. She squeezed in between the boys.

'What's your name?' she tried with the girl. Shy children too
shy to look or talk.

'Is this your little sister?'

'Aye,' said the biggest.

'What age is she?'

'Four.'

'She's big for four.'

They shuffled and scuffed.

'I'll see you again.'

'Papist,' one of the boys hissed after her, silence waiting for
her to turn. She didn't. 'Fenian,' they said, still tentatively testing
the name. 'Papist and Fenian,' into a chant, 'Papist Fenian.'

They were scratching and catcalling at the bridge, must have
been what they heard, must have been what their parents had

said, and the words rang and froze in her ears until she thought she heard them say that Fenians breed like rabbits, but maybe it was only her own imagination thinking the children's teeth looked like rabbits', she thought it was only her imagination.

It was starting to sleet.

19

Stuarty Gibson was the greatest of draughtsplayers

That evening the draughtsplayers met on the night to end in mysterious catastrophe. Bolstered by boredom, held together by draughts, Geordie Biggers, Stuarty Gibson, Black Willie and Tommy Boyce had met every Friday night during all the years since Sunday school when they played on the grassy banks of the glen. The game made its easy transition to adult-hood, and they never missed a week.

Geordie Biggers was always their leader. His social antennae missed no minutiae of the least significant human transaction. Like a rat on a wheel, Biggers pursued his own rural ends with malicious megalomania and sly wit, and was acutely aware of the influence he exerted over bridgemen and draughtsmen. Tommy

Boyce, Black Willie and Stuarty Gibson were his unlikely com-panions. More at home on the hill, Willie rarely ventured abroad, whilst Boyce's drunkenness seemed to preclude all other pastimes. Stuarty was the only one amongst them to follow the path of conjugal happiness, and had that domestic excuse. Their mutual interest was a lifetime passion for draughts.

Lean as a fox, Stuarty Gibson walked briskly and cannily. He smelt the air as a dog smells it. His eyes watched for tracks that animals and men had made before him. It had snowed heavily all day, and in the evening had started to freeze. Stuarty looked up, conscious of someone staring at him. Biggers was there. He was a shadow in the darkness. He stood by the stile dividing the Bells' and Williams' lands. 'There's no blood in you, Gibson, wrapped up and fixing at yourself like a woman,' he said.

Gibson jumped simultaneous to forming his response. He squinted hard to focus.

'It's a cold night that blew up out of nowhere, but a man's got to make the best of himself. You're a hardy perennial, Geordie. I'm more of a thoroughbred myself.'

'Fine chat from you, just out from the fire, when I'm out tracking down sticks,' replied Biggers, whose keen eyesight had followed Gibson from a dark speck moving over the whiteness of the brae.

'That's as well,' commenced Gibson as he approached. A riposte on his tongue, he more clearly discerned Biggers leaning nonchalantly over the narrow stile. Nothing in his demeanour revealed the coldness of the night; he was wearing thin, poorly fitting clothes into which he made no effort to withdraw for the extra shelter. He stood expansive and lean as on the finest summer day. His right foot rested confidently on the snow-covered stone, and his arm stretched open across the wooden post. The full impression was that of the raffish lord who, surveying his domains, feels bored and longs for adventure. In his leaning, stretched-out arm he held a pipe, the angle of which suggested he was on the point of dragging luxuriantly. He wasn't. Biggers didn't have tobacco. Carefully placing the cold pipe in his pocket, he straightened up.

'Brisk walkin'll get the heat in you,' he said with the effort of a man who must always be comforting a weaker creature.

'We'd need to be making a headstart before it's too late,' replied Gibson starting to cross the stile but as he crossed – his legs raised, his body half over – he was momentarily distracted by the look on Biggers' face. It was the strangest sensation, almost fright, but he caught himself on, and realised that the look on Biggers' face was caused by the odd way of the moon on the snow, and Biggers' head tilted like a dog hearing another dog in the distance.

'You can get over all right,' said Biggers, avoiding the offence that a helping hand would give.

'I'm just watching for slippiness.'

There was no shortcut to Tommy Boyce's house in the middle of the glen. The only route was straight across the top field, through Williams' land and down Hutchinson's lane. The top field was in deep hard furrows where Williams had ploughed and abandoned it years ago. When it snowed, the snow lay in the troughs, and when it rained the water collected in large puddles in the tracks. Geordie Biggers traversed quickly and deftly by judging the distance between furrows, but where he glided, Gibson struggled.

'There's a method to it,' advised Biggers dispassionately.

'What sort of help is it to a man that there's a way to it when he doesn't have it?' snarled Gibson.

'Well, I thought it would stop you sliding in and out like an eejit. Anyway, it's well the moon's out, for the nights are getting far blacker.'

'They're pitch black on some nights, pitch black. You couldn't see your hand in front of you. It used to be on the darkest night we would walk the brae and never think of a light.'

'You couldn't do it now. Far darker, I observed it some time ago.'

'If it was pitch black, how could you have observed it?'

'You're a thrad bugger, thrad and contraring.'

'When you state a fact out of place, I like to put it straight.'

They were nearly at Boyce's before Stuarty mustered up the nerve to challenge Biggers, only thing bolstered him was the inquisition he would get at home.

'You kept Felix Campbell's business well to yourself,' said Gibson, whose quiet modest demeanour was attributed by bridgemen to the indomitable spirit of Mrs Stuarty. He spoke now on her behalf. 'Mrs Stuarty says it's a disgrace the way you set Heather up to think Campbell was looking a woman. Getting the young girl's hopes up like that!'

'And was he not after a woman, and hasn't he got one?' trumped Biggers.

'You know what I mean,' said Gibson. The role Biggers had played in coaxing Mrs Stuarty towards Felix Campbell and the wicked tune he'd whistled to their daughter was all Stuarty ever heard now.

'Women are full of fanciful ideas. You know what women are like. Get carried away!' joked Biggers. Stuarty saw how Biggers enjoyed the spectacle of his family made a laughing stock. 'Anyway, sure when would I ever see Mrs Stuarty.' A man's honour was a plaything to Biggers.

'You seen her surely,' said Gibson, and looked again for third-party condemnation to say what he couldn't say himself. 'Even

Maggie Martin says she knows what you were up to.'

'If I only knew all Maggie thinks I know! You know fine well I'm as shocked as the next man at him bringing that whore round the brae.' Biggers' strong language deadened Stuarty's already meagre appetite for the conversation.

'You know I think Heather's a nice girl. He'd have been far better off with one of his own. He'll learn that,' predicted Biggers, a mix of concern and sense, and sinister.

They reached Boyce's after eight. Tommy, Black Willie and a bottle of whiskey sat by the fire in much the same positions as every Friday night. Willie was up close to the fire, and Tommy, a hardier specimen, sat further back and was caught between the heat of the fire and the cold and dampness that came through the door. Tommy was used to being in two worlds.

Biggers and Gibson squinted to get used to the light. Their cold faces and hands thawed and stung.

'Pull yourselves up,' said Boyce. For all his drinking, Tommy still shuffled himself into some fit shape to host the draughts.

'A breezier night the night,' chipped in Black Willie, who was more at home on the hill than in company.

'Hardy hardy,' said Gibson, blowing the cold words into his fingers.

'It'll be worse afore it's better,' said Biggers, laconic at the door.

'You're a bloodless being,' chastised Boyce to excuse his own proximity to heat. Moving aside from the fire, he complimented the healthy appearance of Biggers who, wise to the hazards of compliments, took it as a slight to his usual look.

'The hill's bad the night,' said Biggers, 'you'd think some-thing'd be done with it.'

'Clear as yesterday I see Williams ploughing it,' recalled Stuarty, 'and me thinking, I can almost see me thinking it, what the rare sight it was him out working, and there twenty years on it's the same as he left it.'

'You're a great man for predicting and thinking things after they've happened,' laughed Boyce.

'Sure the set of horses you'd need to turn it,' said Stuarty. 'I don't know what horses you'd not need.'

'Well, there's some goings on over at Ballymully these days,' said Boyce, rising to the occasion.

'Aye, there'll be less of his reading now! Campbell'll have other things to take his mind off the war,' laughed Biggers.

'You'll maybe even think of getting a woman yourself, Biggers!' Boyce wittered whatever drink-distilled words occurred to him. Tommy, desirous of nothing more for himself than the delicious oblivion his liver delivered him, rejected all the obligations in which Biggers traded.

'Fool!' snarled Biggers.

'Campbell's a dark horse,' muttered Willie darkly, and rubbed his black hand over his head. Up close his face was pocked not uniform black.

'They say he's been seeing her for months . . . all those trips up to Cookstown. She was at the end of it,' added Stuarty quietly.

'Sadie's not got over she's Catholic!' exclaimed Biggers, smug about the small preoccupations beneath him. He smirked and waited for Willie.

'Felix Campbell was the last man you'd expect,' said Gibson, abstractedly ruminating whilst Willie stayed quiet in the corner. Seemed Willie had not caught Biggers' meaning.

Long and recent history were well confused in Black Willie's lonely mind. Town, draughts, preaching to bridgemen, these were the bare events that punctuated his daily existence. Any other rhythm that formed his week had been invented by Willie himself. He felt the weather acutely. He could smell rain, and the wind turning, and the growing of grass. His father never passed a cat or a dog without kicking or otherwise tormenting it, and knew more cruelties than there are proper names for. Willie himself kept goats in no condition God ever decreed.

'Aye, if Martha Campbell knew there was a Fenian in her bed . . .' drawled Biggers, and Willie stirred slowly. A great big man, his responses were deliberate and sluggish. 'Fenian?' muttered Willie. Biggers thought of Black Willie's own ma, she too was a Catholic.

'And a dozen weans to her!' said Biggers, and Black Willie spat into the fire.

'Maggie's been over at the house and says that she's installed herself like the Queen of Sheba, and turned the house upside down, and Felix sitting there at the table not passing a word.'

'Maggie'll hardly go back,' said Tommy Boyce to criticise her. It was well known wild horses wouldn't keep Maggie away.

'The boards are out,' Stuarty reminded them.

A crude wooden draughts board was set up at each end of the table. Nearer the fire, Boyce and Black Willie's new game was precisely laid out in its large thick squares. It was pristine without history. At the other end was Biggers' sparse board, its whites and blacks were only a man and a crown. Four solitary pieces for a game entering its fourth week.

'Yours wasn't hard to set,' observed Boyce about the small effort of laying four pieces. Boyce spoke only for chat. It was Willie who had a point.

'Not a lot you'll be doing with it,' said Willie, solemnly nodding at the board as if it was real, the protagonists coincidental. The match was Stuarty's against Biggers.

'What?' muttered Stuarty, lifting his head.

'Not a lot you'd do with the game,' repeated Willie. His speech was terse and internal.

'You'll not be doing anything with it,' corrected Biggers. 'You'd be better concerning yourself with your own game.'

'Sure it's over,' said Willie, showing bitterness.

Biggers sighed but left speech to Stuarty.

'It's the cunning you bring to the game,' countered Stuarty, irritated.

'A bad workman blames his tools,' skipped in Boyce, unwitting of the argument supported by his aphorism. Boyce was too happily crumpled by the fire, and draughts to him was only pleasure.

'Aye,' grunted Willie, 'bad workmen,' and laughed, knew they wouldn't like it. Well, it wasn't his fault their game was in deadlock, too bad they didn't like it, too bad they didn't like the truth.

'It's a game for masters,' sneered Biggers, getting up at the window.

'Aye,' said Willie thinking they were fooling themselves. 'Aye,' he said again, his mind bedded down at some comfortable spot.

'It's rare there's a four-week game,' said Willie dispassionately.

'It's rare all right,' boasted Stuarty, suddenly energised in the corner. 'An old man like me teaching you how to play draughts. There's a time to move forward and a time to move back. That's my technique.'

'More like you'll both get crowns and head for a corner, more like,' criticised Boyce of the interminable strategy of playing aggressor-defender in corners.

'That can go on forever.'

'Back and forward, going nowhere.'

Biggers snapped.

'Like two old women. The company of two old women would be more cheerful! The two of you!' He walked round the table, behind Stuarty and Boyce. 'Cackling like hens.'

'No need for agitation,' said Stuarty, fidgeting and fussing.

'Aye, the draughts gets you out of yourself,' said Boyce.

'Four weeks is enough, I'd think of changing to two.'

'Sure you'd hardly be started a hard game,' said Stuarty, surprised at Biggers losing heart. 'There's no way to change in the middle of the year.'

'There were changes in 1903,' Biggers reminded him. The date's only significance was the meaning the draughtsplayers gave it.

'Genuine reasons,' intoned Boyce, 'genuine reasons. The rules can only be changed for genuine reasons.'

'And only at the end of the year,' muttered Willie.

'Winner won't play winner this time, it'll be the last partners over the last twenty, so it's my turn against you,' challenged Biggers.

'Only if you win, and if you don't, you'll be playing me and if you draw, which is the most likely, you'll still play me under thirty.'

First introduced in '49, the thirty-game rule referred to the results of the prior thirty games and determined who partnered who. Biggers knew the results from the top of his head – they all did.

'The rules are all right the way they are,' said Boyce, sitting down at his own board. Willie pulled up beside him, and with a flourish made his traditional opening move. A steady player, his subsequent game would be cautious and deliberate and a potent strength against Boyce, who was a brilliant but careless player. Willie's record was a testimony to the quiet qualities of patience and resilience.

'Hush, no talk of drawing,' said Biggers, sitting down at the table. Stuarty joined him, leant over and showed his draughts face, serious and inexpressive. For light, Boyce moved a candle between them; it flickered and threw the light back on them.

'Your move,' nodded Biggers.

Stuarty stared at the board and realised that he couldn't remember the move he'd planned all week.

When he eventually made it, Biggers snorted loudly to belittle his effort.

Stuarty didn't respond, just looked up and saw the pitted Bigger eyes and the Biggers snout drawn out and curved, and he thought, as many had before him that the Biggers people were a bad-looking sort with their long thin foreheads and cheeks squared out into jutting wide jaws, and their thick short necks. Their only fineness was their eyes, which looked out wistfully from pugilistic faces. The Biggers aged young.

'Where did the Biggers come from to Tirgan?'

'I don't know, you're the man for the history.'

'Would they have come out from Sixmiletown by any chance?'

'I don't follow the history myself. What's the interest of it?' said Biggers.

'They were chased out, that's the interest of it. They were chased out in the forties for stealing corn . . .'

'Enough of that chat,' snapped Boyce.

'Let him talk,' said Biggers.

'The drink's talking,' said Willie, not following the conversation, still an appropriate rejoinder.

'What did you hear to start story-spreading?' asked Biggers menacingly. Gibson looked up and across the room and shrugged his shoulders like he was suddenly very very tired or very very old.

'Your mouth's too big,' threatened Biggers, and Gibson nodded sadly as if he understood, and from this low base of energy and emotion the game proceeded. Biggers and Gibson were up close to each other over the draughts board, and the room was small

and dark and quiet except for the low murmur of Willie and
Boyce. In this dense proximity and atmosphere they played art-
fully as men who have played for as long as they can remember.
In alternating roles of aggressor and defender, they each moved
their two crowns between two corners, and they knew that with
each being as good and as bad as the other there was no way
either could win. Boyce and Willie started chatting to cover it.

'The games are different from they used to be. It used to be if
you missed a couple of weeks, you'd have lost technique.'

'Aye, like '13,' said Willie.

Boyce paused, he had talked himself into a trap.

'We needn't go back that far,' he said defensively, even
though he had only the vaguest sense of that year's events,
who he had been and how he had come to run through the
country after Sarah McGuigan, a married woman who it
turned out only wanted a bachelor flirting and running after
her. No, Tommy Boyce, genial host and player of draughts,
had lost his sense of old love, the logistics, the passion and
how it had ended – her husband found out. All he knew was
he was always blamed for the draughts.

'You were never in mischief yourself,' he taunted.

'Aye,' slurred Willie, long and slow over three syllables, and
they both knew what Boyce meant, what Willie meant in
response, even though in the whole large wider world there
could have been no meaning whatsoever. Boyce took it hard to
be blamed for a past life that was nothing to him.

'It was a long stoppage,' he said, suddenly conciliatory, and
more involved in their whole history than in his own small igno-
ble role in it.

'The longest,' smirked Willie, and Boyce smirked too, and for
that brief resurrected moment was again the man he'd once
been, and proud of having interrupted the draughts longer than

it was ever interrupted. Only other stoppages were the short-term acts of God like sickness and death and nights when the glen was unpassable. The draughtsplayers always planned and worked within these, and were fortunate at a network of neighbours to communicate misfortune and contingent arrangement. They were neighbours to carry any bad news at all.

Whether it was this stilted staccato, or the chill in the air, or the draughts, or festering on what Stuarty Gibson had said, Biggers suddenly stood up at the other side of the table. 'It's your game,' he said, firm and controlled, and walked to the hearth and rested one hand on it, one on his hip.

Startled, Gibson stared up at him, the wiry thin dark set of him, and the sight turned in Gibson a profound self-pity, a sharp cold in the bones, a soreness at the bad night it had turned out.

'Sure it's nobody's game, it's a draw, I should have said it earlier when we were tiring of it,' he struggled.

'Aye, Biggers, we couldn't record that as a win.'

'Win or draw, call it what you will,' dismissed Biggers.

'Well, that's the quare change over you,' observed Boyce, looking in at the side of him. Biggers kept his head lowered and passive.

'It's tiredness and the weather,' said Biggers.

'This weather gets the best of us,' agreed Gibson breezily. 'I knew myself that it'd lie.'

'Aye, the hill was in a wild bad state,' said Boyce into the room's quietness, just the fire's hush, the creak at the window, his own words straying away from him.

Boyce made a big show of the fire, stoking it, raking and poking. 'We'll get on with ours, Willie, no need to let you think you'll take their result to your advantage.'

Boyce's skilfulness brought Willie back to the game and the others to watch it. Biggers drew behind Willie and Gibson behind Boyce, and with both reflecting on their own slow, dissatisfying game, they watched and thought of the moves they themselves would have played. Biggers thought of the moves he would have made if he had been Willie, and Gibson thought of the moves he would have made if he had been Boyce, and with each being nobody other than themselves they constructed in their minds totally different and superior moves to those acted out in the small real world beneath them.

'Myself I'd have advanced in the middle,' said Gibson to Boyce when Willie had won.

'I would never get into the corner that soon,' said Biggers to Black Willie. Later Boyce poured drink and stoked the fire, and made a fuss of the fuss he was making for them.

'I'll walk you to the top of the glen,' offered Boyce later.

Boyce parted company with them at the top of the glen. Biggers and Gibson lapsed into silence, and trudged back across the field, Biggers measuring out his paces and Gibson falling into every other furrow.

By the time they reached the top of the hill, Gibson's hands were purple blue and the snow was melting in his thin shoes. He could no longer feel his feet. His physical discomfort induced a harsher regret. He regretted his inquisition of Biggers. Both the matter of Heather, and the Biggers' past.

Giving no impression of offence, Biggers started humming to himself, then said he was warmed by the sight of light at Williams'.

'There's Williams,' said Biggers, as much to himself. Gibson lifted his head happy to see human habitation.

'When the drink's in, the wit's out,' apologised Gibson.

Biggers stopped in front of him. 'We never got to the bottom of what you were saying,' he said steadily.

'Nothing at all, nothing at all . . .' explained Gibson, nervously repeating himself.

'It didn't sound like nothing to me.' Biggers turned to face his companion. 'What's the good in dragging things up?'

'You know just the gossip, Biggers, just the gossip.'

'There was nothing of it if I know what you're meaning about,' said Biggers.

'Nothing at all,' repeated Gibson ineffectually, and waited for Biggers to speak, but Biggers just marched on with his head down, and his eyes straight ahead determined to get home. It must then have seemed to Gibson that Biggers wasn't so worried about his small indiscretion as he was about the cold.

The next day, in the town, Williams said he'd looked out and seen two men walking over the hill at about half past ten. It was a Friday night and he was sure it must have been the draught-splayers, for who else would have been out on such a night? He'd watched them walk across the top of the hill, and standing there at the window before he knew what he knew now he'd said to himself they were the quare pair out that night. One of them was higher up the ridge, and the other was further down, and he'd wondered at anybody walking down there with the snow that deep and treacherous. Turned out it was Gibson.

'What the quare pair,' said Williams, intrigued by his own role in the affair. He was not surprised Gibson hadn't made it.

'Out on a night like that!' he said in explanation of events as he understood them, 'even the house was freezing with the fire all day.'

Williams had no doubts about how Gibson died. Old man, worst weather in years, simple explanation. For Williams it wasn't the cold so much as Gibson's foolery at being out in it.

Only much later, when the chill had thawed out in their bones and Williams' testimony had faded, and all other evidence, proximity, emotion were far removed from the circumstances of Stuarty Gibson, how he lived, how he died, it was then the rumours started that there was more to it than met the eye, and more to the Biggers people than had ever been exhumed.

At news of his death, his family were devastated, especially Mrs Stuarty who regretted no kind word between them and the days she never looked at him. Once she had loved him. He was thin wiry as a winter hawthorn, his face witty as a fox, and he was the only person who ever touched her. So lives the unlived life, churns, rots, festers.

And spews forth instantly recognisable.

It was left to Boyce to spread the story of Gibson's draught-splaying prowess, and soon everyone knew that in sixty years of draughtsplaying Gibson had never lost a game, nor cheated, nor lost his temper, nor turned over a board, and most remarkably Stuarty Gibson had never uttered a bad word against any opponent. In this manner did Boyce propagate Gibson's dead talent. No one denied him. Who would deny Stuarty Gibson was the greatest of draughtsplayers?

20

Heather Gibson

'The birds'll get it hard,' said Felix when he met old Jimmy on the lane two days later.

'Heartbreaking,' replied Jimmy. 'Scouring looking for food, and not a pick anywhere. Heartbreaking.' Felix felt his fingers cold, and his feet numb. He slid his hands into his pockets. 'Heartbreaking,' repeated Jimmy. Everybody knew Jimmy loved birds.

'I'll outlast them all,' said Jimmy.

'You show every sign of it.'

'A wild bad time for the funeral, even if the snow's nearly all melted.'

'Aye,' said Felix in response to the abstract.

'I'll outlive them yet,' said Jimmy. His mortal pride was unconvincing.

'What funeral's t'morrow?'

'You don't know?! You haven't heard?!! Stuarty Gibson dead the two days and you don't know!' Jimmy sprang into life. Felix Campbell not knowing was proof apparent. 'Sure, you'd've heard surely!' said Jimmy cautioning himself against good fortune. 'How couldn't you know! Sure nobody's talking about anything else!' he cried.

'What happened?'

'Stuarty slipped coming back from the draughts, and couldn't be lifted. He died from the freezing. When a man's left out in the cold it's surprising quick he'll go. And with a few drinks in him on a bad night. By the time Geordie came back, he was dead.'

'Aye, that's a long walk, and maybe with some drink . . .' Felix trailed off failing to understand. 'Where was he?'

'Bells' big field.'

'But sure he was far nearer Williams' than Bells',' said Felix, compulsive, 'Biggers should have gone to Williams'. Why didn't he go to Williams'? Williams' is far nearer.'

'Geordie didn't know there was that much wrong with him, and you never know what welcome you'd get, Williams would as likely stick a gun out the window,' said Jimmy, and his conviction of Biggers' story precluded further discussion. Felix turned to the practical matter of the funeral, and so they calculated between them Stuarty's age, and his wife's and daughter's, and all the other issues that Stuarty's death brought to focus.

'His wife's bad but the daughter's worse,' said Jimmy.

'Aye,' muttered Felix. Mention of Heather Gibson disturbed him. All the times they'd met in Cookstown, all the coincidences of meeting, in Moneymore, the glen, even the day he walked down to Coagh, each time he turned she was there with something to say for herself, a reason why she was on the lane, an explanation for her journey, a visit she'd had to make at the last minute. Heather was a chatty, friendly girl, brusque but her heart in the right place, that's what they said about her, that's what Geordie Biggers always said when she was brought up at the bridge, not that with her father there they could have said much else.

'She's bad?' asked Felix. Once he had joked that if they kept meeting like this people would start talking; it was not the sort of comment came natural to him, yet he'd tried it in his most casual manner and knew that Heather Gibson would dismiss that sort of sentimentality with a good hard swipe at him. Her reaction had then surprised him. She'd blushed, and played with her dress, and muttered some excuse, which sounded hollow so that he wished he'd never opened his mouth.

'Aye, she's not been well the couple of weeks,' said Jimmy.

'Not well,' muttered Felix. He hadn't seen her since Cookstown.

'I'll see you at the funeral,' rushed Jimmy, who hurried off up the lane, his legs bowed arthritic.

'You'll outlast them yet,' called Felix behind him, and sensed Jimmy smile toothless sad.

'See you at the funeral,' shouted Felix.

It was a cold day at the graveside. A mid-grey sky pressed in upon the world, making it smaller. It drained the world of colour, it chopped the future up.

On good days the church commanded a superb view over the village nestled in beneath the Sperrin Mountains. On good days streets were clearly visible, and the congregation watched the goings-on in Lawford Street and Main Street and the Circular Road. That day the village was obscured. The northern horizon was the vague outline of a manmade structure, the disused limekiln.

The bitter wind sweeping low across the hill lifted jackets and hats, and coloured confetti from last week's wedding, and a loose catechism. The miscellaneous rubbish of churches blew around the graveyard, and the funeral party clutched their clothes and said that a graveside on a bare hill is the coldest place you can ever be.

Geordie Biggers crept out from behind a stone wall as if from nowhere to make his condolences.

'A tragic end,' consoled Felix.

'Tragic,' muttered Geordie, and Felix couldn't help wondering what had happened on the hill.

'Bitter.'

'Bitter, bitter,' replied Biggers urgently, and rubbed his blue cold hands, and hurried behind the extreme motive driving him. The next he was sitting between Mrs Gibson and her daughter Heather.

'There he goes,' remarked Tommy Boyce at Geordie Biggers seated between the women Stuarty Gibson left behind.

'Sitting there with his family it makes you think, it makes you think,' said Tommy with no idea what to think.

'I suppose . . .' said Felix, but Tommy interrupted.

'An awful night,' he concluded assuming the well-worn expression of taciturn men attendant upon funerals. The door was closed. The hush was complete. The minister performed his duty.

After the service, Felix spoke to old Jimmy and people he knew from the town.

'That's his brother from Stewartstown,' whispered Boyce, 'and with the fur round her neck, that's Issy his sister . . .' The Gibsons walked past oblivious. Geordie Biggers moved behind them. The talk resumed.

'Betty Dawkins says whatever he done, she'd entertain no Biggers around her,' said old Jimmy about the threats made by Stuarty Gibson's sister.

'Whatever he's done . . . ?'

'Aye, she doesn't care that it was Biggers ran after to help her brother, she says it doesn't take the bad out of him,' said old Jimmy, and Felix realised that Stuarty Gibson's death distracted from himself. 'One man's poison the other's meat,' he thought guiltily.

The mourners were thirty deep as far as the gates.

Felix watched the mourners form their human circle around a cluster of gravestones. He and Tommy picked their way through the haphazard headstones and stopped by old Jimmy. It was the most congested part of the graveyard, no measured rows of English dead.

'The good ones go first,' said Jimmy, then, as if struggling with the meaning of his own bare utterance, lapsed into silence as on more ordinary days. Passion drained from a small font.

'Thanks for coming,' Biggers was saying, and his approach to the grave triggered a wave of nods. The human circle tightened its ranks. The wind blew godly words random out to the wings . . . God in your mercy on this day . . . accept them into . . . The fast words of a minister with two funerals that day.

At the graveside the proud battling Mrs Stuarty broke down and had to be led away.

'Heather's had it hard enough with Mrs Stuarty, you know what she's like, well meaning and all that. They've been worried about the girl. All that talk about you and her was just Geordie blowing,' said old Jimmy. 'You know what he's like, but this'll hardly help her.'

'Talk about me and her?'

'You know what Geordie's like,' said Jimmy, and Felix

thought of the big plump girl sitting in his room, and Mrs Stuarty on his own chair.

'That's the draughts over,' said Black Willie leaving the grave-yard.

'Bringing her round like that, bringing her round . . .' mumbled Willie not stopping, and Felix tried to dismiss it. In time Willie would find something else, the war, or Sadie Boyce to shout about.

'He'll take the draughts bad,' commiserated Tommy as Black Willie disappeared out the gate and down Main Street. He gave hardly any sign of the loss of draughtsplaying life, nor his black mind already deranged.

They threw on the first soil and started to scatter out.

21

Black Willie – the blackthorn stick

Willie woke up stiff and drowsy early in the morning. He dragged himself out of bed to the fire's red embers, and poked them up grunting as he rose to slide into his shoes worn down with his sliding.

He walked outside and untied the goats, which sauntered off around the back. He smelt the air for signs that any person might have walked by the house in the night. There was no strange smell of a human, and there'd been none for a long time. There were only the smells of the goats, and the hens, and the flowers.

He had dreamt last night about walking the fields with his father. He was pointing out the sights that his father knew and had worked intimately but hadn't seen for forty years. His father was older in the dream than he had ever been in life.

He went inside and threw six handfuls of porridge into a pot hung over the fire. He tipped water out of a bucket into the pot and he thought of the wickedness of the O'Malloran woman up cohorting with Campbell. He spoke to himself that the O'Malloran woman's up there like she owns it, she must be out with his hens and his cows and in his corn, and she must be sleeping in the bed with him. He said, she's a dirty papish bitch, over and over again he said it, and thought of pushing himself into her, and hurting the dirty bitch.

Thirsty for tea, he lifted the kettle half full saving him a journey.

In the dream the meadow below had been teeming with workers, and he and his father stood side by side engrossed in the toil of the workers when a small dark animal darted out of the undergrowth. Holly jasus, it can run, said his father, it can run as fast as a hare or a whippet. Startled, Willie, who had never before seen a monkey nor its picture, recognised it when suddenly a large dog attacked it, waking Willie up.

He cleared a space on the table, and brought down the bowl and spoon.

The porridge tastes good, lumps in my mouth, wet and salty and thick. I'm sliding my feet in and out, and making time with my eating, and I'm humming hymns after I'm eating. My eyes have seen the glory of the coming of the days, and the sun was out and shining when Miss Grey the old witch hunched over the pulpit to sing hymns in the Sunday school in the glen, and we were all laughing and singing of the coming of the glory of the days, and the sun was out and shining, and I more than the rest of them was singing that loud at the top of my voice that they could hear me all over the glen, and beyond to the town.

When I'm eating my brother Duncan's likeness is on the wall in front of me. There was never no photo of me but they used to say that I looked like him, and was the spit of him, and even with him out in America maybe even look like him still.

My head's full this morning after the shouting out on the hill last night when I could see them all below me in the fields like small insects, smaller than that, listening to me. The Campbells know what I'm saying. There's bad mixed blood in them, bringing the papish bitch around here when the troubles are on at Desertmartin, and the Fenians are marching in Derry. In the old days there'd have been none of it. They'd have thought twice Da's day.

He thought of Tommy Boyce joining the Ulster Volunteer Force and how they were all just standing round useless as scarecrows.

He lifted his coat and walked to the shed. He collected the bucket at the back of the shed, and thought of the goats and the sweet taste of goats' meat, which he hadn't tasted for months, and he thought about the O'Malloran woman. He thought the woman's a devil and that he mustn't think of her for he would think devil's thoughts. She would possess him as surely as the devil with horns standing in front of him as he'd seen before him in bad times.

He looked up and saw Tommy Boyce's tractor chuffing off in the distance. I'll smell him if he's up here in my fields. I'll smell him on my hand, I'll curse him, shoot him if he comes near me. His corn is cursed, dried up and dead. He'll see the end of my pitchfork. I'll stick it in his ass. He'd be as well sticking up his arms like a scarecrow in the field.

I like the spring even the coolness more than the heat. The daffodils come out in bloom in the middle of March. I can smell the daffodils in the air, and I can smell foxes running across the land that Boyce's dogs are chasing.

Willie trudged to the well.

He tied his bucket to the rope and lowered it into the water, finest in Ireland, and felt satisfaction as the bucket made contact with water. When the bucket was full, he jerked it up. Fetching water in buckets was second nature to him, he never thought of it, not even today. Then suddenly the rope snapped and was slipping away. Holy Christ, Holy Christ, cursed Willie as the bucket hit the water with a sickening distant thud. Holy Christ, Holy Christ, muttered Willie and his hand was bare except an old bit of done rope rotted in the well's dankness.

Willie flew into a rage. His face was dark with temper, the veins at his temple protruded and pounded. Holy jasus, holy Christ, cursed Willie, who even for want of staying away from Catholics cursed every Catholic curse there ever was. Willie cursed the whole gaddamned trinity. He stormed across the field muttering his hatred against Mary and Joseph, flagellated by Fenians lying down at some blessed Virgin painted all over Ireland on roads and houses to make Protestants sick to their stomachs with their proliferation. He cursed and blasphemed but his curses were not profane for he was a man without religion.

He was walking and cursing in time with his walking, in time with his tramping over the new spring grass Tommy Boyce was growing for hay and over the corn starting to grow and the potato drills newly dug for the spring. He was walking through the river with the water up to his knees when he should have been on the bridge where it was dry and high as his father had built it. But he wasn't caring nor noticing about wetness, nor his legs heavy and waterladen and tired. His waterlogged legs were what saved Sarah-Ann.

He sat in the bush only because he always sat in the bush to rest a bit, and to see what he might see of neighbours who couldn't see him. Only he sat further in, more hidden than usual, so that no one coming down the lane or up it could see him, and none of the Martins looking out over the brae. Dressed as he was in his soot-blackened clothes with his soot-blackened face and his soot-blackened hair, no one could see him, and Sarah-Ann couldn't see him, only feel his presence if she was a woman good at feeling presences, but she was preoccupied that day. That was Sarah-Ann's mistake. She came round the corner oblivious to danger or adventure.

She looked pretty as a picture in her faded florals, which Rosey Bradley had stitched for her in return for eggs. Her rich auburn hair piled high on top of her head was clean and shiny from powder, and her cheeks were rosy from natural glow and rouge.

It was strange but Sarah-Ann started singing and humming as she approached the corner and her voice was not so much beautiful as unusual and lilting. She was singing modern but wearing the old-fashioned things women wear whose husbands are ordinary, poor and mean. She wasn't even a wife.

At the time she was simply singing and thinking about Felix and why she loved him, but she did.

There were the same noises there always were: birds chirping and a faint noise of Felix turning horses, coaxing them carefully on a tight turn where the ditch wasn't cleared. And there was a faint noise of Willie breathing heavy from his gross overweight. Willie sat big and uncomfortable in a small opening in the hedge.

These were the sounds and sights on a late afternoon in the spring of 1917 when Willie Thompson was sitting in the hedge wanting and waiting. These were the sights and sounds and thoughts before the trouble started.

The trouble was brutal and quick.

It was over before Maggie feeding hens thought she heard a woman scream.

Maggie tore out the yard to see the commotion. She found Sarah-Ann lying limp in the middle of the road with the blood streaking down her face and legs and arms in the awful sort of spectacle Maggie's nerves had long feared.

'My God,' said Maggie who crossed herself, as if Catholic, at brow and chest, in that vague outline of suffering. She crouched down and turned over Sarah-Ann's head. Her face was white and bruised, beaten to pulp, and her black eyes were wide open to the sky. Maggie thought she was dead when she noticed a flicker at Sarah-Ann's temple and saw Sarah-Ann's large body rising and falling. No great medical woman herself, these signs gave Maggie confidence. 'She's still living,' she sighed, watching to make sure that what she saw was actual motion and not just something out of her imagination. 'Aye, she's still living,' said Maggie in some low hymn to life.

She was contemplating whether to stay, or run and get help, when her daughters Maisie, and Daisie appeared silent and identical at the corner.

'What in under God . . . what in God's name??!!!!' screeched Maggie. 'Get home, out of my sight!.'

'He's coming,' said Maisie, her arms hung loose by her side, her face closed down.

'Who?' screamed Maggie.

'Campbell,' they said in their voice for good morning.

'Well, she's alive,' muttered Maggie.

'She's alive,' mimicked Maisie crouching down beside her mother. That's how Felix found them.

'What in God's name?' he roared.

'She's still living,' said Maggie. 'I just found her.'

Felix fell to his knees and saw her chest rising and falling and her lips cut. 'I will die, I will surely die,' he muttered, and clasped her.

'You'll die not a bit of you!' snapped Maggie, and pulled him back. 'Go and get the doctor, you'll die not a bit of you.'

'The bastard, the fucking black bastard,' thundered Felix, and Maggie felt fear at a grown man ferocious at a woman so lifeless. Maisie and Daisie started to sob.

'Shut up!' ordered Maggie. 'We'll get her up to the house and you go after the doctor.'

'He'll hang for it,' gulped Felix. 'He'll hang for it.'

'Don't be a fool. Go and get Tommy to run for the doctor . . . It's a doctor matter before it's a police matter,' said Maggie, happily evoking the twin pillars of her secular faith. 'We'll bring her to the house and get her clean,' she added. For all her airs about constabulary and medical men, Maggie was a practical woman. She charged Maisie and Daisie with the task of washing and bandaging her. They stood stoic and helpless.

'There's nothing to bandage her with,' said Maisie and Daisie, who wore the same frock and the same apron and their black hair cut identical. Seeing them was to see the world twice.

Bolt of lightning, Maggie ripped a strip off her apron, 'Like that,' she snapped in demonstration of their simple task. 'I'm off for help.'

'We'll wash the blood off her face and her legs and her arms, and then we will clean up the cuts,' said Maisie in the monotone voice for words unfamiliar to her.

'We will,' added Daisie, superfluous.

Big, strapping and mostly silent, Maisie and Daisie ripped thin strips off their worn-out aprons, then moving as one dipped them in the stream at the side of the road, drenched them in water, moulded them into poultices, held them dripping down over their hands and forearms, then wrung them tight. They crossed over the road, knelt down to Sarah-Ann and dabbed and washed her eyes and her mouth and her nose, and every other part of the large body that lay large undisturbed and reposed.

Maisie and Daisie lifted up her pale spring dress and tied it adroitly around her buttocks and upper thighs in a small tight knot so that the wind wouldn't catch up the dress and expose that Sarah-Ann O'Malloran wore no knickers.

Not a word passed between them. They were gently rubbing the blood off her bare bruised legs when their mother returned with Sadie.

'What a sight,' said Sadie, ambiguous about whether she meant Sarah-Ann or Maggie's big girls.

Maisie and Daisie's silent antipathies lasted lifetimes and they ignored her. 'Aye, she's bad,' intoned Sadie, who observed Sarah-Ann's face gashed and concussed and her groceries bloodied.

'The wild state I found her,' said Maggie to exert her authority, 'even worse than she is now. Well, don't all stand there like a long drink of water, we'll get her to the house.'

'Where's Campbell?' asked Sadie, astounded by her own oversight.

'Off like an old cod,' said Maggie, 'like a silly old cod to the police.'

'The silly old cod.'

'The silly old cod,' muttered Maggie's daughters, who crossed over their arms and entwined their hands to form a sturdy human seat into which Sadie and Maggie might lift her.

'What about the men?' asked Maisie, strangely involved in the world's affairs.

'Only ever across the fields and at work when you need them!' complained their mother. 'We'll have to do it ourself.'

'Sure them two strapping girls are lifting her the best,' said

Sadie, and silently regretting Sadie's presence Maisie and Daisie stared straight ahead, then Sadie and Maggie lifted her into the arms of Maisie and Daisie, who raised her up and in cumbersome fashion carried her up the lane.

'The Waterman's got a cart,' said Sadie, and they huffed and puffed towards the Waterman's with his great waterwheel turning, and he in his shed at his mechanics, the reason he was universally known as a great fool and eejit of a man who spent all his life making energy from water.

'God's truth, woman, what's wrong with you?' he asked crossly when he saw Maggie.

'There's been a beating.'

'Holy jasus,' said the Waterman and ran out the barn to the unforgettable sight of Maggie's two big dumb girls holding the unconscious beaten body.

'Where's Campbell?'

'Off gallivanting like an eejit to the police and her dying in our arms,' said Sadie, her arms folded in neglect of any sort of dying. They reflected on Campbell's folly.

'A right eejit,' frowned the Waterman. 'Who done it?'

'We don't know,' said Maggie.

'We don't know,' said her daughters.

'Surely somebody knows.'

'Nobody knows.'

'Sarah-Ann will know.'

'If she ever comes round.'

'There's hardly a body who could have done it.'

'Who would do such a wicked thing?'

'Campbell thinks it was Willie.'

'It couldn't've been Willie, he wouldn't have the heart for that.'

'No heart for it,' chorused Maisie and Daisie.

'Well, whoever done it, we'll hardly need worry now who

done it, it's done,' said Sadie, and the Waterman in his steady Waterman manner commenced harnessing up the horse and cart.

'You'd need to hurry yourself,' said Maggie to hurry the Waterman, who seemed to her an infernally slow man.

'You'd need to hurry yourself,' said Sadie with the impatient quick-temperedness of a woman observing the deliberate movements of a slow patient man. Sadie went at everything big or small as if her last breath depended upon it.

'More haste less speed,' philosophised the Waterman.

'Stop your codding,' warned Sadie.

'We're nearly ready,' said the Waterman long before he should have been and in such quiet modest Waterman manner that Maggie and Sadie begrudgingly admired him.

Maggie and Sadie quietly bedded down the cart and placed Sarah-Ann in it.

'You'll bring her to Campbell's,' said the Waterman.

'Sure there's nobody up there to look after her, we'll take her to mine.'

'Whatever's best,' said the Waterman, which is how Sarah-Ann came to go to Maggie's house. She was taken to Maggie's because of all women Maggie was the kindest, and by her own admission her own worst enemy for all her life loving men more than they ever deserved, and in the end had nothing to show for it except three weans, a boy, Frazer, and two girls, Maisie and Daisie, who during their long lives never did anything the other didn't do, nor think anything the other didn't think, nor speak anything the other didn't speak. They rarely ever spoke before Sarah-Ann's beating, and rarely thereafter, but it was more than before, and all blessings are relative.

Sarah-Ann came in the Waterman's cart accompanied by the Waterman, and four women making the journey on foot, except

Sadie the smallest who sat on the cart giving instructions. At the house, Maisie and Daisie adeptly hoisted Sarah-Ann on to the bed, whereupon she woke and tried to pull herself up but fell back dazed.

'What's happened?'

'Drink this,' said Maggie, and Sarah-Ann took a sip and fell back into a deep sleep, that strange dormant existence men call coma, and not knowing better or worse, call worse, for of all human conditions it least resembles life.

'Make us a drap of tae,' said Maggie, suddenly exhausted.

'I can't,' said Maisie, eating sodas in the pantry, the cause of her large size and her mother's and sister's as well, but not their brother's, who was extremely lean from living all his life by the maxim that you eat to live not the other way round.

'I can't,' said Daisie.

'Do it,' said Maggie sharply, and Maisie looked like a dog suddenly banished after all its life in the house.

'We can't,' they chanted in genuine protest, and whilst tae-making is arguably the simplest of tasks, in all their twenty-two years Maisie and Daisie had never performed it. The reason wasn't sinister. A 'single mother' before they existed, Maggie was over-protective, and had forbidden her daughters to go near the stove.

'It's time you learnt,' said Maggie, and in one sleight of her hand towards the kettle, Maisie brushed aside her mother's lifelong warnings.

'You'll scald yourself,' scolded Maggie, rushing at her with a cloth. 'Lift it with a cloth.'

Tea was made without further incident, more than Daisie's forgetfulness to put tea in the pot, but hardly a setback to the start of great tae-making days. Maisie and Daisie's hadn't formed poor habits, had never, for example, failed to clear out old tea leaves, or rinse the pot, or stand it until the bottom burnt out.

Two hours later Felix came with the horse and trap to take Sarah-Ann.

On the way home, she drifted in and out of consciousness, but even then her recovery started; cellular activity regenerated, body fibres fused, damaged tissue renewed. Occurring in their small indivisible way, these microscopic events performed their miraculous task of remaking Sarah-Ann as she was before, and went unobserved except their result, which was magnificent.

That night Felix made a large fire in the room and laid her on cushions. She asked for water, and he slept beside her on the floor. She woke before him in the morning, and felt her bones stiff and her face sore. She remembered nothing only the shock of Black Willie's huge frame descending from the hedge with all the gravity and gracelessness of a blackbird falling dead from the sky. In the second before screaming and unconsciousness, there was only blackness and the cessation of noise.

Early evening, Felix took a hurricane lamp to the bridge. Sarah-Ann's basket and all her paltry goods were strewn everywhere: tea and butter in the ditch, a piece of material on the road; all covered in blood. Jutting out of the hedge, its size, shape, markings fixed the weapon, Willie's blackthorn stick, with its owner as assuredly as if his face were painted on it. Felix told the police. He displayed his evidence, carefully pointing out the stick's markings, and the stick's quality to an officer, also a farmer who knew. Knotted at the top and smooth in the middle, the stick's head was the shape of a fine fox terrier's.

'Who?'

'Black Willie.'

'Black Willie?' queried the policeman as if Willie's unbroken blackness were no strange landmark of his own. 'The criminal mind, and what exactly is that?'

'Inclined to these types of things,' said Felix.

'I see,' said the officer noting laboriously in longhand. He would interview the victim, he said, and Felix made such a fuss he had to be escorted. He experienced this escort as a great ignominy.

The next morning, Felix went up to Willie's. The door lay open and flapping in the wind. As he entered, frightened goats ran out nearly knocking him down. The interior was dark, covered in soot, and its minute windows let in only the barest light. Felix strained his eyes in the darkness to see that the table was laid with bowl and spoon, and the kettle was burnt out on the hearth, and that dirt and soot covered every surface, every wall, cup and spoon. The only relief from blackness was a bow tied above a photograph of a young man standing in front of the village hall. The bow retained a vestige of redness.

Felix commenced his study of Willie's possessions. He opened the dresser and reviewed his supplies of food, his stock of delph, his tins. He read the papers on the mantelpiece, extracts from an old farming journal. He stared at the photograph of Willie's brother Duncan.

Finally satisfied that Willie's possessions had yielded their fullest evidence, he commenced their destruction. He smashed the chest of drawers, the dresser with Willie's delph and the table. He broke the small glass covering the photograph, held up the unframed faded image, and tore it up.

He read the letters in the bedroom. From Duncan and a woman in Belfast, they made the normal enquiries after health and harvest, but told more about their writers than they did about Willie. Felix placed them in his pocket and looked around. Willie's only remaining furniture was the bed. He walked out the door without touching it.

Outside the goats watched him fearfully. They stood at the gable as he walked into all the outhouses where he made a mental inventory of Willie's equipment and stocks, then turned to the goats, staring like they had never seen a white man. The sight of them roused sorrow for goats with no master. He thought he would feed them, but changed his mind and caught one on a rope. The goats would be his reparations.

Arriving home he was surprised to find Sarah-Ann up and about awaiting his return. She was eager to get back to Cookstown and seemed only concerned that she had not been able to get all the bloodstains out of her dress, which had great patches of dampness all down the front and over her breasts where she had doused it in water, then vigorously rubbed it with salt trying to get out the blood. She looked down over her dress like a young girl preening herself the first time, then rubbed on blithely regretting only that on that particular day she happened to be wearing that particular dress when almost anything else in her cupboard, her purple skirts and dresses, would have better disguised a bloodstain. As it was the day was such a fine day she had chosen the pale light blue spring dress to keep her cool on the long walk from Cookstown. She looked down as if the dress were the only unfortunate so that Felix, who until that moment viewed it only as exhibit, was struck by a dress so unsuited to event.

'I thought it would be nice for a spring day,' she said, self-conscious of the whimsy of a dress made of thin cotton with thin straps and tie strings at the back, 'for the warm day,' she added, embarrassed at the choice she had made as if Felix could see her yesterday agonising over what to wear. In the end her daughter Mary had chosen on the grounds it was the most grown-up, a criticism Sarah-Ann found she was sensitive to and therefore compelling. There and then she had donned the dress now stained in blood drenched in water ripped in three places.

'What do you think?' she asked Felix, who couldn't help thinking that of all the ways to get out the stains she had chosen the messiest and least effectual. Both she and the room were covered in water. A bucket of blood-stained water stood in the room. 'Dresses isn't something I know anything about,' he said affectionately, thinking it would have been easier to wash out the stains before putting it on.

'But what do you think?' she pressed him, and Felix, admittedly no expert, and with little to go on – Maggie was so hot from her fat she wore hardly anything, and Sadie was so small she wore anything she could fit into – he hardly felt qualified to say that he thought she should have worn something thicker and warmer.

'It's not too bad,' he said, taking the bucket. He got fresh water out of the rain barrel at the side of the house, then he gathered up the front of her dress, immersed it in water, scrubbed it with soap.

'That's better,' he said. It was much firmer, a man's hand.

'Has he hit anybody before?' asked Sarah-Ann, who even before she came to Ballymully had heard of Felix's strange neighbour covered in soot in his sootcovered house with goats in one corner and Willie in the other, and she had easily imagined him, how his every pore and vein were dusted in black, and every thread and stitch of his clothes. That was all she had to make of her attacker.

'Not that I know of,' answered Felix, whose greatest shock was that Willie had absconded, and so Sarah-Ann was left to her own devices. 'Not that I know of,' she thought, standing in front of the fire holding up her dress thinking. When she'd finished drying it, Felix asked what she would say to her mother.

'Nothing, I'll tell her nothing,' she answered and smoothed down her dress. The only good thing about the dress was the speed it dried.

On the way there they met Biggers coming along the road jaunty and sprightly with the urgent sense of purpose Biggers imbued his every activity.

'Biggers,' greeted Felix, acutely aware that only a week ago everything would have been different. Then Biggers would have been judge and jury. Now Felix and Sarah-Ann's crime, whatever it could be argued to be, was relieved by the actions of Willie.

'Smaller than I imagined,' muttered Sarah-Ann, with some sense that Biggers was hardly big enough for the place in society he allegedly occupied.

'A runt of a man,' muttered Felix, and more and more Sarah-Ann realised that the blackness she experienced was not so much as it felt, some aberrant convulsion of body and brain, but had something human behind it.

'You haven't seen Willie then?' stated Felix boldly.

'I've seen nobody,' answered Biggers, who turned full brash to Sarah-Ann. 'You'll be feeling the cold,' he said at her dress, and Sarah-Ann grimaced.

'I was looking for him,' threatened Felix.

'I'd heard,' said Biggers, condescending that not even the greatest follies surprised him. 'You've not seen Heather since the funeral. Over the week now that you haven't seen her when you used to see her all the time. She's taken it bad, you know. She'll need somebody to look after her, and the farm'll need somebody to run it. What she needs now is to settle down to marriage,' condemned Biggers, who turned to Sarah-Ann. 'Felix used to have an eye for her, aye, he had a right eye for her, maybe still has . . .'

'I was in at the police,' interrupted Felix angrily. Blood on his hands or not, Biggers wasn't changed.

'I heard that too,' nodded Biggers. 'Just one of them things, just odd him going off like that . . .'

Felix left angry, wondering if Sarah-Ann could ever live openly amongst them.

Once in the familiar surroundings and trappings of home, Sarah-Ann realised how cold and shivery she was, and how extraordinarily tired. Her inclination was to lie down on the bed and not get up until the pain went out of her bones, and the picture out of her mind. The picture was raw. There she was lying on the side of the road. The dress made it worse. It slid up the side of her legs and exposed her naked as the day she was born. She should never have worn it. 'You'll be feeling the cold,' said Biggers at her frippery flouncy dress, common sense sneering at vanity, and she'd wanted the ground to open up and swallow her. At home she'd put on layer after layer and lay down for a moment's rest before her mother and the children discovered her home.

There was no need to tell anyone. Anyway, who and what would she tell? One minute she'd been walking round the brae in the middle of day with a basket of groceries under her arm and a bounce in her step, the next the world was a silent stunned blackness. She relived for a moment walking towards the corner in the bright day with the light breeze blowing through her pale blue dress and the birds chirping and the sound of the river close by hidden in bush. The river was rising or falling so fast water bailiffs cannot keep track of it and the day was young; still there must have been some clue to the future. She retraced her steps. In her mind already there making the first impression in the pale blue dress Felix never saw not covered in blood, not drenched in water, she saw her body sprawled out face down on the road, and the dress up round her, and the blood pouring out of her. Maggie must have seen she'd worn no knickers.

In Ballymully, the rumour was that within hours Sarah-Ann's bruises had all faded and her cuts had all healed. Unaware of her pedigree, the locals were astonished at her rapid recovery, which much more than the beating fed their imaginations, and Sadie Boyce, so much a participant in the whole affair, quickly attributed to Sarah-Ann supernatural powers. Another time, said Sadie, she'd have been burnt as a witch. 'A witch at the stake,' she said, nodding her head side to side, which after Sadie's own idiosyncratic manner of proclaiming Sarah-Ann's great strength and health was the most backhanded of compliments.

22

The decision

Like many local dwellings, the Shaws' cottage marked a careful geography between farmland, glen and mountain. It backed directly on to the steepest part of the glen, and unlike Felix's or Tommy Boyce's there was no field to distance it from the sharp descent. Common belief held that for hundreds of years it had been the site of human habitation, and that once thriving communities of up to six or seven families had congregated there, and had excavated tunnels deep into the glen. Trace of these escape routes was long gone. The Shaws' cottage itself was unoccupied. For a quarter century its only inhabitants were cows seeking shelter, and birds building nests, and the occasional man standing out of rain.

After leaving Sarah-Ann, Felix went there directly. He walked slowly round the front. He pushed open the door. He stood still near the door. The cottage was dark from small dirty windows, and the air was rank. The cottage's old rotting rafters were swollen and sweated. The thick walls retained weather and water. There were a couple dozen bales beside the chimney, and a rake propped against them, and string tied round them. The damp straw and cow dung mixed together pungent. A bird flew up frightened. Felix held his hands down by his sides. His feet pressed firm on straw. He looked up then and, in his mind, saw Biggers in front of him vivid as he ever saw any human being. The dark came through him. When the dark rose from his eyes he made out the chimney breast in front of him and the back window at the left of him. He looked out at the scene familiar to him. The yard was grown over with grass and weeds. Nettles the size of small bushes grew up at the site of the former dung heap. Amongst their impenetrable foliage Felix knew from childhood lurked all manners of rubbish, rusted metal pots, kitchen utensils, old farm tools and the pristine white bread tin Jimmy Shaw lost forty years before. Many times he had searched for it.

His mind turned over compulsively for how he would take matters into his own hands. Breaking up Willie's furniture, he'd thought of nothing but Willie and tearing him apart, but a day on there was no sign of Willie and the impulse was thwarted. He had to find him first. Shaws' was the obvious place. It was run-down and dilapidated, but still had its windows, and doors, and an easy escape to the glen. Felix's eyes darted about, scoured over windows and floor, searched out every inch of the room. What would Willie do? Where would he go? Willie had no family to speak of, and as few friends. Putting himself in Willie's shoes, Felix realised that there was hardly a soul who would let

Willie over the doorstep. Felix clenched his fists. If Willie was still in the neighbourhood, if someone was harbouring him, he'd kill them too.

An eye for an eye, quoted his father, and his mother acquiesced. Committed to life only by the small domestic duty that lay ahead of her, she had stood at the window seeing nothing, asking for nothing, waiting only for his father to come for the tea she put out for him. Together they had delineated the world by the small part of themselves they had in common. Death could not separate their unhappiness.

When he was young he had believed the world governed by inexorable rules, but now he saw how in the worst adversity the Irishman will profess the view he professed the day before. No horror changes it. Everywhere he found his evidence. Man seeks peace and makes war, pursues ideal where there is only compromise, conceives happiness amidst suffering and misery. What more evidence? Rumours of carnage filtered back from the front and sickened him, how the real world events were tawdry, but after a few days up in the hills war's actuality retreated, became again the domain of his books and papers, and fantasy completed what he didn't know. In that realm, there were no real dead people, no farmers from Coagh, Moneymore or the Loup. There was only glory, sacrifice, martyrdom. When the Russians pushed forward, he rose almost faint at the sheer scale of it. He lived between glory and shabbiness, sought ideal out of horror, imagined glory out of ghouls. Man clings to ideal, and becomes sick in the process. Why? How much better if he had no ideal, only a brutal appreciation of the world, its limitations and horrors, its abominations and griefs. Nothing would be disappointing, little would affect him.

A fly crawled across the back of his hand. He wondered why it would crawl when it could fly. One swat it was dead. How small he was in the world, even there in the glen where flies are more tangible than a man's own motives.

The strain was unbearable. Through the thick deep darkness of the world there was a slow nervous stir. He heard whimpering and knew it was he who whimpered, he felt pain and knew it was he who pained, and he pushed out a long deep breath. It was his breath. Some hours later he stepped out of the house, and walked through the brambles and nettles at the front, and over the small mound of rubble of an old abandoned outbuilding, and through the gate into Shaws' meadow. Waterlogged in the spring, the meadow was high in bulrushes, and he was aware of the bulrushes rubbing against his legs, and the ground wet underfoot. He headed in the direction of the clump of trees at the edge of the meadow where once his grandfather had planned to build a house, and he slipped through the hedge on to the lane running between thick whinbush on the glen side, and the trees. The lane was always that bit drier than any other part of the farm, and the whinbushes and trees on each side sheltered it from the wind, and their roots crisscrossed intricately near the lane's surface. Felix had often stopped to admire the spot, and to remember the ambition of a man who'd once thought to live there. The clump of large trees was majestic, its roots stretched out thick into the earth, and whenever he passed them he felt himself more human. Felix felt the ground hard and definite below, and the sky clear and fresh above, and the whole physical experience felt right, in the fullest and sweetest relief action brings after indecision.

23

Madonna, over the mantelpiece

The next morning Felix strode across the fields to check the cattle. They were out of winter confinement, and the hard-baked dirt and cow dung of indoors peeled off their broad sides and their soft warm bellies. Seventeen, twelve cows and five calves, he counted reassuringly. He put great store by numbers. Later, he would bring them hay.

He set off for Sarah-Ann's. A small house, much smaller than his, thatch instead of slate, dozens of geese, pecking and hissing, amongst a small forest of pine trees, so rare to find pines in this country. Children came running out of the byre, and a pig behind them. When they saw him, they stopped dead, and when he spoke, they giggled and ran back into the byre. To him they were only a gaggle of tattered children, scurrying off in the opposite direction, whispering conspiratorially in the corner, which, in his paranoid nature, he knew was about himself. He knocked on the door, and Sarah-Ann, thinking it was the children, shouted, 'Stop your fooling!' When she discovered it was him, she was mortified.

'What a state to find me!' she startled, and tried to smooth down the apron tied up around her neck, and her dress riding up her legs. 'Come in! come in!' she urged anxiously, her discomfort heightened by Felix's own grooming. She thought he would have been lying low, feeling sorry for himself; instead he was all bright and fresh, with his shirt pressed and his shoes polished to perfection. 'Come in, come in,' she motioned again, forcing vigour in her voice, but her tongue was constricted dry at Felix catching her with her hair hanging lank and her face bloated. Leading him into the house, she apologised again, 'Had I even thought you were coming . . .' she started, but didn't continue that she would have dressed up, run a comb through her hair. She rubbed her hand tight against the side of her hip, pushed the hair out of her eyes, tugged at her ill-fitting dress. She felt herself tingling with unwashed tiredness, her hair exposed against her skin, she felt from the inside the dress's slack, crumpled layers around her.

'You made your way back all right yesterday,' she said, and inside railed at him. Yesterday he could hardly wait to be away from her. His protests that he walk her home had been pitiful.

'Aye, it only takes over the hour fast walking,' he said as if it was the most natural thing in the world, and Sarah-Ann withdrew. Suddenly, she couldn't even look at him. Stubbornly, angrily, she thought that whatever he'd come for, whatever it was, she wasn't going to help him. If he had something to do, he could do it himself, if he had something to say, he could say that too. She sat silent and wondered what he would say about Willie and beating and Ballymully, would he even acknowledge it? She wasn't going to. She wasn't going to make any effort at all. The same went for her mother, sitting next door straining to hear the stranger.

'Who's it?' barked her mother, Theresa. Her voice was blunt and harsh, but distinctly powerful.

'A visitor,' called back Sarah-Ann, aware that, with Felix now in the house, her mother would discover their secret. The pause from the room was her mother digesting the stranger's lack of identity.

'Who?'

'Felix Campbell,' answered Felix, disconcerted at the exchange and the presence of someone else in the house, but he said it too soft, and again, 'Who?' From the pitch and direction of the voice, Felix imagined its owner was lying in bed.

'Felix Campbell,' called Sarah-Ann. Tentatively saying it, waiting for a reaction, expecting none, Sarah-Ann knew how her mother, pinched and lined, starved of affection, would wrestle with the uncertainties the Protestant name aroused in her.

'Who's he?' came the voice, and Felix shuffled in his seat. Again, 'Felix Campbell,' came the reply. Felix felt the stir of his name in the house; it reverberated back silent and angry from the anonymous room.

'What's going on up there?' came the voice, and Felix sat there disconsolate that, at best, his name in this house could be no more than apology. Everywhere he turned there were religious artefacts, Marys and crosses, beads and mass cards, and over the mantelpiece a Madonna and child. In their unfamiliar symbolism, he felt wavering feelings of hostility and exclusion that these things, so foreign to him, were on prominent display. He tried to picture his female accuser.

'I'll shut the door to give you some peace,' said Sarah-Ann to draw over them captured at the door, and her mother inside fuming. Sarah-Ann felt the drama of shutting the door against her, and her failure of her. She was an old woman, her faculties pared down with sorrow, blunted with age, but since Frank had gone to the war Sarah-Ann had relied more and more upon her.

'She's in bed tired from looking after the children,' said Sarah-Ann, which sounded to Felix like a reproach. He felt for the tobacco pipe in his pocket and thought of the speech he'd rehearsed.

'You're feeling well?' he asked again. 'Good,' he said, and stood up to take off his coat. Up close, he saw the Madonna was held up with string, and he thought of reading somewhere that the Virgin's pre-eminence was no earlier than the fifteenth century, therefore relatively recent, therefore barely holy at all. 'A fine day for walking,' he said amidst the gloom of the room, then stared straight ahead over the mantelpiece, and placed together his fingertips, tip against tip, as he used to do as a boy, concentrating on his loneliness.

'Here, I'll take your coat,' offered Sarah-Ann impatiently. The moment she'd left him yesterday she had flooded into tears. 'That's my mother coming,' she whispered aloud, as the next-door woman appeared exactly as Felix had imagined her. Dressed in old tattered clothes, with her teeth out and her grey hair dishevelled, there was no divergence between the woman he had heard and what stood before him; a woman past middle age but not yet elderly, her breasts hung down low under her gown and her varicose veins were visible just below the knee. She was as his dead mother incarnate.

Felix stood up, just missing the ceiling. Fearing some ritual of worship he failed to observe, he nodded vaguely in the Madonna's direction.

'Where did you say you came from?' she asked, standing at the doorway making conversation, overtly polite, overtly innocuous, about Ballymully and the environs, but beneath that conversation, not far from the surface, ran that heightened awareness, peculiarly Irish, peculiarly intuitive, of the other person's religion. Theresa didn't need to know his name. Reflexive as telling a dog from a cat, Theresa knew Felix was Protestant, she knew all quite as if he had said out loud, 'I am Protestant, my family are Protestant, my neighbours are, it is the religion from which I derive my identity, it is the starting point for my sense of nationality, British not Irish.' Easy as telling a dog from a cat, without any mention of name, Theresa could tell. Perhaps it was his eyes? Perhaps these, in the proportions of Protestant eyes, were closer together, or further apart. Amongst popular opinion this has some credence. Perhaps Felix's grey-black eyes, with speckled grey intensity, fulfilled these proportions.

'You've had some trouble over your way,' said Theresa, thinking who was he this Felix Campbell, she wouldn't have let him over the doorstep, 'trouble with burning houses and intimidating,' she said watching him, not as she expected him from the sound of his voice, but far older, thinner and harder. His grey steel eyes suited his face.

'Trouble?' queried Felix, before he realised she was confusing Ballymully with Ballymolloy, miles away.

'Burning houses, and intimidating,' repeated Theresa, who knew the Protestant enclave, full of orange sashes and UVF arms.

'Naw, Ballymully's a quiet place, neighbourly that way,' he answered.

'Aye,' she barked. 'Liar!' she thought. Felix Campbell was transparent to her as an old worn sheet in the daylight. 'Do you know down this way?' she asked.

'Only as a rabbit and fox country, there's always one or other coming over this way hunting,' he said, the room's heavy atmosphere pressing down on him.

'There is a big trade in rabbits in the war, there's a big demand for them,' contributed Sarah-Ann, trapped between them as any snared rabbit. 'They're shipping ten thousand a week,' she could have said of the furs that war made a market for.

'They say they're shipping ten thousand furs a week.'

'As many as that, I never thought it was so many,' nodded Felix, relieved. He could talk about rabbits.

'But you're not after rabbits yourself,' said Theresa, thinking he's fifty if he's a day. All she could see was the orange collarette around his neck and the black bowler on his head.

'I keep a few cattle.'

'And you've a bit of help, your wife?'

'I do it myself.'

'He doesn't have a wife,' said Sarah-Ann, pointed for her mother who couldn't resist her own rudeness. 'Aw,' sighed Theresa coughing and spluttering. As far as she was concerned his visit was over. But Felix didn't move. He sat gazing somewhere into the empty hearth.

What's he doing, thought Sarah-Ann, who stood up to brush her hair, and to imagine then that her mother and Felix Campbell locked in silent battle was only experiment. Who would yield first? Who would move first? Who would sit longest? With his resources she knew it'd be Felix. Hah, thought Sarah-Ann, I can bear anything. In the corner of her eye, she saw his shapely legs, and the thick manly weave of his trousers.

'What happened your arms?' asked her mother.

'I cut myself on some briars,' replied Sarah-Ann. The impudence, scalded Theresa, inwardly; she could slap her for brushing her hair so brazenly. Theresa rubbed together her bony bare ankles.

'It was nothing,' added Sarah-Ann, and turned away. Through the window, she spied her daughters, Theresa and Mary, at the well pumping water. Theresa was on a box holding the handle and Mary was doing all the work. The sight filled her with joy. Ah, even in adversity, the world is full of variety, the heart moves on.

Abruptly her mother lurched out of her chair.

'You know rightly!' she stormed as she blazed out of the room. 'You know rightly!' she railed against all the tensions she could not tolerate. The world knew rightly the breaking point she was at. It was freezing cold out, for what she was wearing.

'I had to wait to speak to you,' started Felix. 'Are you all right?' he asked. It was not clear if he referred to what had just transpired or if he meant to enquire how she was after the beating.

Sarah-Ann responded coldly.

'Did you get the stains out?' he asked.

'I just threw the dress in the corner, it's hidden in the wardrobe.'

'I'll take it with me,' he said, he was a collaborator . . . 'I'll wash it, it'll look as good as new.'

'Oh, I don't care about it, I never liked it anyway, I'd be better throwing it out,' she said dismissively. After yesterday, with him brooding heavily beside her, she had no interest in the dress.

Felix must have understood. He said no more about washing, but started on about how he was going to fix the house, put in some stairs, get the pantry fixed. As he explained all this, Sarah-Ann felt increasingly exasperated. Plans for the house, that was why he was here. And her expecting some declaration of love! She felt his tight grip on the world, closing out hers.

'Your mother . . . ' he queried; eye level with the Virgin, he noticed Her slightly sooted, 'is very religious?' Eye level, he could have reached out and touched Her. 'Will I say it? he thought. After everything, if he didn't speak now, he never would.

'I got you a dress,' he said, 'a dress out of Scotts.' He looked sheepish as he said it, and grew more uncomfortable as Sarah-Ann, trying to make sense of it, almost rudely enquired what he was talking about. 'You mean,' she said finally, if not still tentatively, 'that you went into Scotts, Scotts here in Cookstown?'

Felix, feeling foolish at his impulsive decision, admitted his sin, and Sarah-Ann interrogated. What was the dress like? What size was it? What colour? When would she get it? Part it was the excitement of the dress itself, more it was the process of purchase. To negotiate the stuffiness of Scotts, to encounter Miss Ruth and Miss Sarah, to place an order for a dress, to make that most intimate of purchases, Sarah-Ann instantly recognised what it all meant. Felix didn't need to make the speech he'd rehearsed.

'Since I met you that first day coming round the brae, I have dreamt about you every night, and thought about you every day, even during the months between seeing you on the glen road and meeting you in Cookstown . . .' started Felix as if he was reading out some speech. He spoke into the distance of the room, as if that space far away absorbed him, as if he were only the ventriloquist projecting into the void. The tone of Felix professing love had all the cadence of a Sunday school recitation. Love sounded like fear.

Town wasn't busy, the cold kept people away. Sarah-Ann looked affectedly in one Scotts window, then in the other, then returned to the first, all the time posing conspicuously for any staff member who might notice her, and casually dismiss her, one more dreamer. Through the window she could see the well-cut folded skirts and blouses, the expensive clothes, but what she most admired was her own bright reflection. There she was, a woman whose lover had bought her a beautiful Scotts dress. She glowed from the inside. With her head high, with the imaginary book on her head, she held her figure straight, she glided over the carpet into the shop. Everything, the mahogany cases with glass doors and brass fittings, the counters with marble tops, the cash railings on the ceilings, shone and gleamed. Polish and flowers and soft expensive fabrics perfumed the air. 'Can I help you, madam?' asked a young girl of about twenty. With her tiny sparrow features and her matronly manner, the exact copy of her mother's, old before its time, she was definitely one of the Scotts girls, either Miss Ruth or Miss Sarah, training never to leave the family business. You most certainly can, thought Sarah-Ann, who wondered then, as she had all the way there, how Felix, who could hardly purchase his weekly newspaper without some snub to himself, transacted his business? Miss Ruth or Miss Sarah must have been nothing short of masterful, thought Sarah-Ann, they must have spoken in the right tone of voice, at the right volume, with the appropriate respect, not over fawning, not over familiar, their conduct must have been perfect.

'You most certainly can, I've come to collect my dress, which my dear friend has bought as a present,' affected Sarah-Ann, who knew the Protestant girl had no clue who she was. 'I have no idea what it looks like, it's a present.' She thought of all the times she had seen the Scotts girls out with their parents, walking two by two.

'Oh yes, you're quite right, your friend was in only a few hours ago, and delighted we were to have him, it's not all men are gentlemen these days, when you meet one you just know,' parroted either Miss Sarah or Miss Ruth after the patter of their mother.

'It's lucky there are any left at all,' mimicked Sarah-Ann, who could adopt any priggish posture she cared to. 'How,' she said, 'would you even recognise one these days?'

'Exactly! Even just to hold a door open seems to be too much for some of them.'

'I know, storming on past you!' added Sarah-Ann, enjoying herself.

'I'll tell you something, there would be a lot more manners if the women didn't let them away with it!'

'It's the women's fault,' agreed Sarah-Ann. 'Tell me, what sort of gentleman are you looking for?'

'Who me! Not me! I've more to be getting on with than looking after gentlemen!' she protested. 'About your dress, if I just introduce myself, I am Miss Ruth . . . Miss Ruth Scott.'

'I was hoping to wear it today.'

'We'll see first if it fits,' responded Miss Ruth, leading Sarah-Ann to the corner, where she produced a red dress, with long tight-fitting sleeves and a smart flowing skirt, very much in keeping with the elegant style of the day, but not the sort of thing Sarah-Ann, used to homemade tailoring, had ever had opportunity to wear.

'Oh, it's beautiful,' exclaimed Sarah-Ann, knowing as Miss Ruth obviously already did that there was no hope of her fitting into it. 'And if it doesn't fit?'

'Well, the gentleman thought it would,' said Miss Ruth stiffly, giving the impression that, even at the time of his purchase, she knew 'the gentleman' had no clue. 'We'll measure you up, and get our dressmakers to make up another one.'

Sarah-Ann followed her, a thin emaciated girl hopping as a sparrow through the shop. Beside her Sarah-Ann felt like an elephant in motion. 'But this here's beautiful!' she exclaimed. In the corner stood a mannequin in a white silk blouse and a deep tartan silk skirt.

'Yes, it's a copy of a dress worn in London this season.'

'Or this, this is exactly what I need!' pronounced Sarah-Ann, turning to a rich deep-blue suit behind it. The jacket was beautifully fitted, the skirt long and lean and elegant, much like the dress, but for once Sarah-Ann was drawn to the more subdued colour.

'You'll have that then instead of the dress . . .'

'Oh no, as well as, I'll have both the dress and the suit! And I'll wear the suit now!!' Sarah-Ann started to undress right there in the shop, she took off her coat, she unbuttoned her cardigan, she was about to take off her blouse, when she realised she had deep black bruises all over her body. She spied Miss Ruth's dismay.

'Miss . . . miss . . . !' protested Miss Ruth. 'Our fitting rooms are here.'

'Oh yes, oh yes,' sniffed Sarah-Ann. Ten minutes later, she stepped out in the dark rich navy wool suit with its detailed stitching all along the jacket and its beautifully cut skirt, which fell just two inches above her feet. She swirled into the middle of the shop, and another assistant, must have been Miss Sarah, appeared from the back. 'Oh it suits you wonderfully, such a beautiful colour and that lovely intricate stitching.'

'Intricate, isn't it?' said Sarah-Ann enjoying the word's beauty on her tongue. 'You don't do shoes, do you?'

'We do, of course, we have a great selection of shoes.'

Sarah-Ann reflected. 'No, I'll do without,' she said. She couldn't see her feet, by the time she'd get home, any shoes would be ruined. 'You can put that with the gentleman's bill, Mr Campbell's.' Miss Ruth seemed uncertain, stole a glance at her sister.

'As for my old things, I've no need for them, so that's everything.' There was no need to dally more.

Triumphant, Sarah-Ann headed off in her new wool suit. She glided home, as if on air, resolving to herself that now she was in love she would need more new things of quality, she would need dresses and suits, and gloves and hats, and things for summer and winter, for warm and cold days, for going out and staying in. She could no longer afford to be caught out on the brae like some young immature girl wearing a strappy dress with no substance. It's a mess, she muttered cheerfully, full of enthusiasm to turn her wardrobe inside out, to inspect each and every garment, to sort and match them. Unaware that her feet touched the road, Sarah-Ann held up her skirt like a young bride tripping up the aisle.

'Nice,' said her mother sarcastically. She knew it had something to do with Felix Campbell.

'I got it in Scotts.'

'Well, he's gone and got you that!' condemned her mother.

'He's wanting me to live with him,' confessed Sarah-Ann, and Theresa's bluster evaporated. The power of Sarah-Ann's rich deep-blue suit faded away, there was only herself in the room, there was only her mother, an ageing woman, who had never quite reconciled herself to the stepdown in social status that befell her upon marrying Micky O'Malloran, the 'cattle breeder without cattle' as she called him.

'The children would come too.'

'Then you'll not come here again,' declared Theresa. As a mother, the advice had been given, the work had been done. She shuffled in her seat, she wiped her nose.

'No,' said Sarah-Ann, who understood. Her mother's faith was her life's fullest devotion. She knew that for her to hitch her fortune to that of a Presbyterian, or Baptist, or whatever he was,

was, in her mother's eyes, the ultimate betrayal. With Sarah-Ann, under her arms, or strapped to her back, or tied to her front, and, with the sort of large ba Sarah-Ann was, there had been no doubting her stamina. She was more like the O'Mallorans than her own side, who were strong as bulls but didn't have the staying power.

'As long as you know,' confirmed Theresa, bitterly.

'Well, as long as you do,' she repeated. On the roads of her youth, she was familiar, almost famous. Theresa O'Malloran walked home when the light faded on a Saturday and the sabbath approached with nothing to do. Her movements were so punctual, said her neighbours, you could set your clock by her. It was said every Saturday until, by virtue of repetition and the lapse of long hard undifferentiated time, men, even those who lived after her, called it the 'walking woman's time'. By these feats of great walking, and the birth of a large daughter, she gained fame, but her punctuality made her immortal.

'I do know,' whispered Sarah-Ann going to the door. She could hear, from the living room, the noise of her mother, fixing and turning at all her small domestic business, maintaining her constant vigil over that tiny world, and, from the outside, she could hear the children, shouting and screaming. Outside was bright and cold. The scrawny black dog shivered on the step, and yawned and looked at her for human invitation.

24

Caught bathing

Felix propped his head against the side of the red cow's big warm stomach and started to milk. He rhythmically coaxed the two back teats, he felt them flow through their supple strong skin. 'That's the girl,' he soothed to steady the good milker. 'That's the girl,' he whispered as if she were not the gentle cow out of Tommy Boyce's bull but some wilder beast. 'Steady steady,' he cajoled as the red cow nuzzled lazily and contentedly at the water. He could feel the healthy rise and fall of her manifold stomachs and the rhythmic swell as she drank. The heaviness of her udder testified her contentment. At the end of the winter, with the cattle back in the fields, he too was set free. No more carrying water and fodder, cleaning out byres, bedding and tending. Some days he started in the dark and finished in it. The cattle too got fed up. The moment they heard him in the morning, or felt the slightest movement, or some sense of Felix's presence, or his smell, they started roaring. Some days it went on from morning to night. Felix would hear them, even as he sat down at the table. 'Aye, I'm still here,' he'd say when he returned to the yard. 'Aye, I went nowhere,' he said.

It had been a long winter. Late snows had delayed taking the cattle out of the house. The prolonged drudgery of carrying to them was followed by a couple of anxious weeks when he wasn't sure he'd have enough hay. Hay was at a premium. To have had to buy this late in the season would have been a disaster. As it turned out the weather dried up just in time, and he was able to put them back out on the grass.

Felix stared deep down into the cow's belly then lifted his head as he finished the back teats. The cow turned dolefully towards him; he thought he could see what she saw, a pathetic creature beyond pity or sorrow. 'That's the girl,' he urged as she lowered her head into her bucket of water. As he squirted the milk into the bucket held between his knees, he could see in it the taint of new grass. It was more pungent than hay-fed milk. Last summer he'd drained the bottom meadow and the big field on the hill. Around the new drains the grass was lighter and drier, further out it was darker and coarser. Felix patted her side as he switched teats to the front. 'No, not yet . . ' he muttered as the cow turned as if it were going to come out of the byre. Felix drained the last dregs of milk from her udder and lifted the milk bucket out of the path of her big hooves. The cow turned docile, and Felix opened the door the day was facing bright into and watched her walk through the gable gate. 'Aye,' he ruminated. Often now, as he went round his business, he couldn't help thinking how exciting Sarah-Ann's life was, and how dull his in comparison. To walk in and out of town, to tend after cattle, to talk only to the dogs: the possibility now that he would spend the rest of his days alone on the hill was desperate.

'Peggy, Sheila,' he called to the dogs. A small brown terrier came running round from the back of the house. 'That's the good dog,' he praised Peggy, whose name was carried down the generation of dogs. 'Aye, Pup, there you are,' said Felix to an old black and white mongrel. The Campbells always had a 'Sheila', a 'Peggy', a 'Glen'. There was always a 'Pup'. 'It'll have to be the day, Pup,' said Felix. He'd put off going to Sam's because Sunday was bridge day, and he thought he would do it on Monday, but the longer he left it the harder it was, and Monday came and went with another excuse. By Tuesday evening he realised the only way was for himself to do the work.

In the middle of the night, with the sweat dripping down him, and the dust flying round him, it was as if he were physically there beating out stones to make the new entrance but when he awoke in a panic there was not a single stone out. He needed Sam Birch to get the new entrance made, the stairs put in, the hallway blocked up.

His plan was to build a wall between the hallway leading from his room to the parlour, to make a new entrance to the parlour from the front. This would be Sarah-Ann's living room. Felix felt calmer as he thought of it. That would be her house, this will be mine, he thought, she would live in her house, he in his, there was no point making it confusing.

'I'm doing up the houses,' he'd say casually to Sam, knowing that the expectation of event differs from the experience of it. The only predictable thing was the conclusion Sam would draw – Sarah-Ann was coming to live.

Sam was known as the thatcher, but his house showed no sign

of his craftsmanship. His roof was pinned down to the ground with an untidy arrangement of stones tied with string. It seemed that the man who thatched other men's houses had no interest in his own. As Felix negotiated the dogs, he realised that Sam wasn't in his shed.

His sister appeared at the doorway.

'Felix Campbell, by God,' screeched Dolly Birch with an unexpected display of enthusiasm for the world outside her, 'what brings you here?' Dolly's black hair stuck thinly round her face, her apron was stained and grubby, an unhinged pin dangled from her breast.

'I was looking for Sam.' Felix had never before seen her with her hair hanging loose.

'Well, he's not here,' pronounced Dolly triumphantly. 'Even an hour ago you'd have got him, but now he'll not be back for the rest of the day.'

'Sure it'll wait to the morrow,' said Felix, as contained in mood as Dolly was uncharacteristically exultant.

'Sure we never see you these days,' said Dolly.

'I hardly think so.'

'It's a fair while,' remarked Dolly, 'how time passes.'

'Sam'll be busy these days.'

'Wild busy, he's always busy, sure you'll come in.'

'Naw, I'll leave it now, I'd need to get going.'

'A terrible business,' peddled Dolly, 'a terrible business,' she continued seamlessly. Felix knew she meant Sarah-Ann.

'I'll go on.'

'What's your hurry?' protested Dolly. Her small-boned but scrawny face was tense.

'No hurry.'

'Well, what'll I tell Sam?'

'It's just a bit of work to the house.'

'I see,' sighed Dolly, who then saw everything clear in her head. 'Sam'll maybe come over this evening,' she called behind him.

'That's the good Pup,' comforted Felix at home, 'that's the Pup, we'll get you your food,' he promised as he slouched off to the pantry to get the bowl of scraps of old bread and milk he kept for the dogs. 'There you are.' He laid the bowl in front of Pup, who lapped it greedily.

Felix downed his last dregs of cold tea. He threw the last old tea leaves into a bucket in the pantry. He lifted his mug, spoon and bread to one side of the table, he folded and refolded his paper, he set his tobacco up in the hole in the wall. He was anxious that Sam would come.

By eight it looked less likely, and he went out to check the cattle. At the big hill field, he spied them there settling down for the night. Cattle are hardy animals, they do not suffer like sheep, and normally Felix would have turned happy with this sighting, but from the hill, he could see the blue-grey cow had taken herself apart from the herd. She must have been calving. When he got there, she was already licking a great fawny brown bull calf. Felix pulled from his inside pocket a large white handkerchief and an old piece of cloth. He stuffed the handkerchief in his jacket pocket, and with the old cloth started to wipe away the clear sticky afterbirth. When he left, the calf was already suckling.

At home he brought down his large washing basin and placed it on a chair in front of the fire, where the kettle was heating up. When the water was beginning to bubble, he got up and slipped his waistcoat over the back of his own chair, then carefully, fastidiously, placed his trousers, shirt and socks on the unupholstered Queen Anne. He lathered his neck and hands with the soap Sadie had once given Maggie, who had then given it to him. 'Another grey one,' he observed in his chest hair, he was almost celebratory. Felix took down his trunks. He was enthralled that his cock had been used.

Just then came a knock, the hammed fist on the door. Felix jumped up like a scalded cat. 'Sam, hell and damnation, it's Sam,' he cursed, grabbing whatever clothes he could find, and making for the pantry. There, with shaking wet clammy fingers, he struggled to pull on his shirt and button up his trousers. 'No shoes, where the hell!' he muttered, then opened the door just a fraction to see if Sam was at the front window. Goddammit, he thought, goddammit, the window has no curtains! He dived in for his shoes and grabbed the basin. The door knocked again.

'Aye, you were wanting me,' intoned Sam ungraciously at the door.

'Aye,' answered Felix, flustered, feeling Sam alive to the fact he didn't have on any shoes. 'This afternoon, I spoke to Dolly, she said you were out, sure, it would have done to the morning.'

'Not at all, I came straightaway I got home.'

'Well, you'd better come in,' offered Felix, seeing Sam was already in.

'Aye, I just came to see why you needed me, and then I'd head on.'

'Well, you'd nearly not have got me.'

'I thought that,' said Sam making no apology for the late hour of his visit.

'I'm going to do the house,' said Felix, fretting whether to lift or leave the wet soap lying in a watery puddle in the middle of the floor. 'Aye, what for?' demanded Sam, and in these most inhospitable circumstances, with the soap lying melting on the floor, and with his feet unshod, Felix was obliged to tell Sam his plans. The house would be in two, two entrances, two pantries, two stairs, and the living room and parlour where they were now adjoined would be divided by a wall.

'Aye,' said Sam. Work was work. Who cared if it was the Fenian woman? Who cared if he caught Felix bathing? With his own furtive bathing pleasure, Sam didn't feel he could point the finger at anyone else.

Late getting to bed, Felix pulled down the cold blankets, heavy and damp as a fog, and jumped in. 'They'd laugh at him if he told them,' was how he comforted himself as he lay on his side with his legs curled up towards his body and his arms clenched in. His feet were like ice. He pressed the left one to the heat of his other leg, then the right one, then he did so alternately feeling the friction of his feet rubbing against his skin and the hairs dragging down. His head could feel the cold air stirring round the room. He tucked it in further, and curled up his toes to tug and pull at the blankets that were riding up. His toes were numb and hard and stiff like prongs or tongs, which he used to swathe the blankets round his legs until they were securely bandaged, then he lay absolutely still.

Eventually his body started to warm. He stretched down one leg as if he might test it for warmth or circulation or some other bodily strength. Outside himself, the window at the bottom of the room rattled, the wardrobe too, as if they were part of the cold.

25

Return to Scotts

Walking the short distance into Cookstown a few days after, Sarah-Ann passed a field in which a couple of cows were grazing idly and a man was lying near the gate in a posture of unique and utter repose. He reclined on the ground with his head flung back towards the sky like a young man lapping up the fresh air. The manner of it, abandoned and carefree; the context of it, a damp field on a grey spring day; the spectacle of it, an ageing man, gave Sarah-Ann a frisson of excitement. She stopped to watch. The man was worn, but not old, or rather not elderly. Fatigued, there was still something vital in him, which aroused in Sarah-Ann some expectation that she would witness some extraordinary incident. Perhaps the man would jump up and sing! Or fling himself to the ground! Or prostrate himself face down in the grass! When he moved it was only to pull his shirt off, then from his sitting position he rested again. Every so often he rubbed the soles of his feet against the grass. Sarah-Ann could almost feel the sensation of the damp luxuriant grass against the soles of his feet, and between his toes, and tickling gently the bottom of his calves. Because it was damp the green of the new grass would stain his feet, the bottoms of them would be green. He then stretched out his heels with a sigh.

After a time he reached down for his socks. Whether by this motion or some other slow recollection, Sarah-Ann recognised him. It was Sean Boyd. Prostrate in the field, struggling with his socks, was none other than the cad who had so ruthlessly duped her. How could it be? How could they be one and the same? Somehow his bodily gestures, or expressions, repeated many times over, confirmed him as the man she had known, the man she'd made love with. Where a second before she had seen him carefree, all she saw now was a ragged dejected specimen. She felt nothing for him.

In town she had time to stop at Scotts to look through the window and to browse inside. Once in, with Miss Ruth fussing, she soon found herself caught up in an agitation of needing and buying, an indulgence which before Felix's dress, she had never enjoyed. Now she felt the force of its full compelling cycle: first she admired as if distanced from the object, then, with the insidious power of things, the desired object, some delicate ribbon or bow, made itself closer, until it assumed a part of her, then possessed her. This revolution, from first to last, lasted no more than a few seconds. 'I'll have it!' pronounced Sarah-Ann as Miss Ruth unfolded some garment, and spread it out or held it up. In twenty minutes Sarah-Ann found herself consumed again and again. It was as if Miss Ruth's wares had a life of their own:

petticoats danced, knickers skipped, collars twirled. Sarah-Ann found she couldn't resist them.

When Miss Ruth told her the bill for six pairs of knickers, she answered breezily, 'Just put it to Felix Campbell!' The words were no sooner out of her mouth, Miss Ruth was no sooner repeating them, when Sarah-Ann began to panic, but it was with a delicious delinquency she affirmed his name.

Molly's, the town's only tea shop, was already near full. Women shoppers, who came to the town no more than once or twice a year, sat bulky and steamy round the shop's small round white-clothed tables, whilst Molly herself, or the person Sarah-Ann presumed Molly to be, worked amongst them. The disappointment was that the only table left was wedged between the window and the door. In her fantasy she'd envisaged sitting with Felix up in the far corner from where they could view all the comings and goings. Sarah-Ann hesitated a moment at this corner window from where they'd see no one, and glanced across the tables for some sign of someone leaving. No, they're all settled as Moses, she thought of the mainly farmers' wives in to buy children's shoes, or some household good, or, more rarely, something for themselves. The corner'll have to do, she thought as she manoeuvred amongst the backed-up chairs. She worried how Felix would like it.

'You're here,' Felix almost whispered at the door. His conspiratorial tone implied he'd had to search for her. He hadn't wanted to come to Molly's, he'd told her as much, he couldn't see the point of it.

'Where else?' she sort of whispered back, with pleasure. 'I even found us a table.'

'I left Sam at the chimney,' he said, brusquely sitting down. The implication was he couldn't stay long.

'The best place for him, I'm sure. It's very nice, don't you think?' she asked for reassurance.

'We'll see,' he answered as the prelude to twenty minutes of Felix staring in and out the window, almost flinching each time the door opened and closed.

They had the appearance of couples you sometimes see who have no longer anything to say to each other, or have something to say but no way to say it, or to say it would be destructive. Public places, tea rooms and waiting rooms seem to attract them. The presence of others, the comfort of strangers, assuages their pain. Felix stared indeterminate in front of him as if his eyes were glazed, as if seeing nothing. How long could they sit, he emptily wondered, how long? For the practice or habit of it, for something to do, one of them reached occasionally for the pot. 'It's cold,' said Felix eventually and Sarah-Ann frowned. She was more used to places and people. She placed it back, glancing as she did at what looked like a mother and daughter stiffly arranged at a nearby table. 'How do they get on?' she posed abstractedly, and casually noticed the girl was wearing the boots she'd seen in Scotts. 'Stone cold,' said Felix of the tea as mother and daughter got up.

'That's it,' thought Sarah-Ann. His sullen moodiness ate away at her, and made her think of all the ways she didn't like to think of him. Even entering Molly's was an ordeal, she had watched him excruciatingly self-conscious and had felt like shaking him, and telling him no one cared. Sarah-Ann pushed the bag further under the table, she straightened again the cardigan she'd draped over the back of her chair, and turned to find herself speaking. 'I got some underwear at Scotts.'

'Scotts! You bought underwear at Scotts?'

'Aye,' she declared recklessly as his face clouded over, and his throat choked, and his whole body visibly tautened as if to draw in the tight wad of pounds, shillings and pence that must already have disappeared.

'But I don't understand,' he muttered.

'You don't understand what?' she asked aggressively. For the first time in Molly's, she felt quite serene.

'What you were doing . . . how you thought . . .' Felix could feel slipping away from him all the five hundred and twenty-seven pounds he had saved in the world.

'Scotts sell underwear, don't they, they sell it every day, and even girls like me need underwear!' Sarah-Ann trumped at her self-description as a girl.

'How did you pay for it?' he asked, suddenly cautious.

'Well, you got the dress there, and I thought . . .'

'Thought what?'

'That I'd just get it the same way.'

'Well, I can't stay here,' he said then with the utmost restraint she almost hated him. He stood up with precise controlled movements, he looked at her as at a dog.

'I don't want the tea,' he muttered under his breath, and she nodded passively as if she were not the persecutor of his every measured monetary emotion. 'I'll wait outside.' Felix shuddered with affront. It was his money! Only he could spend it! Only he had scrimped and saved and hoarded it. His mother had left him any small penny he had saved. Five hundred and twenty-three pounds and seven shillings. She'd held it secretly in the bank, which is where it had stayed. His plan had never been to touch it. What had now happened? Sarah-Ann had spent in an afternoon what he wouldn't have spent in a year.

Inside Scotts, Felix mumbled something about coming to settle the bill, realising that only money could have willed him to this new humiliation. Poor Miss Ruth stammered that she would have to check with her mother. 'Well, at least they were unused,' spat Mrs Scott caustically when she arrived to autho-rise the transaction she hated most. Far better to make no sale in the first place. 'Could we go over it?' he asked modestly, trying to find out what had happened. The dress and a suit she said were outstanding. 'And that's my account closed,' confirmed Felix, wondering then with trepidation if she were going to present some new bill. 'That's correct,' sniffed Mrs Scott, as Felix vowed he'd never set foot in there again.

Had he done the right thing, he questioned himself as he came out. Was there any alternative? Had he missed some opportunity not to pay for the suit, which he would later regret? Presumably she already had it, presumably she was at this moment swanning round in it. It might even, he thought with a flash, be the very outfit she was wearing that day!

'You bought a suit.'

'What if I have?'

'Is that it?' he questioned disparagingly.

'It is,' she said; as she spoke, she patted down obsessively and unconsciously the blue skirt she'd been so desperate for. 'Worth every penny of it,' she responded coldly.

'Are you trying to break me?!'

'I got it the same day as the dress, I don't know how I got carried away,' faltered Sarah-Ann, who couldn't explain or put into words the turmoil of emotions that had propelled her. How could she explain to Felix Campbell, who was as constrained in every human gesture as she was undisciplined? 'I've just always liked dressing,' she said, and rubbed again her skirt as if rubbing away the one lasting impression of childhood: that of her mother hacking away at the hem of her confirmation dress. The rumours or innuendoes or something vague about her childhood appearance had never been explained. 'You spoke your words better than anyone,' was her mother's only recollection of confirmation, but in Sarah-Ann's nightmare her dress was hacked away and the blood poured right down over her legs.

Felix stood stoic. Part of him wished to rage against her, another wished to reassure her that the suit was lovely.

'You could come in two Saturdays,' he said.

'I'll see.'

'Will you come?'

'I will,' she answered flatly.

'I had to cancel that account at Scotts,' he said, thinking she had her war pension.

'Aye,' she said departing.

'Sam is fixing the house,' he said to detain her.

'So you said . . .'

'It'll be ready then, it'll be nice when it's done.'

'Aye,' she nodded, and vowed as she left that she'd show him what she thought of him, but as he walked towards Moneymore Road she felt a powerful urge to go after him. Only the thought of Miss Ruth and Miss Sarah stopped her. No, she thought she would not go to live with Felix at all. The only trouble was she wanted to tell him immediately. Only trouble was she'd have to wait to next week. Only trouble was in the meantime she got a parcel from Felix containing a single pair of the knickers she'd chosen. He must have kept them back! He must have said to Miss Ruth, he must have hid them in his pocket! Sarah-Ann laughed and laughed.

26

Desire

To send a pair of knickers might, one imagines, take a certain sexual confidence, borne of experience or long intimate relationship. Yet Felix had spent only a few nights with Sarah-Ann. Theirs was a short sexual history. And since there had been no woman before her, any confidence in his gesture must be discovered in something other than seasoned response. It must have had its origins in instinct, or strength of feeling. In three weeks, far less even, Felix, the virgin of forty-five years, had discovered his erotic and passionate nature.

It was Sarah-Ann aroused it. Could it have been anyone else? The strange thing is that, after the first night, when Sarah-Ann first led him by the hand, beckoned him up the ladder, took the shirt off his back, there was between them an immediate ease, which she could not help comparing with her first experience of Frank. Or, even, with the more worldly Sean Boyd. In the bedroom, Sarah-Ann found Felix possessed of all the tentative and gentle assuredness she could ever have claimed for her love.

Which is not at all the same as the coquetry of sending to your lover a pair of knickers. Admittedly, Sarah-Ann had chosen them. Admittedly, Felix was assured that the flimsy, lacy, expensive underwear, which he excitedly fingered and wrapped, was to Sarah-Ann's liking. In finding himself possessed of a pair of lady's knickers, Felix could hardly be credited with much initiative. To give them their due, that was the realm of Sarah-Ann and Mrs Scott, these two had made Felix's circumstance. What was Felix's triumph alone was the decision to send them. For this he had no precedent. Arguably, no one in Ballymully had ever wrapped a pair of knickers for their lover, nor carried home from Cookstown, in their inside pocket, a delicate piece of lady's underwear. During his long walk home, Felix furtively, pleasurably toyed with the lacy knickers he had in his jacket. Only when he was safe in the house was he able to inspect them. They were smaller and finer than anything he had seen Sarah-Ann wear. The material was some sort of silk, reinforced, it seemed, at the gusset with another layer of material, again covered in silk, and the lace trim round the edge was sewn through with pale green satin. As he had his tea, Felix placed them on the table, just near enough for him to admire them, but far enough to prevent any accident of spilling food, or staining them. He arranged them in the centre of the table, facing him in the direction in which a woman, Sarah-Ann, would have stepped into them. Fastidiously, he patted them out to their precious shape. He deliberately didn't stare at them but diverted himself by reading his paper, then every so often looked up for the pleasure of rediscovery.

He realised how small they were, only a few inches wide, and he wondered how they would fit Sarah-Ann's firm solid thighs and rounded hips. For two days he carried them in his pocket, and laid them on the table, and brought them up to bed with him. The inspiration of what he would do with them stirred in him slowly. He had no intention of secretly stowing them. Nor any idea that he had to make up to Sarah-Ann for the incident with Scotts. What prompted Felix was desire.

As he took them for posting, he felt a certain sorrow that he would have to hand them over, and a great and delicious pleasure at Sarah-Ann's response when she got them.

For she was the other side of Felix's prowess. After forty-five years, Sarah-Ann was the woman who unleashed in him a life that had seemed fatalistically and finally closed to him. Too likely, Felix could have ended up like Black Willie, or Tommy Boyce, without the least experience of love.

27
The bachelor men

Not only middle-aged bachelors share Felix's appreciation of domestic order. There are daily renewable benefits: putting your hand to something you need; admiring a newly scrubbed table; sitting down to a fresh brewed cup of tea. What are the seductive pleasures of the world to these tiny experiences making up the fabric of the domesticity you might never need be diverted from, as some presumably never are; perhaps for them all their days and all their nights are filled with the pursuit of the best set of curtains, or the proper arrangement of pipes, or some other such seemingly ordinary material quest. What else would fill a man's day if he didn't concern himself with such things? What else would he do? Felix didn't hang curtains, there were none in his living room, and it might be true that he never ever noticed, but the pertinent facts are these: he had spent all his life at the honourable activity of his forefathers, he had farmed the land to the best of his abilities, he had calved and milked, drained and ploughed; up until recently, each and every day could be accounted for by the fulfilment of the tasks and work that had been laid out for him. Never did he question it. The land presented itself for the work he invested in it, the crops were planted and harvested by the seasons, the cattle lived and died to their cycle, all he did was fulfil it. Indoors, he maintained the rhythm of his outdoor life. He put back from where he had lifted, he tidied up what he had disrupted, he replaced what he had used. He did it all so naturally. He was used to being on his own, and, every much as Tommy Boyce and Black Willie and Sam Birch, was accustomed to the bachelor life. Happiness never occurred to the bachelor men. They owned their land. Where they walked they forbade others to go. Their prejudices of religion and politics they held to them like a priceless treasure. The rest of the world be damned.

Felix settled down into his hard wooden chair, which Sarah-Ann had tried to find a cushion for. 'I hate cushions,' thought Felix glumly, wishing now that she'd never put it on his chair. If she'd never put it there, he'd never have gloomily and petulantly asked her to lift it and she'd never have had to get cross with him, and think less of him. 'The darned thing,' muttered Felix, kicking it nonchalantly as if with a prod it might show some sign of life. The ragged cushion fell on to the floor where Felix poked it again with the toe of his boot. 'What a thing to bring into the room,' he thought. 'A damned useless thing,' he swore and kicked it again across the room towards the door. He flung it at the door in the direction of the parlour, then with a last ferocious kick turfed it into the hallway. Dust and stour flew out of it.

The incident had started innocently enough with Sarah-Ann, excited and playful, coming into Felix's with a cushion she'd had out on the step. A cushion, she'd declared as she came through the door, would make his room more cosy. She was flushed with the agitation of the work she was doing, and with the expectation of the arrival of her children next day. Too, in a skirt and blouse, she was dressed in the sort of clothes she would never normally have worn in the house, but with Felix she remained, as at the very beginning, conscientious of the impression she made and aware too of the scrupulousness with which he attended his own grooming. Every morning and evening he washed. The routine of it mildly irritated her, but she copied him and regretted only a little the character that would never allow itself to sacrifice duty for pleasure. 'Never mind,' thought Sarah-Ann, as she lay in bed watching him wash. 'Never mind, I'll have a pot of tea alone.'

Unwashed and ungroomed, she sat down at the table with a large pot of tea, and milk and sugar, and to top it all off, a full loaf, which she idly and happily sliced off in large thick chunks then spread with jam, and broke off with her fingers to eat heartily without the least concern for the cares of the day. Felix could do what he pleased, she thought, as she sliced another chunk, as she buttered and jammed and dunked. That was better than pleasing Felix Campbell, of dressing for him, of trying to anticipate him, and understand what he meant when he asked her to live with him. All that mattered was the tea in her hand, the bread and jam, and the quiet dull atmosphere of Felix's room, smelling of Felix, and hardened like Felix without concession to comfort: the windows without curtains, the floor without a rug, the rough bare table. The only distraction was all the clocks keeping slow or fast time. Sarah-Ann idly wondered if Felix knew which were correct. Perhaps none, she thought.

Two were chiming in unison. They had the imperiousness of things. Of clocks hung up on the walls, and hanging with dust, with the spectre of Martha behind them. One was a small brown-faced clock, with unclear figures and an unattractive case; the other, a grander affair, had a mahogany casing with roman numerals. The grander chimed in seven, the other half past eight. 'Ah,' thought Sarah-Ann, 'the time'll not matter.' Even as she had walked to Felix's on the Saturday, it was with a subdued sense of the remoteness of the land she was entering, of its foreignness and loneliness. From the gooseberry bush she had seen that the house had been disturbed. New stones at the front showed a different colour of grey from the originals; their scattered appearance gave the house an agitated air, as if some-one had lifted it, shaken it, then set it down again. The entrance to the parloured side of the house was large but oddly incon-gruent with the rest, as if an old human face were suddenly possessed of a bright new nose. A red pitched roof for the entrance, the red door, a large window at each side of the entrance were in contrast with the grey colour of the rest of the house and the very small windows. The appearance was akin to a doll's house.

When she'd finished her tea, Sarah-Ann took her chair out to the step.

'It's hard,' she thought sitting on the step, 'the chair could do with a cushion,' which is how the cushion from the parlour commenced its innocuous journey across the self-imposed border of Felix's room and the rest of the house. With the greatest ease Sarah-Ann fetched the old ragged cushion and settled back imperially.

Felix came from the field. 'You're on the step,' he said awk-wardly.

'For a breath of air,' she said, thinking how he was, fragile and

233

remote. 'He doesn't want me here,' she thought, and turned away.

'The day's nice,' he said for nothing better to say, then made off quickly with Sarah-Ann watching his head bowed for carrying hay.

For all his grand plans, Felix didn't know what to do with her. With the arrangements for the house nearly all finished, with the plan for her children to come the next day, he had become more and more withdrawn. Sarah-Ann realised it was hopeless. The speed with which he got out of bed in the morning told her as much.

There and then Sarah-Ann decided to leave when she spotted on the lane, patting down her hair and wrapping around herself her thick black shawl, the vision of Sadie. Sadie stopped at the corner and looked down over herself, and seemingly satisfied lifted her small narrow back straight as a field marshal, and her small head as high. Witnessing that proud, stoic gesture, Sarah-Ann felt a sudden tenderness.

'You great ugly brute! Get down! Down! Down!' barked Sadie, dressed in a man's shirt and old skirt.

'Glen!' ordered Sarah-Ann at Felix's great big black dog. 'Get down!'

'Down! Down! Down!' yelled Sadie, guttural from the base of her throat. 'You great big brute!.'

'Come here, come here,' shouted Sarah-Ann haplessly. Felix's dogs respected only one master.

'The most goddamned unbiddable dog! I never seen more unbiddable, that dog'll kill somebody some day,' squealed Sadie as Sarah-Ann tried to restrain him.

'His bark's worse than its bite, he'd not touch you.'

'Not twice it wouldn't!' snarled Sadie. 'I'm in good mind to report it.'

'Here, I'll lock him up,' offered Sarah-Ann to placate her. 'Come on Glen, in! In!' ordered Sarah-Ann with no confidence that the great brute would follow her. 'You great beast of a thing!' she shouted at Glen so that Felix would hear her too; she couldn't wait to tell him what she thought of his dog.

'There, that'll put an end to his misery,' muttered Sadie when Sarah-Ann, flustered by her exertions, returned out of the byre.

'I didn't think he'd go in for me.'

'Sure a big strapping thing like yourself,' observed Sadie. 'Sure look at you, last time I seen you, you were some shape, but you'd hardly look like there was a scratch on you now.'

'I didn't know you were there.'

'There!' scraked Sadie. 'Of course I was there! You were lying on the ground covered in blood, I thought you were dead. When I think of it, I even wonder if I had not come upon you whether you would have lived at all.'

'I thought Maggie found me.'

'No, it was me! When I heard the commotion, I just went running as fast as my legs would carry me,' said Sadie, unconsciously drawing attention to her stumpy short legs; 'as fast as I could get there, sure you wouldn't do that to a dog,' commented Sadie, who only seconds before would have had anything done to Glen.

'Who did it?'

'Aw, I wouldn't know that.'

'Felix thinks it was Willie.'

'Felix thinks a lot of things.'

'What do you think?'

'I never think anything but Willie lives just up there,' said Sadie and pointed, 'you can just see the top of his house, those are the trees round his house, and that's his field. Anyway, I hear far too much about Willie,' cut off Sadie as Felix turned the corner at the bottom of the byres. He must have been down in one of the meadows.

'Maggie's not with you?' he asked casually coming across the yard, but with this he subtly pointed out the deficiency of Sadie's solitary visiting presence. 'I thought Maggie'd be with you,' said Felix thinking what excuse Sadie would come up with for her presence. Neighbours didn't invite. They came under cover of day in day out exigency – a cow calving, saving hay, a message from town – to justify their neglected social presence. Sadie had no such excuse.

'Down! Look what the other brute's doing now!' Tiny was gnawing at the wooden gate post. 'That dog'll ate somebody some day! Them dogs are a disgrace, they'll kill somebody some day, they're that unbiddable.'

'They're not that bad,' answered Felix, feeling defensive about his dogs, which never did anyone any harm, and he thought angrily to let Glen back out of the house that Sarah-Ann had cooped him up in. 'There's no need to lock him,' he said as if addressing neither of them in particular, but Sarah-Ann took it as a snub to her.

'Aye, well you might think so!' snapped Sadie. 'It's well seen you don't care what he does to your visitors.'

'I think of my visitors as much as they think of me.'

'Well, you're not changed!' trumped Sadie, and Sarah-Ann wondered what she could do. 'Maybe you'd better come in, Sadie,' offered Sarah-Ann.

'Aye, I hear you're to live on this side,' stated Sadie getting into her stride. 'Well! Well! Well!' sized up Sadie, jutting out her too prominent chin, and rolling her bulging eyes, and firing her unreserved tongue. 'When I saw you lying there on the ground that day, I got the shock of my life, but look at you now, and to think that you would fall for somebody like our Felix.'

'Who did you think *he'd* fall for?'

'I didn't think he'd fall for anybody, or that anyone would ever fall for Felix.'

'Well, who knows,' said Sarah-Ann, who perhaps imagined that Sadie called him 'our Felix', it didn't matter, Felix was part of Sadie's narrow landscape and, whatever Sadie felt for him personally, his fate would always touch hers.

'Aye, you've got the room nice,' cooed Sadie, who turned then to touch the plant in the window, talk about the plant in the window, look over the brae, say what a great view it was, so that from Felix's house nobody could come around the brae without Felix seeing them.

'I was just saying to Sam who ever thought of such an idea. I was just saying to Maggie that it was some arrangement, it's years since that room was used, the last time I was in this parlour, aul Martha was laid out in one end of it, and aul John in the other,' said Sadie, who, an hour later, was still talking.

'Well, Felix,' said Sadie solemnly as Felix walked in carrying his chair from the step.

'Well,' responded Felix frostily.

'Well, you've got company now!' declared Sadie.

'I've never been one for company.'

'Some are all for the company, but I'm not one of them,' droned Sadie, and in this vein she and Felix discussed their differing capacities for company, and whilst they mentioned no new thing, nor reached no new conclusion, still their conversation had purpose; it successfully circumvented their status as enemies.

'Mrs Stuarty's wild failed,' said Sadie, whose mind turned over endlessly for the thing to entertain her.

'Wild fast,' said Felix, who could talk just like Sadie. There was already gossip that Mrs Stuarty no longer paid the bills, nor sold the duck eggs, and that only days before had resigned her floral duties at the church.

'Aye, went down wild fast,' droned Sadie as Sarah-Ann imagined the demise of the Mrs Stuarty Gibson, whom she'd heard from Felix had been suddenly and unexpectedly widowed.

'And the daughter as well, she's as bad,' said Sadie, who suddenly turned to Sarah-Ann with some explanation which was not without guile, or malice. 'Aye,' said Sadie, 'Heather was a strapping great girl.'

Felix said nothing.

'But her mother, I was talking to her only the other day and couldn't help but think what a great big woman she once was,' continued Sadie, who blinked rapidly to align and absorb her world.

'They're the ones who'll fade the faster,' chirped in Sarah-Ann as Sadie got up and came to the table for milk.

'I've always wondered about it, you see these people that look like they won't draw another breath, and then go on for years and years,' said Sadie, and to make space for her at the table, where he thought she wanted to be, Felix pushed aside the paper.

'Then there's the great big man with all the life in him and just falls down one day,' she said, and got up again to get milk, and, with long practised movements she didn't have to think about, only her body, which was used to too tall tables and milk too far away form her that other people would only have had to stretch for, Sadie clambered clumsily on to the chair. What other people stretched for, Sadie had to walk for.

'And then these 'uns who say their mother and father lived to a right old age, and are good long livers like they'll be good long livers themselves!' she said, and Felix looked between Sadie and the brae, and Sarah-Ann stood at the stove, and each of them with self-interest contemplated the demise and age of their parents, and relations, and the good or bad or mixed implication. Felix would die in an instant over his supper. Sarah-Ann would die in her bed when she couldn't turn over at ninety, and Sadie would die younger than anyone was ever supposed to. Is that how and when they would die?

'My ma's side were all over ninety!' said Sarah-Ann.

'Sure you'd not want to live that long,' said Sadie, 'you'd know nobody and nobody would want to know you, and the state you'd be in!'

'Never mind ninety! The state I'm in now!' said Sarah-Ann to reverse and heal her mistake in mentioning her own long-living family when she knew Sadie's died young.

Sadie insisted she would return to help with the children next day. 'It's no bother, sure I can come back, I'll be back, what time would you want me?' asked Sadie intensely. 'Say five? Say if I was back here at five, they'd be arriving and I could be waiting, and have the tea on, and the house all nice for them, it would be no trouble at all, if I only knew what time you'd be back,' said Sadie, and Sarah-Ann, for a moment feeling oppressed by these attentions, had a glimpse of the new world Sadie envisaged for herself. 'Sure what else would I be doing?' protested Sadie, who explained that if it was her she would be homesick in a new place full of new people, and new things, and strange unfamiliar noises. She was, she recollected, already the size of her mother when she had been sent off to her grandmother's. It was hopeless. Each night she had pined for her mother climbing up on her stool.

'We'll hardly want her here tomorrow,' stated Felix dryly when Sadie left.

'Why not? She can help,' smarted Sarah-Ann, who was yet unsure if she would still be here in the morning. 'Anyway I'll just bring in the cushion off the step,' she said.

'Bring it in where?'

'In here,' answered Sarah-Ann, not understanding.

'But it goes in the parlour.'

'Well, it can go here for a while, a nice soft cushion won't do any harm.' Sarah-Ann strode out to get it.

'It always went in the parlour,' muttered Felix behind her.

'There!' she exclaimed, returning with the cushion.

'I'll not have it here!'

'Well!' thumped Sarah-Ann, opening up her hands wide to let the cushion fall flat through them, then she turned on her heels.

Felix remained fixed to the spot. He was incandescent with rage. Why couldn't she listen, he reared, why , why? He loathed and hated anything to do with cushions. The same went for buttons, loose ones, he couldn't bear them, even the very sight of an unattached one. Before, when he lived alone, when his parents were living, if he spied one lying on the ground, or on a side table, or on his mother's dresser, he had to turn away, suddenly and violently. His mother's tin of disgusting old buttons, all shapes and sizes, all colours and shades, all jumbled and mixed, half of them sticky and stuck together, others stained and dirty, provoked in him almost a physical sickness. There were some so revolting they had even attached to them small threads that had come away from their clothes.

Felix flinched at the thought. He prodded out with his foot at the discarded cushion. 'Disgusting!' he mouthed as if to himself, but partly somewhere it was, too, an urgent appeal to Sarah-Ann, now his witness, his imaginary audience for every action and thought. 'Filthy!' he uttered again, blaming her for the soft-bellied, floppy inanimate object before him. 'Useless bloody thing!' he frothed as he toed it, as it collapsed through the air, as it descended, helpless, and burst on to the floor. The pitiful sight only enraged him more. One more violent kick, it was nothing but a shell, its guts were spilled all over the floor. 'Fucking use-less thing,' stormed Felix in the white heat of his hatred.

Sarah-Ann's presence returned only slowly. 'My God, she'll see it,' he realised, as he picked up all its putrid feathers. If he could just clear them away, if he could just get rid of them, he plotted, she need never know. Unfortunately, as he began pick-ing up all the stinking old feathers, he felt again a renewed sense of his wider humiliation. In every motion of scraping up feath-ers, he felt Biggers' malicious eye watching him, and Sam Birch's stupid smirking face looking down on him, and Maggie Martin's sniping tongue cutting away at him, and, strongest of all, bear-ing down on him, the physical pressure of Tommy Boyce's drunken hand on his shoulder. 'Go steady Felix, steady!' urged Tommy.

He nearly got all the feathers, what was left wasn't worth scraping after. Those he had collected in the basin he threw a cover over, and left in the pantry.

Then Felix waited. Like a child. She'll return, he thought. As he waited, his mind returned to some semblance of order. He wondered what Sarah-Ann was doing, when she'd come back. With all her strengths, with all the powers and gifts he attributed her, he imagined her. 'God, she might be gone!' he suddenly yelped, and ran out the door. She was not in the parlour! She was not in the house! There was no Sarah-Ann!

Felix stared down the lane. The first stretch, twenty yards, was perfectly visible. The next stretch, maybe forty yards, lined by beech hedges, had gaps through which he could see anyone coming. But at the gooseberry bush corner the lane's hedges were higher banked, and the lane itself irregular, and it was dif-ficult to spy anyone coming or going.

Felix's hawk-like eyes, unblinking and tense with concentra-tion, scoured back and forth over the hedges of the lane, and over the exposed side of the brae road. Back and forth darted his eyes, back and forth his mind over the scene with the cushion. Staring didn't make her materialise.

What occurred next in Felix's soul is barely explicable.

Sarah-Ann was gone, yet Felix didn't even think to go after her. He sat on the step, and saw the sky static, and felt loneliness bolt him. Through a small chink in the dense trees, he saw the grey darkening sky, heard the wind's faint rustle. It seemed to say, who was Sarah-Ann? Who was the other person? Some ghost spirit that he was too frightened to look upon, or speak to, or touch? Some phantom of his own imagination transforming emotion to ghost, ghost to emotion, then leaving him hopeless and stranded? Felix felt his chest constrict, and his tongue grow dry in self-revulsion.

Suddenly, out of isolation's hiding holes and despairs, he imagined some distant sound. It could have been anything, an animal moving, the wind in the trees, a bird flying. Felix strained harder and harder. There it was again in the distance falling back to darkness, leaving him listening and straining, then converging again, breaking, until sound and dark merged into human voices. They were female. One was Maggie's. The other was Sarah-Ann's. Their conversation was high-spirited and giddy, cackling and laughing, but as they reached the last stretch of lane they fell silent. Felix awaited their approach, he crossed and re-crossed his knees as if trying to find the proper posture.

'Well?' fired Maggie brusquely. As he waited for Sarah-Ann to speak, Felix swallowed and re-swallowed the mercury taste of his saliva.

'It got dark quick,' he said.

'Wild quick,' retorted Maggie sarcastically.

'I could make some tea,' he said, standing up stiffly. In his own ears, the offer sounded weak, plaintive and base. 'My daughters are coming tomorrow, and Sadie'll be coming,' snorted Sarah-Ann as she walked straight past into the house.

'You must be freezing sitting there,' followed up Maggie.

'Aye,' he answered.

'Cooler the night,' she sighed, 'but not a bad night,' she continued as if only to herself, as if Felix were only incidental. 'Sam did a good job.' She paused then as if she wanted to say more, like there was something on her mind.

Felix barely heard her. He sat staring out at the lanes they'd emerged from, he heard the wind in the trees, and the rustle next door.

28

Her Protestant boy

$\mathcal{S}$arah-Ann first became suspicious in the early autumn; her breasts felt plumper and her head felt lighter. When she was seven months pregnant, she told Felix she was five months due. She lied from experience, and a habit of hers acquired during one of her earlier pregnancies, either the third or fifth, definitely one of the odd numbers, when she had mentioned in passing how her baby was moving funny inside her. Her offhand comment on a day she felt queasy returned to her as a rumour that Sarah-Ann O'Malloran's gallivanting had jiggled up her baby, and irreparably damaged it.

In any case, she thought it no lie. Women are always terrified they're pregnant, or terrified they're not, and between the terrors of women, the incidence of pregnancy is perfectly indiscriminate. For Sarah-Ann five and seven months were the same. In defining truth, she simply balanced uncertainties.

She achieved huge proportions. Her legs swoll, and her buttocks swoll, and her breasts, and all her bodily parts increased their size to their fullest dimensions, which for some would have caused the greatest discomfiture, but Sarah-Ann bloomed and glowed, and with radiant eyes, hair and skin fulfilled to satisfaction the absurd expectations of pregnant women who more often are white wan and seated on toilets.

Her body, large and round and sumptuous, seemed to Felix as attractive as always. Nimble and supple as ever, Sarah-Ann bent down and pulled out from under the bed the porcelain chamber pot, and lowered herself on to the night-time throne. The sight of her – not that he ever really saw her, more imagined the pot under her, and her large white firm thighs, and large white backside upon it – inspired Felix to abstract ruminations concerning the physical properties of delicate porcelain pots to bear the weight of large pregnant women. Sarah-Ann sat on it in her white cotton nightdress, which she fanned out around her in a perfect concentric spread of cotton, an action that had nothing at all to do with modesty but more to associate her, in psychology and character, with the long ago O'Malloran indulgence of painting famine doors bright purple. Over the years, Sarah-Ann's grand vanities tempted her to many things, crisp white cotton nightdresses and days spent laundering and pressing them, and wearing no knickers.

Those beautiful purple famine doors were revelatory.

Felix felt the bed tilt when she got in, and rise again when she got up.

In the morning the pot was overflowing, and had to be carried out. Some days she was so unsteady and dizzy that she spilt a drop on the stairs, or into the holes in the floor where the cats supped their milk. Sarah-Ann half subscribed to the wisdom that the finest of skins, complexions and health are achieved by drinking your own urine.

The pregnancy evoked in Felix wonder, incredulity, even terror. When he was away from her, and out working alone at the things he'd spent all his life out working alone at, he felt wonder at how a man like himself could have got into this predicament and wonder at the mechanisations of creation, the perfect symmetry and randomness of it, and he saw that even the cows in the field seemed to rise up from the green earth, and the brown ground as out of nowhere, yet were the most perfectly formed and finished displays of creation. Felix saw sheep and cows and rabbits and a fox running across the land so fast from the instinctive urge to life it was just running life incarnate. Out there in his solitude. And then, after wonder, he felt incredulity, which was a more personal response to the role in the grand march of creation and fatherhood, his strange incredulity at her on the pot every night, the sound of her floods so remote from his highfaluting concepts.

He occasionally indulged himself in self-congratulatory day-dreaming where he imagined her pregnancy to be the greatest self-achievement, not in the least caring that, of all human endeavours, the conception of new life is at once the most remarkable and the most simple, requiring little, if any, talent on the part of the progenitor, even less control, discipline, morality, decency. The conception of new life is impervious to human concerns, and it sometimes fitted him better to feel the marvel of God who propelled him forward according to His will.

The pregnancy tested to the limits his capacity for waiting. He vacillated between saintly patience and distress.

Felix set about preparing for the forthcoming occasion. He arranged that the cupboards should be stuffed with food, the barns full of turf, and all other physical comforts over-provided. When the house was full of bread and milk, eggs and butter, and all the sparsely rationed tinned meats and salted porks he could lay his hands on, he felt they were ready to receive the newborn. Fat lot of good him being a good cows' man, thought Sarah-Ann, observing the house stuffed up with foods that she redistributed to neighbours.

Sarah-Ann couldn't take for granted that she was bringing into the world a fifteenth Catholic. But the neighbours were certain. Sadie Boyce was sure it'd be brought up Protestant, someone else that Felix would turn.

'Not a bit of him,' said Sadie, 'a Campbell'd never turn.'

That's how the pregnancy was controversial. Neither the mother's exceptional size nor the father's late age detracted from the incontrovertible fact that Felix was Protestant and Sarah-Ann Catholic.

Historians suggest that the religious Reformation of seventeenth-century Europe was played out within the very small confines of a very small island, but there's little comfort in that other than to dilute within a wider bitterness the bitterness of Irishmen.

The question of religion did occur to Felix, but in his heart he knew it'd be Protestant.

Sarah-Ann knew what he thought.

'Well, the Campbells will maybe have a line yet,' said Felix.

'As long as they don't have the O'Malloran temper.'

'If they're Ulstermen, God couldn't stop their tempers.'

'Maybe they'll be Irishmen.'

'Sure if they'd born in Ulster, they'd be Ulstermen.'

'Sure they'll know better themselves,' responded Sarah-Ann, who didn't want to disturb the intense romantic feelings the pregnancy invoked in Felix. They talked all night about the baby they might have, and the one after that, and the ones after, so that by the time they had finished there were dozens, maybe hundreds, of descendants. There were the magnificent and the magnanimous, men of genius and men of spirit who can perceive sadness in the glint of a half-glimpsed eye. The sane and the mad, and the sane who are always fearful they are mad and the men who all their lives would live mostly in their minds were all called forth from their future. Most had five senses, but for the way things are others had less, and some died by their own hand, or the bitter hand of another. The ambitious and cruel, the stupid and crass, and those who see sadness in the glint of an eye, all were wittingly borne, originated from one and the same origin, one and the same man. They talked themselves a full imaginary line. Felix said there would be farmers and soldiers for his people were farmers and soldiers. Sarah-Ann said there would be philosophers and poets for she believed her people were philosophers and poets.

'Oh, it'll be a wonderful baby!' exclaimed Sarah-Ann.

In late pregnancy, Sarah-Ann thought more and more of the sort of world her child would enter.

'You've moved Willie's stick,' observed Felix.

'I threw it out.'

'There'll be no case without it.'

'And none with it.'

'What do you mean?'

'It's over and done with.'

'I'm not over and done with it,' he said, but Sarah-Ann didn't answer. He thought what else he could say, but abandoned thinking and just asked the same question. 'How can you be over and done?' She didn't speak.

He stood waiting and watching her resuming her cooking

with her jaw held taut and her mouth held tight and her hands moving with speed showing nerves. Unused to the strength of other people's feelings, he didn't pursue her. He walked out the door saying he would prefer to live alone on the mountain, and heard the sound in his ear of her shouting after him that for all she cared he could spend all his days with the wind and the heather and no company.

'Aye, I will,' he shouted after him.

The girls were playing and fighting in the yard, and he walked across it and saw the sticks the children had thrown all day for dogs, and the strings they'd tied to an old plough at the gate, and the teeth they had pulled off the plough.

'The plough's broken,' he said sharply as he walked past to the cattle waiting for hay. 'Who broke it?'

They stood silently looking at him.

'They've broke the plough,' he called into the house, but Sarah-Ann didn't call back, and he didn't shout again.

Later that night, when the children were in bed, she softly said, 'There's no point in going after it, I'd rather forget it.'

Felix sat at the table, and stared at the stove, and did not respond, except for his facial expression, which was indeterminate between anger and hopelessness. The sight of him depressed her, and she slumped in with his mood. She was normally stronger to resist him.

A few weeks later Geordie Biggers announced his marriage to Heather Gibson. Twenty years younger than Biggers, Heather brought with her the family farm, and livestock, and a sturdy house encumbered only by her mother's day in it. She herself was a handsome girl, reputedly kind. After her father's death, Biggers had consoled her, he had organised Stuarty's financial and practical affairs, he had sorted out the farm. Marriage must have seemed the natural step.

But the public mind had stored itself up for the event that would illuminate Stuarty Gibson's tragic end, and in drama and possibility the marriage of Geordie Biggers to Stuarty's daughter was subordinate only to Felix Campbell bringing round Sarah-Ann O'Malloran. It brought to vivid mind the spectre of the father, it recast the daughter as traitor, it made the neighbours shudder. They contemplated every nuance and offence they ferreted out. Even Biggers' self-proclaimed sufficiency of women, that too was a lie.

Brought up on a poor farm far from the road, Biggers' influence derived from cunning, wit, bitterness. He must have felt the tension of possessing power without symbol. In marrying Heather Gibson, Biggers not only quadrupled his landholdings but acquired a large farmhouse with orchard, pond and porch and aligned his social status with that of Mrs Stuarty. Now anyone making to town, or the bridge, or Ballymully, would have to pass him standing in Gibsons' yard observing their business, boasting his own. Now, in brick, mortar, stone, they could not deny that in extremis they turned to him, in extremis they lived by him.

Felix was singularly uneasy. He relived the innocent age of Heather Gibson's ubiquitous presence: tea in Cookstown, chats on the lane, suggestions she find a good man. Naively and stupidly he had given her the wrong impression, now in his mind, the day she came with her mother marked the end of his innocence.

Felix and Sarah-Ann's son was born at the spring equinox. During the birth Felix absorbed himself in the peripheral activities; the fussing, the noise, and Maggie and Sadie each more important than the other running in and out whilst he stood awkward around the fire needlessly and nervously stoking it until he could no longer stand the heat of the great sweltering fire and the boiling, hissing and steam of the great three-gallon kettles. He sweated, his face was red and blotched, and the backs of his legs were hot; he was convinced of his utter redundancy.

Sadie resolved his predicament. She shooed him out of the house. 'You're better out,' said Sadie, squinting at the weather. It was blustery and thundery. 'You'll get something to do,' she said shutting the door after her and thinking that that'll give him something to think about. The click of the door told him as much.

She never changes, that woman, he thought, and wondered not for the first time at the irony of Sadie, who before Sarah-Ann had rarely crossed over the threshold, now being stuck up in his house whilst he was banished to the yard. He went into the byre, where he sat on a milking stool. He pulled out of his pocket a small hardbacked book, and a pen. He wrote the date, and made the following entry: '*As bad an equinox as we've had. The rain started at six. The glen waters are well up. Fermanagh's flooding for days, and the wireless says ten inches in parts of Tyrone. Maggie is over for the birth, and Sadie's here as always. If it's a boy we'll call him Jim.*'

He closed his book and trudged slowly back to the house and made to himself his favourite argument of equinoxes: when no man enjoys a longer day, or suffers a longer night, then the weather is bad, which is how it's paid for; this is nature's hard lesson that there's no such thing as perfectly equal, only the fairest and unfairest distribution of resources. Maggie ushered him in. There were cloths and buckets and basins everywhere.

'It's a boy,' burst out Sadie, 'a teeny weeny weeny boy, the littlest thing you ever seen,' Sadie was jigging round the hall, 'with teeny weeny hands and feet and legs and arms and head.'

'Aye,' said Felix, the woman's mad.

'Twenty-two years since there was a ba in Ballymully,'

pronounced Sadie gleefully. 'Twenty-two years,' repeated Felix to Sarah-Ann, 'since we've had a ba in Ballymully.'

'You standing there doing your sums! And dressed for the occasion!' she laughed at Felix in his best suit and a cravat. Sarah-Ann handed over the tiniest creature Felix ever laid hands on.

The baby's name was a sticking point. Felix suggested William, but Sarah-Ann wanted Patrick after her grandfather, and in favour of it Felix recalled some Protestant Patricks but worried that it would be shortened to Paddy. Yielding to his fears, he said Patrick was unimaginative. 'And how imaginative is Willie?' she asked, put out by his cleverness. He proffered Jim, which he said was a nice name, and easy to say and spell, and nothing fancy in it. Or Duncan, he said, but she would hear none of it, any Duncan she'd ever known was an idiot. During the stalemate the baby was called 'ba' and fed and gurgled and hummed, all quite as healthily as any named baby.

'I come from a religion that has no symbols,' protested Felix. 'What's the baptism then?'

'Every man's relationship with God is direct, no need for symbols and priests and rosaries,' he argued, and she smarted at her holy water and beads, which lay on the window sill, and for all that they were not visible from the bed they held all the heat of the room, and all the heat of the house, and all the heat of themselves. There was no heat left.

That first night he wouldn't hold her. He got up silent from bed, and walked down the ladder. She had no strength to go after him. She went over to the window, and looked out and prayed she would never again rue the day or its richness.

After a few days, Felix started to intersperse his bas with Jims, and Sarah-Ann did the same with Seans, which was not a favourite name but ideologically satisfying. Ideology was her mistake. Felix, who was irrationally opposed to any mention of Sean, said there was no question he'd be named anything but Jim. Too late Sarah-Ann realised that with a bit more wit she'd have had her Patrick.

They didn't speak for two days. Felix slept in a chair, never entered the room.

'Not everybody believed in the war,' she said one day, in the full knowledge she was telling him what he already knew: that bridgemen had been fooled, and would have spent their time better at home.

'I've no time for them that take the British security and give nothing back but their slabbering,' he said, and was content enough to say it. Neighbours and farmers and shopkeepers say and still say and know and still know that a Fenian will hide his true colours but not for long.

Sarah-Ann sat at the other side of the table, and said nothing, and it was early evening but as light as if it were the middle of the day, and she could see his face, every line of it, and saw for a second what she'd seen that first time, the big smooth face of a Protestant. For a second she felt she might hate him.

'How could you think that? It's stupid,' he said, the hard cut of him gone.

That was the spring of 1918.

It was the spring that Willie came home. He was seen in Moneymore, where his skeletal appearance, with his trousers hanging off him in twine, and his jacket hanging off him in more twine, and his face like a shadow, ignited a rumour that he'd been lying low with his old crony, Peter Donaldson. 'The bones are sticking out on him, there's not a pick on him, he must be starving,' said Sadie to Sarah-Ann, who knew what starving was. As a girl, she had seen cottiers at the side of the road, just a tatter of clothes, a pile of bones, and she had turned her head and walked on because there was nothing she could do, because she too was tired and hungry. Once one of those poor wretched creatures called out, at first she didn't hear properly, and approached him. 'A great ass on you,' he said as she neared him, 'a great bloody big ass,' he cackled and she retracted. What was more shocking was not what was defeated in him but what was crudely beating with life. Sadie's testimony of Willie was every bit as shocking. He had not even the recognisable feature of blackness. The frugal Donaldson appeared not to have indulged the criminal's habit of heating his feet in the hearth. During months of this harsh regime, Willie's soot had worn off. He was as pink as a baby, as pink as Jim, said Sadie, and the talk of the town for wearing a hat that barely disguised he was as bald as a coot. Even if he hadn't done what he done, there would have been talk, said Sadie, who knew the story of Willie.

Black Willie's house was wrecked, and his goats were gone. Goatless, he fell into apathy. He could hardly struggle out of bed, lay long past daylight. He should have been up doing things, ploughing and sowing, turning and tossing, draining and hedging. He should have been out and about, making the most of the good day. Light and air entered at the torn thin drape at his window, birds sang, swallows and sparrows. He took it hard, the wanton waste of good days. Every day's not a good day, hardly ever good days.

In his da's day they'd have killed you. There was no lying on them days. They'd have had you out feet first, shouting and roaring, cursing and blinding, they'd have dragged you out feet first, many's the time they did, it's what made him a good riser.

Bad weather was easier. Thick dull days followed heavy rain.

Sensitive to every draught, he submerged himself under quilts and heavy coats, consoled himself that with the rain there was nothing he could have done anyway.

That first night he'd waited in terror of footsteps, but nobody came, nor the night after, nor the nights after that. They could have had him a hundred times over, but they were biding their time, picking their moment, waiting and watching. Willie didn't care if they got him. Heavy coats fastened him.

From the gable he spied down on them, black figures moving over the yard. She was stouter and shorter and slower, and Campbell was lighter and taller. He knew their movements, her getting wood, lighting the fire, then smoke rising, him herding cows, cleaning the byre, lifting dung. Their inter-related movements intrigued him. He fancied Campbell's big face planning and plotting, her urging him on. Muted strangulated voices rose from the distance. He imagined he heard them.

Town visits were perfunctory. He crept down the hill, almost crawled, then out of range of their vision scuttled to town, where he quickly and nervously transacted his business.

He lay in bed, felt fear, crept amongst hills. He noticed that the longer he lay, the worse he felt, but the realisation in the form he had it didn't change his behaviour. He almost recalled no other existence. His life was impoverished, and lonely to near madness. He knew nothing but goats. He was still far too thin. When he was existing on that water-based gruel Patterson served up he'd fantasised about food, great greasy mounds of it, but after months of semi-starvation there was no interest in eating.

His hair fell out, and he thought it was casting, thought it was natural like dogs shedding hair, but after days of thick clumps of hair in his hand he realised it was too much for casting. He knew what it wasn't. Naturally anxious about what he didn't know, he considered how he might find out – a futile exercise of imagining himself in an external world of doctors and Baptist ministers. Willie hated doctors. He couldn't stand the minister. Ungrounded by knowledge and communication, he lay anxious and restless in bed, and anxious and restless in front of the fire.

He started rubbing in buttermilk to preserve it. The effect was to cohesively bind the hair, which then fell out more in a unit. He stacked the long sticky clumps on the dresser, and a mound of hair, far too much for casting or balding, grew up. It was almost the room's only personal effect, and he cried one day when he saw it, just a paltry tear, hardly wet, but it was crying all right, and inside his face was contorted, as if it wasn't at the outside, and if there wasn't a drop of saline water, it hardly mattered in distinguishing crying or not. Through consummated crying Willie saw his hair on the shelf not his head, and saw it was dead. In that first awareness Willie, who had rarely distinguished one body part from another, felt a sensation of stinging, a searing red pain that shrieked through his skull, traversed some open cavity. From the thick round fat that had padded him, from never being touched, kissed, and no tenderness, from all that lack of human sensation, Willie was momentarily united.

The pile of hair grew higher. Large matted lumps lay on the bed in the morning. He muttered a quiet lament and ran his hand over his raw head, and hoped every day that there'd be some improvement, stubble or growth, some stimulation of scalps. There was nothing. By late summer he was bereft of hair. Large flies settled on the ceiling, spun over the bed, and dunged. The slightest move, they scattered.

He had some vague recollection that his father's line all had good thick heads, so it must have been his ma's side. Must have been. He thought he saw flies dung.

The thought of going to town became unbearable, with everyone looking and saying Willie was bald. But if he didn't go he'd run out of provisions, exist on spuds and water, and die slowly without hair. Until he miraculously conceived that there was no need to die, so easy that he who had never previously conceived wondered how he hadn't thought of it earlier. Willie conceived of a hat. A hat would restore dignity. A hat would resolve death. Breathlessly he approached the dresser praying that Campbell had left it. The hard bowler was there. He picked it out of broken crockery, held it up to the light; it was squashed, covered in dirt, but not that much wrong with it, thank God, it would do. The hat would do for the town. Under its cover, he perfunctorily and efficiently performed his business, bought provisions, settled his accounts. Under its cover, it protected and gave Willie identity.

Battered by the elements, thumbed and patted by Willie, the bowler looked like a giant beetle attracted by his darkness. It was never practical. Heavy showers filled the brim with water, trickled down his face and nose and lips. With a nervous tic he licked it off, lick lick lick. Willie felt like a fish. 'Ireland's not the place for hats,' he thought, 'not the place,' when it's so wet and cold and drizzly, but he wouldn't take it off, or try a cap, or copy Berty Waters' trick of simulating hair with straggles. Berty piled them up.

It retained the spherical shape of bowlers, upsetting the Orangemen. No matter Willie wasn't an Orangeman, no matter he wasn't a lodge man, it was outrageous the sacred hat of their forebears worn like some common everyday hat. 'It's a sight,' they said, 'stuck on him like a beetle, never cleaned, black like the rest of him.' 'A bowler's for marching,' said Berty, the local master, 'for marching and parades, next thing you know, he'll be out in the sash.'

Contemplating their duty, a ragged crowd of farmers and shopkeepers gathered. 'Where would we be if we all just stood back and did nothing, just laughed and guffawed?' they asked poker-faced and answered themselves, 'Nowhere, that's where we'd be.' No one laughed, no one guffawed. It was an abomination of bowlers. Berty, a tactless man, swore to settle it. He raised the hat without forewarning.

'The Orangemen are upset,' said Berty. 'There's a lot who think the bowler's just for marching.'

'There's a lot who think a lot of things,' said Willie.

'You'd maybe buy a cap.'

'Aw, no cap,' intoned Willie, 'no cap, no cap.'

'The cloth caps aren't dear these days, I bought this in Lizzie's.' Berty raised his eyes in deference to his own headgear.

Willie paused, and for a long time shuffled from foot to foot. His eyes followed Berty's as if making some serious assessment of caps.

'A cap's dear when you've got a hat,' he concluded.

Berty reddened at the undeniable fact.

'It's more respectful is the meaning of it, running about in a bowler like some laughing stock.'

'Naw, a bowler's more respectful,' said Willie which Berty reported to the Orangemen, who were incensed. A bowler's not respectful when it's not worn for marching.

Poor Berty had poor defence. He simply said, 'At the time, it made sense.'

'At the time!' they bellowed. 'Nonsense! Sense is sense, and time will never change it!'

Felix was the last to spy him. He was drinking tea one day when he heard Willie shouting, whereupon he rushed to the gable to see the spectacle of Willie searching for the goats Felix's new family had already eaten.

A few days later, Felix startled Sarah-Ann leaving the house.

'That's some outfit for the lane!' he teased.

'Would you have me down at heel, dowdy and drab?' countered Sarah-Ann, who had imagined Felix was over the fields. 'Is that how you want me?'

'I was only saying . . .' Sometimes Felix didn't know if she was serious.

'Keeping body and soul together,' laughed Sarah-Ann.

'And a brand-new suit, another one!' he teased with some point, and Sarah-Ann trilled, 'Isn't it lovely!' She twirled and turned at the top of the lane. 'How otherwise am I to keep a man like you?!'

'That was a bad day I sent you to Scotts.'

'It was the best thing you ever did.' Sarah-Ann twirled again. 'Or maybe you'd rather me naked?' Felix was then obliged with the facts of Sarah-Ann's mixing and matching, hoarding and scrimping so well that her few paltry items were as five fishes to the multitude. 'A bit like myself, stretched out in all directions.'

'You've more clothes than you know what to do with.'

'And not even married.'

'That's different,' he said serious.

'I know, you're a stuck-up dried-out Presbyterian.'

'Baptist,' he corrected.

'All the same, and all the same for not marrying.'

'I'd do anything I could.'

'Well, I'd better go for my walk with hardly the pair of shoes to take me.'

'Not only naked but barefoot too!' he jested, trying to make light in his own mind of all the Scotts bills filed in his room.

Sarah-Ann set off quickly down the first stretch of the lane. She was not a minute to the gooseberry bush corner, another couple of minutes took her to Archie's, where she looked in out of habit to see what Archie was doing and pass the time of day, but seeing no sign of him made on down the hill towards the river. At the fork in the lane, she turned up Anderson's Lane, which runs along the river. Ballymully River is barely more than a fast-running stream, but its character is temperamental, it gathers pace here and there unevenly and builds up in deep pools. It has huge unbroken boulders and fine rounded pebbles. Stopping to look at it, Sarah-Ann felt it immediately calming and peaceful, and thought of Felix's love for it, his measurements and observations of it. Felix has no friends, she thought, blankly standing at the side of the river, but it was only a vague reflection; she was vague and distracted, and standing there rooted at its bank, just like anyone trying to garner up all life's experience into the one pure moment, and abandoning it to the slightest disturbance. She had her journey to make. At the corner, behind the trees, she crossed over a makeshift bridge, a narrow wooden plank raised above the river, and walked up the overgrown lane at the other side. Soon it turned into a dirt track skirting along the upper western end of the glen. This part of the glen is wide and majestic; Sarah-Ann didn't stop to admire it, she turned away from the glen up the approach to a house. This, a bit of flattened land wide enough to turn a horse, was littered with all sorts of rubbish, but each side was planted out resplendent in laburnums. Their flaming yellow flowers in full bloom filled the air with their sweetness. Sarah-Ann paused before the house's blackened gable.

'What do you want?' came a gruff voice behind her.

'Sarah-Ann O'Malloran,' she said, she didn't know why.

'I don't need you smelling around here, this is private property,' said the gauntest, bleakest human being hobbling maliciously towards her. His huge starved eyes stuck out in his head.

'I don't . . .' she started but could smell the fear on him, and realised then that he thought Felix was with her. 'Felix isn't here,' she said boldly. 'I'm on my own. I'm not afraid of you,' she said as his scarecrow figure propelled itself forward with a strange kicking motion, his right foot turning out as he kicked.

Willie stopped. He poked the ground viciously with his foot. 'My goats,' he said to the vicious earth that consumed them.

'I know nothing about goats.'

'No bones, if they'd starved there'd be bones.'

'I never had goats.'

'What's that?'

'I said I never had goats,' shouted Sarah-Ann.

'I had goats.'

'I know,' she said compassionately and averted her eyes, and looked absentmindedly towards the house, how lonely it seemed; she glanced back at Willie staring oblivious towards the laburnums. 'The laburnums are lovely this time of year,' she said abstractedly.

'Aye,' he muttered from the depths.

'Out in full bloom there is no more beautiful tree,' said Sarah-Ann, and for a moment Willie just stood there, then without a word, without even a glance, hobbled towards the house, disappeared into the yard, she heard him shuffle inside. Sarah-Ann took the few paces to look from the gable down into the glen. One way was all the upper scope of the glen, another was the bridge, and the brae, and the road leading to the town, Ballymully was as clear as day. That's what he sees, she thought, that's where he watches the yard to see us cutting sticks and putting out washing.

Sarah-Ann turned into the yard, she walked up to the door of the broken-down hovel, she put her head in the door. 'Well, I'll be going, Willie,' she shouted through the door, she didn't know whether he heard her or not, he didn't respond, for all the sign of life, he might have been dead. 'I'll see you again' she called into the emptiness, she wouldn't go in, whatever had happened between them, it was now time to go home.

Maggie was waiting for her. 'That was some walk,' she said tartly.

'I needed a walk.'

'You hardly need go as far as Willie's,' came back Maggie.

'No,' answered Sarah-Ann meekly, and felt the deep secret shame flow over her. She had wilfully visited the man who attacked her. That she was as bad as him must be the conclusion of it.

'Well, it's nothing to be ashamed of,' said Maggie practically, 'though what Felix will say is more than I know.'

'What will he think?' asked Sarah-Ann anxiously.

'He'll think you're away in the head,' opined Maggie. How easy Felix'd have had it, thought Maggie, if he'd chosen me.

'Well, he'll say whatever he wants,' said Maggie, 'it'll blow over him, you'll give one of your great big smiles, and melt his heart the way you always do.' Maggie was patronising.

'He's not got a bite,' said Sarah-Ann.

'So they say,' answered Maggie, thinking she's a canny one, who had never once said against Willie the one bad word that could have been expected from her.

'God knows what people will make of it if they ever find out,' warned Maggie bleakly.

The next time, Sarah-Ann took some food, a tin of stew, which Willie gulped down whilst she waited. 'You'd be better with the fork,' said Sarah-Ann.

'Runs through the fork,' swallowed Willie. 'Look! Runs right through it!' He held it up accusingly.

That's the way with forks, she thought. 'Right,' she said, conciliatory, 'it would be better with a spoon.'

'Or better not so runny.'

'Right,' she said.

'I never saw any reason for a fork,' he said, and Sarah-Ann was about to respond but thought better of it.

'I brought you some bread, that'll be easier, you can keep that in the house,' she said, but Willie's conversation was done. He was concentrating on his food, he only looked up when he had finished, he belched and made as if to join Sarah-Ann sitting on the bank of the laburnums. 'All the food's run all down his front,' observed Sarah-Ann, moving up the bank away from him.

Twice a week Sarah-Ann went to Willie's. She told Sadie she was going for a walk, an implausible story that Sadie was well motivated to believe. With Sarah-Ann out of the house, she could assume the full matriarchal role. 'Sure I'll see you when I see you,' said Sadie, dismissing her, and picking up Jim. 'Sure Jim'll be fine with me' said Sadie.

It was Geordie Biggers told Felix. 'Up and down every other day so they say,' said Biggers.

'She goes wherever she wants,' responded Felix with a confidence he didn't feel. He could almost hear the resonance and pattern and rhythm of Sarah-Ann's voice in his words. He looked towards Biggers' house for any sign of Heather and Mrs Stuarty confined within it.

'Up and down to Willie's! That's a walk for you!' said Biggers.

'How's Heather?' asked Felix, aware that Heather was never let out of the house.

'Aye, that's a lot of walking,' ruminated Biggers, ignoring any mention of Heather. The implication was that, unlike Felix, Biggers had his woman under control.

'Heather should get out more.'

'Up and down to Willie's!' taunted Biggers with all the Biggers malice he was renowned for. Felix had sat with Biggers in Sunday school, he knew Biggers the bully at school, he had lived his taunts at the bridge. 'Aye, up and down,' started Biggers at the gibe he would never complete. From his seemingly inert position, Felix lunged forwards and punched Biggers right between the eyes. 'What on God's name!!' cried Mrs Stuarty, running from the house.

'How are you, Mrs Stuarty?' enquired Felix, nodding in her direction.

'What on earth!'

'I'd better be going to the town,' said Felix.

'I'll get you for this,' shouted Biggers feebly behind him.

'I looked like a fool,' railed Felix at home. 'Traipsing off to Willie's when I stood there in Moneymore police station shouting like a fool for hours at Sergeant Black who wouldn't arrest him, and me like the fool gathering evidence, and bringing in the stick . . . and not even telling me! I had to find out from Geordie Biggers, who stood there gawking at me like he had never heard anything better. How long's it been going on?' Felix was demented.

'A few weeks.'

'A few weeks! You've been traipsing up and down that hill for a few weeks, and me so much the innocent I didn't even notice, and me so much the innocent I thought I knew everything about you. I don't know anything!' he shouted. 'What on earth possessed you? What made you think of it?'

'Willie was hungry.'

'Willie was hungry,' he mimicked in a little girl's voice. 'Was he thinking of hunger that day he met you, was that what was wrong with him then?'

'He hadn't got a bite.'

'And how did you know that if you didn't go near him?'

'I heard it from Sadie.'

'I knew it was Sadie, and me, all this time, biding my time, and thinking that if Sarah-Ann doesn't want me to do anything about it, then I won't, out of respect for you!'

'I didn't think. I didn't think.'

'No, you didn't.' Felix started to calm. 'How on God's earth I wish that you would.'

'I wish it too,' she said to appease him.

'Has he got no food?' asked Felix incredulously.

'Hardly any.'

'Well, he can go to the town.'

'He's no goats.'

'He doesn't deserve goats!' protested Felix, who then burst out what he couldn't help confessing. 'I got Biggers!' he announced jubilantly with all thought of Willie dismissed. 'You should have seen him crawling about on the ground like a coward. God he had that coming to him!' triumphed Felix, who started to laugh and guffaw and indulge himself in all the absurd details of him a grown man punching Biggers with Mrs Stuarty coming running out into the middle of it. 'The sight of him,' he laughed.

'Honestly,' teased Felix good-naturedly, 'all the trouble I've been in since I met you!'

Over the years, Sarah-Ann's visits to Willie were less of a necessity, more of a habit. Sarah-Ann waited whilst Willie ate his food greedily, then, when he had finished, when he had digested and ruminated, they sat outside on the laburnum bank watching and contemplating the view of the upper glen and its huge great amphitheatre spreading out in every direction. Seated apart, saying nothing, staring out into the distance, they looked out over the same world. The visit had a natural duration. Willie would shuffle his feet, and blow his nose on to the ground, Sarah-Ann would fidget with her tin, and fix at her cardigan, then both would rise, and Sarah-Ann would say, 'Well, I'll be going now.' That was the visit over another day.

As Jim grew up, Sarah-Ann took him, and when he was older, when Sadie would let him out of her sight, she sent him on his own. The first time he was seven. He was a fair-haired boy with big white teeth and a large bare forehead. His eyes were blue in the daylight, and black in the shade. When his hair got wet, it went into a lick at the front. Sarah-Ann watched proudly as he left the house.

'You've got the spoon?' she checked.

'Aye, Ma!' he said, exasperated.

'Just checking, Willie'll be cross if there's no spoon.'

'I know, Ma.'

'And give it to him right the minute you get there.'

'I know that too, Ma.'

'And don't let him lick the tin.'

'Aye!'

Sarah-Ann watched him at the top of the lane. He was swinging Willie's tin back and forth and kicking at stones. 'He's going to be a big man like his father,' she thought proudly as he disappeared down the first stretch of the lane, in between the hedges, round the corner, she could hear where he was, or imagine she could. 'Well as long as you know,' she called. She had no fear for Jim. Like his father, he knew his own mind, he knew what he was doing, and kept his own counsel, but had none of the extremes of character that still tormented Felix. She had learnt to cope with them, and to thank God Jim wasn't the lonely boy Felix had been; he had all his sisters, and Sadie, and Maggie. There he is off on his way to Black Willie's, she thought, there he was, her Protestant boy.

29

Asleep, 1956

*I*n the early new year, Felix was reading quietly by the fire. The house was calm and closed up for the night. An old dog snored in the corner, the fire crackled and spit, the gas lamp sputtered unevenly. On the table the wireless hummed barely audible as it hummed night and day at Radio Ulster. When it pipped for the news, he stretched to turn it up, and sat intent to hear every word, and the weather forecast to follow. Cold, dry, bright tonight, turning colder and windier, with easterly winds getting stronger, and the odd light shower. He could have told that himself, he thought, and pulled his chair out of the draught up near the fire. At his movement, the old dog rose. 'You've had enough eating all day, you're fit to burst, just look at you, you wouldn't know a rabbit if it ran over you,' muttered Felix as he got up to the table and broke off a lump of bread from a loaf. 'Butter?' he wondered. 'There, you'll not get fat on that,' he said comfortingly. 'There!' The old mutt, black, white and bloated, no breed at all, ate the buttered bread in a gulp, and skulked back to her corner. 'There'll be no more where that came from,' he said, satisfied, and pushed back the bread and the butter to the far end of the table. 'Far less would do you,' he said, 'the half of it would do you,' he thought, and promised that tomorrow it would do without, but knew that tomorrow would come, the old fat hound would look up at him, and he'd think what harm, a small bit of bread, a small scrap of comfort. 'It's a dog's life,' he teased, as the dog stretched lazily in the corner, then licked desultorily at its ears '. . . to the Home Service for the rest of the evening,' announced the wireless. 'There,' said Felix; he fondled his pipe, its reassuring fullness, its smooth stem, in his fingers and palm it lay seductive. He turned down the wireless to its backdrop drone. Soon it would file reports from Africa, China, America, India, Russia, the Middle East, all the countries had new names now. Aye, he thought, glancing over at the bags and baskets of turf and sticks in the corner, there's enough in.

Already a small wind was rising in the air. The wind brushed against the slates on the gable roof, and against the window pane. There was the whisper of the wind on the slates, and the whisper of a woman's voice on the thin half-hung door. It was the strained voice of a woman, whispering prayers and reciting. Now and then, Felix distinguished Mary, dear Mother of God, now and then, silence, now and then, she called out for her children.

He got up and pushed open the parlour door, with the gentlest physical pressure, his hand like a breath against the thin fragile door that opened out as an arc towards her bed in the corner. The room was a tomb. He tiptoed to a chair at the window where a huge fern grazed his face as he sat down to absorb her sleeping. She slept deeply in the early evening but woke at bedtime. He reached up tentatively to turn down the gas. He'd never got used to it. She was the practical one. She took charge of changing the mantles and cleaning the lamps. When he'd got the new wireless, she'd tuned it in at Radio Ulster, where it stayed, and she changed the large batteries it used excessively. Her bed was in the middle of the room, with its foot towards the fire. It was surrounded by paraphernalia: a large wooden box for her clothes at the end, a solid oak table at the top, the bed seemed long extended and functional like a battleship. Dressers and cupboards and tapestry boards at all the sides of the room. They only used the downstairs now. The upstairs and back of the house were closed up. He slept in the living room. All he had to do at night was step from the fire to the bed, and all he had to do in the morning was step from the bed to the table. He stored his clothes in one corner, and his table in the other, and pushed his bed tight up against the wall. Anyway, he didn't sleep. He did not have that God's oblivion. As time passed for going to bed, and as the night descended further into itself, he felt a rush of strangeness over him as if he were stranger to himself. He couldn't pray like Sarah-Ann. By day, she was her old self. Always busy, always flitting here and there. She still went across to Maggie's, and down to Sadie's, and was at Jim's nearly every day. Jim had three sons and two daughters. They were always in the lint ponds, and the glen, and Ballymully River. Their mother was a distant relative of Sadie's, who took to them, nursed them, walked them, told them all her stories as if they were her own. He could see Sadie as if she were there. She was digging her thin arthritic fingers into the sides of her seat, she was hoisting up her small arthritic frame, she was manoeuvring her contorted body to the table. How could life have sustained itself in the life-sapped, sparrow size of her? A cow called from the byre. It was the old blue and grey cow, more grey now than blue. In the morning she dandered out bored and dazed. She looked at him, then, steady, picked out the few dozen steps over the gravel laid in a pile in the yard. She walked up over the rounded mound of gravel eroded into this shape for no purpose, nor point moving it, and descended the other side. She roared in the byre. She roared and roared. She would be inside the rest of the winter. No fresh air blowing over her great blue-grey back, and her huge impressive sides. Felix rose and went to the window. He could make out the hedges, the cattle at the clump, and the field's smooth roundness. It was a mirage. In the day, the field was pitted and rough, churned up by the cattle into thick ruts, where the rain lay in the large imprints of cattle hooves. The fields were in muck. There was the dark outline of the cattle lying together in the clump of trees. Their huge bovine heads, dark and steady, were lifted from the ground, then lowered. The cattle were resting, not sleeping. There were no more whispered prayers. The cattle were resting, not sleeping. He knew the lights in the distance. This was Williams', above to the right was Boyce's, near the town was Biggers'; he always thought of her in the family house, after the wedding, putting up curtains, and without a word, even a 'How are you, Heather?' he looked away quickly, just long enough to observe that from a big stout girl Heather Gibson was failed away to nothing. Was that the summer Annie left? It was a glorious summer, one long hot day after another, one balmy night, you could sit out all night in a shirt, you need never think of a jacket. 'All children leave,' she said, 'they would have left anyway.' He could no longer hear the cow, she must have stopped roaring, she must have bedded down on the straw, she must have pressed her large bloated stomach into the ground, and laid down her big gentle head. He lay down on the floor facing her. In his mind's eye, he always saw her at the bridge. It was spring. Then the sweet waft of turf was on the lane, the laburnums were in full bloom, the honeysuckle crept bright along the hedges. All summer he had yearned for her. 'Sarah-Ann,' he whispered, 'Sarah-Ann, Sarah-Ann.' Her face was as alabaster. Her fine-boned hands were pure white over the quilt. Her hair was smokestained red in a lick at her forehead, and strawberry white over at the crown. Soon she would wake, soon she would ask if he wanted tea, and they would talk. She could talk for hours about the children. When they worked she brought them tea to the field. She brought heavy sweet tea in thick chipped mugs, she brought bread and eggs and ham. It wasn't the food. The pleasure was sitting in the field, with Sarah-Ann beside him, looking out over the hills and the sky and all the great vista of Ballymully. As for the children, she loved them, she hoarded biscuits and barley water for them, and in the evening she stretched her thin bare arm over the high wooden headboard of the old bed and searched out her store precisely. What fancies she had! She loved a proper tea at table, with matching cups and saucers and spoons, and a nice cake on a cake plate all laid out, and a jug and white linen tablecloth crisp, ironed out of Martha's box, who ever would have thought it? Whilst he Felix was bound at the table, forbidden to move or even rise, he might read for a while but the moment the table was ready everything else must be laid down at the moment that she would draw out hour upon hour talking. Even now they laughed at what on earth they'd been thinking as they walked round the brae. They couldn't wait. 'There! Now every-thing's ready!' Sarah-Ann exclaimed at the table, and poured tea, and passed cups and spoons, and a knife for spreading jam and syrup on pancakes. Dressed in her finest, in some long dress out of her box, her delight in dressing up was child-like, and he was in his suit. He still had his suits all lined up in the corner, maybe they were faded, maybe they were musty, he saw one in *The Times* one day, the same that was out of fashion. In Cookstown, they stared. Not even Sadie wore shawls these days. 'Ready! All ready!' she enthused like a young girl at the table, and he laid down his paper, and tucked away his pipe. 'I'll brew more' she said. He needed no encouragement. Then Sarah-Ann was happy. She loved ceremony and show, and making the effort. She'd been proud to step out with him in his suit, and hadn't cared about the neighbours and townspeople, and had had Sadie eating out of her hand and the girls running after her. When the house was silent he thought he could hear them still. They were pretty, Sarah-Ann's daughters, spirited like her. He thought he still could hear them over the living room shouting and calling and coming noisily into the parlour. He started as the clocks struck quarter to ten, and from habit looked at his watch. The house was full of clocks, they chimed night and day, they chimed in the morning and out the evening, and he changed them twice a year, forward and back, for the summer and winter, and declared, 'There's the clocks changed another year,' and Sarah-Ann laughed, and said as she did every year, 'You're far too interested in clocks, they tell you nothing.' He had to agree. What was his mother thinking of? 'She just liked them,' he said out loud, as if explaining, 'she just liked them, that was all, nothing sinister.' He thought then Sarah-Ann stirred, he thought she snorted into her pillow. 'Are you awake? Are you waking up now?' he asked, and placed his hand across the blankets. 'Maybe you'll sleep to the morning, you need the rest,' he said, but he was only whispering, only whimpering. The house was full of ghosts. 'There'll be no more suicides out of this house,' said his da, disciplined and stern, as Felix eavesdropped from the porch. The front door had to be closed to allow the inner door to be opened, the walls closed in, the long dark momentary experience between opening and closing. There he was a boy fumbling. There he was imagining himself elsewhere. It was long past bedtime; he could hear his da on the stairs, he could hear his joints squeak at each motion, and the angry scraping of his toes hitting the iron stair rods. He was afraid of his da finding him. He imagined himself elsewhere looking back at Ma walking across the yard with the ashes to the ashpit and Da on the stairs. Felix stared back. The ash was billowing. The house was filled with smoke. 'You'll have it your own way now,' said Tommy Boyce at the funeral, 'you'll do it the way you want, you'll do it your way out of the journals.' And he had. Here and there he made changes, here and there a hedge out, a drain dug. Now it was all by machine. Jim did it now. In the summers they had worked together. The girls were still there but soon followed Annie. He knew Sarah-Ann blamed him. How nearly he had been a bachelor man! How the night dragged in! He would have gone to the room for a whiskey, for a large glass of Bushmills, but thought he would wake her. He raised his hand on his face, traced down the long deep marks running from the outer corner of his eye down his jaw, sunk into his cheek. He felt the scar on his cheek from ringworm, and the small cleft in his chin. Now the cold seeped into him, the fire was near out, to put a stick in it would make no difference. 'All children leave,' she said, 'they would have left anyway.' She meant 'even if it wasn't Ballymully.' Hah! He didn't give two figs about religion. He placed his warm hand in her cold ones wrapped round in the rosary, 'I turned the wireless off, the news is all the same, I should have listened to you,' he said. She was now very pale, very still. He raised her hand to his lips, he curled up beside her, and with the exhaustion of the day was aware of fading out from land and house and memory, and he thought that I am lain in bricks and mortar and my Sarah-Ann beside me, and land and house and family became a dream with nothing to separate them. He thought thickly until even thought and living dreams faded out. In the morning the window was drenched in condensation, liquid breath dripping down the pane. It was only his.

*

He never learnt how they knew. From the parlour, he had a vague sense of them shuffling round the living room, whispering and muttering, and mumbling what to do. He didn't move to go to them. At the far point of his consciousness he rehearsed how he would tell them. 'Sarah-Ann's dead.' The words rattled round him. 'Sarah-Ann . . .' he mumbled, as Maggie and Sadie appeared at the doorway. 'Dead,' they finished. 'Aye, died in her bed, the best way to go.'

They had things to do. Maggie stretched and pushed back Sarah-Ann's hair, and Sadie straightened her blankets. 'You'll not touch her now,' they said. They were self-appointed mistresses. 'You wouldn't want a hungry wake,' they said. Ashen-faced and agitated, Felix sat where they put him. He only heard them whispering, 'It'll be Roman Catholic.' 'Aye,' affirmed Sadie, 'that's how it will be, a Roman Catholic funeral, they'll bury her with her husband.'

'We have things to do,' Maggie softly told him, as she and Sadie took over.

'To get ready for the first of them,' added Sadie. 'The first of who?' wondered Felix. 'The first of who?' he later muttered.

'The first of anybody,' soothed Maggie, confidently anticipating the onslaught, not for one minute expecting Black Willie. Funereal in his ordinary clothes, an old black bowler, his face as black, she spotted him out the window. 'Would you ever believe it! How did he know!' Sadie scarpered to the window as Willie, without speaking or looking at anyone, pushed open the door and solemnly entered. 'How did you know?' demanded Sadie with such vigour and rudeness; Maggie admonished her.

'Do you know?' enquired Maggie suspicious. Black Willie, his huge immobile bulk, ignored her.

'He knows nothing!' spat Felix, suddenly fired to life. His outburst, which startled Maggie and Sadie, made not the slightest impression on Willie. 'Well,' pouted Maggie, as Felix just as abruptly fizzled out. 'You can at least take a seat!' commanded Maggie. Willie hoisted himself into a large armchair, and took off his bowler as a sign of respect. His bald head was soft pink against the blackened fretted rest of him.

'God, when we last seen it, you had hair!' sputtered Sadie.

'Dwarfs,' mumbled Willie vehemently, and Sadie faltered. Blue veins rose at her old-woman temples, time froze. 'What did you say?' she scraked up to him, as Maggie tried to placate. 'Nothing, nothing at all,' motioned Maggie, 'remember your place, it's a wake.' She turned hostess to Willie. 'Willie,' she said, 'have yourself a sandwich.' In the face of Maggie's authority, Sadie scuttled after Willie, who for over an hour ate sandwich after sandwich.

'He ate them all!' hissed Sadie, as Willie, silently, without fanfare, rose from the chair and made for the door. 'When?' he asked bluntly.

'Last night,' answered Maggie, 'how did you know?' Willie turned heavily on his stick, then thumped it against the door. 'Them doors of Campbell's are rotten,' he croaked lumbering out. 'Aye, how did you know?!' shrieked Sadie hoarse behind him. 'He watches all the time,' she snorted. Black Willie was already stumbling home.

'Well, that's the first of the wake,' declared Maggie, as Felix returned to the parlour. 'Sure there's none of us getting any the younger,' she reflected, eyeing his sinking form.

'Aye, the first of them,' affirmed Sadie.

At the relatively young age of sixty-three, the widowed Heather Biggers came and went as she pleased. She was one of the first at Felix's. She made her condolences to Jim, and offered to help Sadie and Maggie. 'It'll be the Catholic funeral,' she murmured conspiratorially.

'What would make you say that!' snapped back Maggie, who couldn't care what funeral it was, all she wanted was Heather out of the pantry.

'Well . . .' sniffed Heather, who couldn't care either, all she wanted was to know any drama. 'Well, you've dressed the body?' mollified Heather, who was assured, once again, that all had been done.

'Sure some have that little to talk about!' condemned Sadie when Heather was out of earshot. 'Sure some will make religion out of anything!' pontificated Sadie. 'Aye, who does she think she is!' snorted Maggie, as Sadie arranged her old small frame on a stool at the pantry table. When she was settled, Maggie pushed her in closer, an act of assistance which Sadie, in old age and in the sombre situation of the wake, didn't object to.

On the morning of the funeral, Felix made for the copper beech that grows at the river's sharp bend. There he stopped. In the shade of where Sarah-Ann should be, he took up his spade and cut into the glen.